THE SPECTRE
IN
THE LAKE

With illustrations by the author

The Shollond Trust

Published by The Shollond Trust

87B Cazenove Road

London N16 6BB

England

headexchange@gn.apc.org

www.headless.org

The Shollond Trust is a UK charity, reg. no 1059551

First published by Head Exchange Press 1996

Printed in the United Kingdom by Lightning Source UK Ltd, Milton Keynes

ISBN 978-0-9554512-2-5

Gratefully dedicated to Virginia Parsell, who wrote the song on page 119. To John Wren-Lewis, whose joke about Sat-Gurus appears on page 102. And to George Schloss, who contributed the concluding poem on page 208.

CONTENTS

PART ONE - BEASTON

PART TWO - MANBRIDGE

PART THREE - GODSEA

PART ONE
BEASTON

1

HODGE

The villagers of Beaston, as you might guess from its name, were animals - and that includes birds and fish and so on. All except Hodge, who wasn't sure what he was. Certainly they made him feel that, if he was an animal at all, he was a very poor sort of one. The village idiot, in fact. Not up to their standard by a long chalk.

He didn't like being the village idiot one little bit. It gave him a tight sensation in his chest and a droopy feeling in his arms and legs. But there were advantages. It did mean that he got the simplest - if not the cushiest - jobs to do, like walking along trails to firm them up into paths. Also it left him with plenty of time for just hanging around and looking at things.

On the day when this story starts, he happened to be looking at the village pond. Gazing straight down into the water, to be exact. It was a windless summer day, and for once the pond was free of duck-weed, so that its surface was as smooth as a mirror. He was standing on a large projecting stone at the very edge. This was a good place because the pond was deep here, and the water was clear and interesting crea-tures were liable to turn up in it.

He was watching a trio of sticklebacks playing chase-me-charlie so swiftly that all he could make out were flashes of steely-blue light as they darted about, twisting and turning. Then away they shot as an old acquaintance of Hodge's, Snouty the Enormous Pike, glided majesti-cally into view, blowing one solitary bubble and with fins very slightly a-tremble. As if he were too calm and unflappable and dignified to do anything more showy and unsmooth.

He glided on, was lost to view…

And then it happened! The Thing came!

2

PODGE

Yes, the Thing arrived!
 The Creature this tale is all about (well, not quite all) showed up at the edge of the pond. At Hodge's very feet.

At first, it was a pair of eyes - but what eyes! - and practically nothing else. Great, staring, unblinking eyes they were, so piercing - so transfixing - that Hodge could take in little else, and nothing of a face (if there was a face) to frame them. Hit as if by a burst of powerful radiation he staggered, and almost toppled over.

Then, gradually recovering just a little from the initial shock, he did make out something like a face. But the face of what creature?

Was it a fish, or was it a frog? Or was it neither? Whatever it was, this weird specimen of pondlife was unique, like no other he'd seen, even in his most astonishing dreams, let alone in waking life. A sort of podgy Globe Fish or Bullfrog it was, puffing and puffed up till it was as round as a football. Everything about Fat-face was strange, and fascinating, and vaguely disturbing. It was even beautiful - in a scary, dangerous kind of way. In spite of the heat of the day Hodge found himself shivering.

The name of the Underwater Thing was Podge. That's what Hodge called it, later on. It was a good name because it was descriptive, and because it connected neatly with his name, and also because it left open the question of whether the Thing was more fish than frog, or frog than fish, or whatever.

Podge

The question was a moot one, all right.

For a start, there was Podge's skin. Yes, its skin - not scales as worn by fish. What a contrast between that burnt-sienna surface, dead matt and leathery like the skin of a poisonous toadstool, and Snouty's iridescent and burnished chain-mail!

On the other hand, there was the Thing's mouth. Its too-pretty, too-rosy, too-Cupid's-bow lips, pursed and rather prissy and pouting at Hodge in what can only be described as a coy and arch manner, all too easy in a fish, impossible in a wide-mouthed, thin-lipped old frog.

As for limbs, the Thing seemed terribly handicapped. If it was a fish of sorts it appeared to be finless and tailless, and if it was a frog of sorts it appeared to be armless and legless. More likely these append-ages were there all right but secretly tucked away in the rear, and making up for being exceptionally small by being exceptionally nimble. In fact the Thing, by never turning its back on Hodge, made sure he never caught it with its pants down, so to say. It kept him guessing.

Another funny thing about this fishy frog or froggy fish. Normal and sensible pond-dwellers look ahead and sideways: this one was staring no way but upwards, as if to say, "This watery element is all very well, but give me air!", or even, "Let me out of here!" As for the eyes themselves, they were oval instead of saucer-shaped like proper pond-eyes, and they were fringed with black lashes, and the left one was blue and the right one was hazel. In short, either this was the fishiest of frogs or the froggiest of fish; or else (and more likely) it was neither, and just a monster or freak. A terribly attractive monster or freak.

What got to Hodge most of all, what continued to enrapture him, was the absolute steadiness of those staring eyes - staring at him the village idiot, and no-one else. Not for a split second did they glance away from him, or blink, or flutter.

Most surprising, and disconcerting, and - yes! - flattering. He felt all funny. Never, never before had he been really looked at, by any of the villagers of Beaston. They didn't bother, were far too busy, weren't the tiniest bit interested in him anyway. Always they left him with the impression that the less they saw of him the better. For them a good Hodge was an absent Hodge, an invisible Hodge, even a Hodge that had never happened. And now, if you please, one of them (if it was one of *them*, which he doubted) was going to the other extreme. So fasci-nated with him, apparently, was this mysterious pond-dweller that it just couldn't take its eyes off him for a moment. What's more, it was actually looking up to him! As if he were somebody! As if he were quite something!

Well, you can imagine what that kind of attention, seemingly amounting even to adoration, meant to Hodge! To the village idiot who had always been for hushing up and overlooking, or looking through as though there were nothing to him, nothing to see in the space he somehow suspected he occupied.

Was this the sort of love at first sight which didn't last much longer than that? Or the glad eye, a passion too torrid to keep up? Or perhaps a piece of wizardry or magic which, once the spell of it was broken, was broken for good?

In search of an answer to these dimly formulated questions, he went off to brood in the wood that bordered the pond. And came back after fifteen minutes - with mingled hope and apprehension - to the same spot, and looked down again into the water.

Yes, there was Podge, still. With no eyes for anybody or anything but Hodge, the village idiot!

To say that he was astounded and flummoxed and grateful, and scared, all at once, would be to put it mildly.

He was also trembling once more, for no reason he knew of - as yet.

3

THE CRIPPLE

They say that there are two kinds of village idiot. The sort that are cheerfully unaware that they *are* idiots, and don't look down on themselves at all. Or up to others, thank you very much. Rather the reverse, in some happy cases. And the other sort that realise they aren't up to the mark, and have a shrewd idea of the things they fall woefully short of.

Hodge was one of the latter sort. He was all-too-conscious of being bad at - well, just about everything. You name it, he muffed it. Not only was he unable to do more things than any creature he could think of: he was unable to forget that horrid fact.

As he stood there, that summer afternoon by the pond in Beaston, he ran through the list of his more obvious handicaps. They were severe enough and plentiful enough (he admitted) to account for the contempt his fellow-villages held him in. They had good reason to make him feel inferior, sub-standard, an outcast.

Every animal found itself in its element - whether in the air, or on land, or in the water - every creature, that is, except Hodge. It wasn't just that he was a flop at flying and a dead weight at swimming (he had tried both, with humiliating results), but that even as a runner he wasn't in the running and was soon left far behind, puffed and exhausted and forced to lie down and rest. Slowly he had sunk to the bottom of the water, quickly he had sunk to the bottom of the air; and even here, safe on terra firma, he found himself sinking to the ground all too often. In a word and however you look at it, young Hodge was *sunk*. Life seemed determined to turn him down, flat.

Above the water a dozen swallows, with a sprinkling of martins, were swooping, soaring, curvetting, gliding in a dance without rules or leader, an absolutely spontaneous ballet every moment-to-moment pattern of which was unique, never achieved before, never to be achieved again. For the umpteenth time Hodge watched for the near miss - let alone the mid-air collision - that never came. How did a swallow on a collision course with another swallow know whether to swerve right or left, up or down? It wasn't as if the corps de ballet (as we might call it) was always of one tribe. He'd seen gulls and starlings interweaving like this without the slightest mishap. Nor was it as if this incredible know-how, this genius-in-action were the province of birds alone. Fish were just as bump-free. All Beaston was like that. Why, the cloud of humble midges over there on the far side of the pond was at its yo-yo-like aerobatics with equal aplomb and assurance and safety. To be outsmarted by a swallow was bearable: to be outsmarted by a gnat was too much! Showing off shamelessly they were, and showing him up shamefully - a lout who couldn't stroll round the pond without stubbing his toe on a boulder, or take a walk in the woods without bumping into a lurking tree-stump. When Hodge was around nothing was safe, least of all Hodge the stodge, the clumsy one, the slowcoach, the bungler.

He looked the part, too. You could charitably describe his contours as non-committal. Or else, more frankly, as untidy, knobbly, ill-packaged. By contrast, how lithe, how streamlined were those swallows, how neat and flowing-svelte was Snouty the Pike! And the same went for just about all the other birds of the air and all the other fish in the water. As for the land-dwellers, though they were certainly a mixed bunch, Hodge was surely among the least lissome and elegant. Also, of course, deplorably naked. Exposed to all weathers, stripped of the cosy and exquisitely-coloured and exquisitely-patterned feathers and furs of the animal kingdom. And armourless, so tender and unprotected that a mere thorn could leave him streaked with blood. As vulnerable at twenty years as one of those baby animals at twenty hours.

Yes, that was his trouble, surely. He'd never grown up, he was retarded, primitive. Tearing his gaze away for a moment from the Monster in the pond, he looked down at his hands. What on Earth were those five-pronged implements good for except scratching flea-bites and picking blackberries and grubbing up the shallower roots? Why, even the hands of the frog - the real and unfishy frog - he could hear croaking somewhere but couldn't spot (a heron, of course, gifted with Beaston expertise, would have located him instantly and stopped his croaking) - even those four-fingered frog's hands weren't anything like so primitive and useless as his. At least they were webbed, and just the job for getting round the water with, and preventing him sinking into bogs. As for the hands of birds and bats, how cleverly they'd turned them into flip-flaps for pushing and pulling the air with, and generally reducing that baffling and dangerous element to servitude! Snouty and his brethren, of course, had marked up similar successes, by somewhat similar means, in their element. Nothing primitive about any of those creatures! Nor about that high-heeled and high-stepping lot - deer and horses and their relatives - that he could hear somewhere in the distance galloping around for sheer joy at their mastery - not this time of air or water but the land. Or about any of the other villagers of Beaston, so brilliantly diverse and diversely brilliant in all they were and all they did.

Add to all this the fact that these wonderful forms had been achieved so effortlessly by the tribe, and these wonderful skills learned so speedily by the individual - almost overnight, actually - and it was all too obvious why the animals looked down on Hodge. And why he looked down on himself, and felt at such a disadvantage. Even such miserable skills as he could boast - such as tottering about on his hind legs without actually keeling over - had taken years of painful trial and error to develop. Dim, the slowest of all slowcoaches, the dunce and cripple of Beaston, how wretchedly his life-story compared with the life-story of the swallow that had just flashed by, so close that the wind of its passing brushed his face! A couple of weeks ago this ace of all aviators had been a wingless, featherless, legless glob, in looks and deeds very much like a mere pebble of the sea-shore. Yet, in a few months' time it would be winging its way, navigating by sun and star

to its other home on the far side of the world. A success-story not untypical of Beaston. Whereas after a whole year of growth, he, the new-born baby Hodgkins, had been unable to do more than sit up and wave his arms and legs about aimlessly, and make a lot of mess and a lot of noise. Here was a slow developer all right. And a developer of what, and into what, forsooth? What was the outcome of a full twenty years of Hodge's so-called growing-up, but a case of arrested development, of failure to grow into anything beautiful or clever or interesting?

Disadvantaged and backward, stuck, gormless, a byword and embarrassment in Beaston - that just about summed up Hodge's impression of himself. Of course, being the village idiot, he didn't put it as clearly to himself as this, and he'd quite forgotten his helpless babyhood. All the same he got the message and felt the feeling. And both were disagreeable, as you can imagine.

Such, at least, had been the state of affairs - the state of Hodge - until this critical afternoon of high summer, by Beaston pond. But now, and for the very first time in his life, something tremendous was happening that could never unhappen, something with a bright ray of hope about it, a clean break with the depressing past, exciting and dangerous and improbable and leading who-knows-where? Already the droopy sensation in his arms and legs, and that tightness in his chest, had almost gone, leaving him lighter and bigger and quite springy.

He had reason to feel like this, of course. At last, someone thought so much of Hodge that he actually wanted more of him, more and more, hour after hour! If this wasn't love - a most fervent and heartfelt sort of attraction - then what was it? "He must need to drink me in like that, must really like me so much he could eat me," thought Hodge.

"No! That won't do," he added hurriedly, more than a little scared. The creature did look as if he might be hungry.

And certainly Hodge would have preferred a less peculiar friend - one furnished with fins or wings, or at least arms and legs, rather than no limbs at all. Of course it might be (Hodge reminded himself) that at the rear he sported all sorts of limbs, any number of them and as nimble and energetic as could be, held ready for instant use. Like the hundreds of feet underneath a starfish, only infinitely swifter... Another horrible idea, which Hodge dismissed hurriedly! But beggarly village idiots can't be choosers. Any Thing that falls in love with one like this must surely be a Rather Good Thing, and Hodge accordingly did what he could to return the compliment. You could say that he, too, had half fallen in love, if not quite at first sight, at least by the end of the afternoon.

Now it's a law of Nature that what you love you try to get together with. Fall for someone, and you're liable to find yourself falling into that someone.

Overcome by the feeling that those pursed lips were inviting contact, Hodge went down on his knees and approached his new friend. Very, very gingerly...

The friend was growing, and growing, and staring harder than ever...

And then suddenly, as if in a huff (or was it a panic?) it made off.

Startled, Hodge lost his balance and very nearly fell into the water, but recovered just in time. Raising himself and standing up, he noticed that Podge had returned. No harm done. He needn't have worried lest he had given offence.

By this time it was getting dark, and Podge was getting harder and harder to see. He didn't swim away - dimly his round shape and the glint of those staring eyes were still visible - but there seemed no point in lingering any longer by the pond. Besides, Hodge was tired. It had been quite a day.

With a tentative I'll-be-seeing-you wave to Podge, he made for the wood, and his secret bed of leaves under the greatest of the oaks.

In almost no time he was fast asleep and dreaming of a heroic Hodge, fitted out with the most magnificent fins (or were they wings?) in rainbow colours, shot and fluorescent. Yes, they were wings all right, and he was dancing with Podge, also magnificently winged. A pair of swallows, they were beautiful as dawn and quicker than the wind.

But - horror of horrors! - on a collision course!

He woke up, all of a sweat.

It was some time before he dropped off again.

4

THE PODGING OF HODGE

Bright and early was Hodge next day. Dull and late was the light of that day. As yet there was little wind, but heaped-up masses of dove-grey clouds hung overhead, becoming slate-grey to black over there in the east. There was a great heaviness in the air.

Scarcely pausing for his breakfast of honeycomb and hazel-nuts and blackberries, washed down with draughts of water from the brook that ran through the wood, he made his way to the pond. He very much hoped that Podge would be there waiting faithfully for his Hodge, and at the same time he very much feared he knew not what. Being half in love didn't mean he had the faintest idea of what the loved object was really like, of course, or felt the tiniest bit comfortable with it.

Sure enough, there on duty was the Enigma, less pink and more

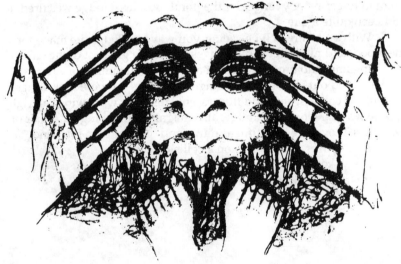

grey than on the previous day. But the stare of those eyes was - if any-thing - more intense and penetrating. And a trifle sad, or even reproach-ful, Hodge thought. Was his watery friend sickening for something, or tired, or (perish the thought) tiring of him? Something needed to be done, he felt certain of it. Action was called for, and that right speedily. Matters had to be brought to a head, scared though he was.

For the second time Hodge went down on his knees, balancing himself on the very edge of the water. And for the second time, dear friend to dear friend, he sought to close the gap that came between them.

As before, Podge seemed to welcome his approach. Again he was swelling as if in eager and pleasurable anticipation. Anticipation of what?

And then Podge *rushed* Hodge.

Rushed is the only word for it.

That Podge rushed him is certain. *How* he rushed him will never be known for sure. No doubt he wanted Hodge to imagine that his backside was like his front - dirty-pink and smooth and innocent-looking. Or plain soppy. The truth, Hodge was pretty certain but couldn't prove, was very different. It wasn't that hidden there were terrible claws and teeth and stings, but (even more alarming) scores of supernaturally nimble legs like the legs of a giant millipede but much, much swifter. And hooked. Legs at-the-ready and poised to come at Hodge, the moment he stretched out his hands towards the water. Legs eager to whizz-z-z-z up his arms so quickly that all he could see was a flash and a pinkish streak. Anyway he *thought* he felt a prickling as of many sharply-clawed feet. Or was it that Podge, more frog than fish, had leaped up at him in one bound? He could never be sure of what happened, it took him so by surprise. Either way, most definitely he sensed that Podge had landed lightly on his shoulders. Where, after a good bit of twisting and turning to make himself quite comfortable and at home - like a dog in his basket - he settled down. Settled down for good and all.

Or was it for bad, and the time being? Well, time would tell.

Anyhow - whatever the consequences - Hodge was from now on thoroughly Podged, taken over, topped up - however you like to put it.

Endless doubts there are about how it happened, fewer about the feel of it, none about its importance for him.

He was different and he felt different. He felt peculiar, both special and funny. No longer the droopy village idiot of Beaston but somehow more wow-ish, and ha-ha-ish, and even I-told-you-so-ish, and now-I'm-somebody-ish, and so on. No longer topsyturvy, the right way up at last. And he felt taller - getting on for a foot taller, to be precise. Vaguely he supposed that this must be how a crocus must feel, as it suddenly pokes its head through the snow and bursts into flower and drenches the frosty air with its perfume.

And if he didn't actually say to all those behind-the-scene, clever-snooty Beaston villagers: "You lot only grow *outwards* and *sideways*, I've grown *up*, so there!" it was because he couldn't find the words, and they wouldn't have understood them anyway... But he had the feeling, all right.

And a very comforting feeling it was.

5

GETAWAY

I t had begun to rain heavily, to pour. Hodge ran for shelter in the wood. The wind, now blowing hard from the east and whistling and whining through the trees, was whipping up the surface of the pond into wavelets.

After a little while the rain, but not the wind, held up a little, and he felt a strong urge to go back to the old spot at the pond's edge.

Here, looking down into the water, he saw what he'd three-quarters expected to see. Namely, nothing but water. No Podge. Not a trace of him. So it was true! Podge had left the pond, left it for Hodge, no doubt about it. Podge was now so thoroughly Hodged, and Hodge was now so thoroughly Podged, that from this moment on it would take something more powerful than steel wedges or dynamite to disentangle them.

And from this moment his proper name was, naturally, Hodge Podge. Or Mr One-off Hodge Podge, if you wished to be polite, and distinguish him sharply from all those nameless Beaston types.

But no-one gets this kind of promotion for nothing, or even on the cheap.

On the far side of the pond - no doubt they'd got wind of the Podging of Hodge - five large wolfhounds showed up, howling and growling and showing their fangs and slavering ominously. This was something new. Hitherto, even the fiercest of Beastoners had either dismissed him with a yawn and maybe a snarl, or else ignored him altogether. That growling was a serious development, those teeth were strong and sharp, and his legs were altogether too naked and unpro-tected. He ran for the cover of the wood, ran deep into the wood. But what use was the densest cover when trying to escape from hounds that could smell a stranger - a trespasser in Beaston - hundreds of yards away?

Beyond the wood there rose, treeless, pathless, rock-strewn, thorny with dwarf gorse - the Great Moor of Kreep. Combing and raking it that wild night was a moaning and roaring wind that bent double the cotton grass of the bogs, and tore at the heather clumps as they held precariously onto the near-soilless rock.

Up from the sheltering wood and into this shelterless wasteland raced poor Hodge Podge. Up and away from those baying hounds into dangers no less dreadful than their terrible jaws. Up into ever colder, wetter, steeper regions, with ever more dangerous bogs and pitfalls.

Three times he fell, painfully, and each time it was harder to get up and brace himself against the wind's push.

If those hounds were anywhere near, their baying had been drowned long ago in the roar of the wind. All he could hear was that continuous thunder. And all he could see was that Great Moor of Kreep still rising, purple-black and huge against a sky that was like the final battle between the Titans of all the world.

And presently Hodge couldn't see even that much. Because, though he wasn't quite dead, he was dead to the world.

PART TWO
MANBRIDGE

6

IN THE CARAVAN

Months have gone by since that night on the Moor. Eventful months for Hodge.

Picture the lounge (if any apartment so cramped and jam-packed deserves the name) in a thoroughly modern caravan trailer. One of the larger sort, the kind that you can still hitch to your car if its horse-power is sufficient, and is fitted with everything from a dynamo to a dishwasher. A white, light, tight, chilly, air-freshened apartment, entirely normal in every way. That is to say, everything rigid in and about it was pressed out of plastic, and everything floppy - such as the curtains and the carpet and the clothes of the two young people it currently contained - was woven out of synthetic fibre. All very smooth and aseptic and guaranteed manmade, with not a chip of wood or a shred of wool or cotton to spoil the general effect. *Manmade* was the operative word.

Yes, this caravan was of Manbridge manufacture, had come from Manbridge City itself, and been set up in the county of Manbridge, just where it bordered on the Great Moor of Kreep.

One of the two people was a young woman dressed all in blue, curled up in the easy-chair, feet tucked away. Her name was Mary. She was gazing across, thoughtfully, at the young man draped on the sofa and overhanging it at both ends. He appeared to be fast asleep.

She had reason to be thoughtful - bemused and amused - for what she saw was an arresting sight. Just about as disturbingly irregular as his surroundings were reassuringly regular.

She was looking at Hodge Podge. A long, thin creature, in the baggiest and coarsest trousers you ever saw (more like a pair of potato sacks they were), and a tight little T-shirt that failed to reach anywhere near his middle. A hideous garment - what there was of it - chequered in fluorescent pink and magenta squares that hurt the eye. It belonged to her, of course - a relic of her wilder youth - but he'd become so fanatically attached to the horror that she'd not yet succeeded in getting it off him and into the washing machine.

The trousers belonged to her dad, Professor Porticule of the

University of Manbridge, who measured 60 inches round the waist. Hodge hated them as much as he loved the T-shirt, but usually wore them to please her.

And the face surmounting that T-shirt? Well, it was very brown and very lean - you could say gaunt - otherwise not at first sight remarkable. Yet for Mary - letting herself go - there *was* something truly extraordinary about those clean-cut features. They combined those of a child - a charming, spontaneous, unpredictable, often mischievous and sometimes maddeningly idiotic child - with those of a wise old man, a master, a knight of the noblest order, a deep one who had access to unimaginable secrets. Nor was this fantasy of hers entirely baseless. What she knew of him as yet wasn't much, but it went some way to confirming her impression that she had on her hands, for better or worse, a far-from-smooth blend of simpleton and sage. Well, say three quarters simpleton and one quarter sage, the mixture to be taken with an occasional pinch of salt. And, furthermore, a challenge to herself personally, who for sure was neither. "I guess I'm just a common or garden middle-of-the-road complexiton," she reflected. "And bored and fed up to the back teeth with being just that," she added, rather wistfully.

No, this simpleton-sage image was by no means a mere fantasy of Mary's. There were several odd things about the look of Hodge Podge that backed it up. The main one was the contrast between those ridiculously sweet, almost babyish Cupid's-bow lips and that broad and lofty forehead surmounted by masses of spiky and ungovernable lack-lustre black hair, sticking out at all angles. She had tried but could do nothing with it. And, though he seemed to take no interest in his appearance, he resolutely refused to let her give him a crew cut. Anyway there they were, the lips contradicting the story the rest of the head was telling.

At this point he opened his eyes and stared at her, expressionless, as though he were still dreaming and she were an unremarkable character in his dream.

The left eye was as blue as the deep blue sea, and the right was hazel. No doubt about it.

Yes, she had reason to wonder what she had taken on. But whatever it was, she was determined to go through with it, anxiety be damned and come what may. When Mary Porticule set her heart on something it stayed set.

7

GROWING SIDEWAYS

From the strangeness of the creature confronting her Mary's thoughts naturally went on to the strangeness of his entry into her life - into her life and her dad's. The Professor was spending the long summer vacation studying the vegetation on the edge of the Moor, and she was looking after him. Also she was riding about on Jones, her little horse, and trying (unsuccessfully) to paint the bleak and ever-changing landscape in oils, as well as putting in a spot of singing practice.

At least those were the things she was doing till this astonishing third party showed up, early one morning after the worst storm she could remember. The Professor and she came upon him there on the high Moor, flat on his back in the drenched heather, naked, all muddy and scratched and blood-smeared, his mouth wide open. A fly took off from his cheek.

They thought he was dead. But no, the Professor felt a heart-beat of sorts, and there was enough breath in him to cloud the mirror that Mary found in her satchel. Also she detected a shivering.

The Professor's idea was that he was a gypsy lad (the travelling folk had been seen around recently, in the country skirting the Moor). Mary's more romantic idea was that he was a feral child brought up by wolves (the Moor was said to have a pack or two). But whether he was lost, abandoned, a refugee from some community or institution, or (for that matter) a drop-out from another planet dropping into this one, there was no knowing. Time might tell. Meanwhile, first aid. They carried him back to the caravan - she, desperate to get some hot milk into him before it was too late; the Professor of botany winded and exhausted (Hodge was no featherweight), and eager to get back to his beloved dwarf gorse bushes. Which he did just as soon as he decently could, leaving her to coax Hodge into drinking pints of milk, and sponge him down, surround him with hot-water bottles and load him with blankets.

Soon he was shivering less, visibly and audibly breathing, and in a deep sleep that lasted for hours and hours.

Extraordinary though the story of his advent was, the story of the weeks and months that followed was, as Mary saw it, even more extraordinary. His rapid convalescence, his quite amazing eagerness and ability to learn to talk and read in almost no time at all (in fact, to learn just about anything she could teach him), and his photographic memory - all this left her spellbound. About his past she could discover nothing. If he understood Romany, the language of the gypsies, he wasn't letting on: he made no response to the few words of it she knew. It was almost as if he had no past to speak of. Had he something to hide, or was his a case of genuine and total amnesia? She thought the latter, but was never absolutely certain. Often she toyed with the idea that he learned so much so quickly because he was being reminded of what he knew in some now-lost childhood. Spent where, she had no idea.

Then there was his abounding curiosity about every bit of gadgetry she could find in the caravan and the Land-rover attached to it. More like addiction it was, an insatiable appetite for gear of all descriptions. The peculiar way Hodge handled everything that could and should be handled - and some other things too - was unique. She got the message - much more from observing the way he fingered and fondled what he touched than from trying to understand his attempts to describe what he felt - the message that he *flowed* into what he touched, and *incorporated* every tool and implement he laid hands on. It

was as if he actually *grew* each tool in turn, as if it sprang to abundant life in him and as him - blood and nerves and all - for the time being. As if its subsequent ungrowing or amputating were a somewhat painful surgical operation. In fact he was quite capable of bringing a saw or hammer to the dining table - so attached had he become to these bodily extensions - and of going off to bed clutching a knife and fork so firmly she could hardly tear them from his grasp.

On the positive side, his knack of feeling himself into every handleable thing meant that he soon learned to use it so skilfully that already he was more dextrous than she was, and as a rule did a better job. To say nothing of the Professor, who couldn't knock in a nail without bashing his thumb.

For sure Hodge was no imbecile. Very much the reverse. Already he was becoming quite useful to have around. All the same, he kept on revealing sides of himself that seemed deficient, dim, even infantile. Was he determined not to grow up, or was he incapable of doing so? For example, why did he pretend to hold the Moon between his thumb and forefinger, the way young children do before they learn about distance?

Also, why was he so childishly addicted, at least once a day, to turning round and round on the spot - pirouetting like a dervish - with one hand pointing at the silly grin on his face, and the other at the walls of the room? Did he really suppose that what he was trying to tell her - that he'd set the room racing - was true?

Mary had heard of near-idiots who could tell you in two ticks what was the cube root of 9,251,745 (if any, which she doubted), or what day in the week February 29, 2734 A.D. would fall on, (again, if any). Well, Hodge wasn't that sort of genius-moron. He could barely count his fingers - not to mention those eerie toes of his. Here was a specimen of a sort she'd never heard of, who was at once extremely intelligent and extremely stupid; who was extremely quick to learn and extremely selective about what he chose to learn; who was quicker than Formula One at what interested him and slower than a state funeral at what did not. Also as bright as sunshine one moment and as lowering and dense as a thundercloud the next. In fact, not unlike this autumn day on the edge of the Great Moor of Kreep. Consequently, at least in her experience so far, he was immensely intriguing and likeable, and irritating and exasperating, by turns; and a touch anxious-making, too.

Yes, indeed. All told, the young man draped on the sofa there, now sound asleep again, was a funny one. An oddball, with something of the screwball about him.

Little did Mary know how neatly the term screwball fitted our now well-podged Hodge, the refugee from Beaston!

8

FUNNY PEOPLE

He opened his eyes. His large and wide-apart eyes. What magical, disturbing, mysterious lumps of stuff those things are, Mary reflected. Fruit-centred cups of blancmange, from some witch's kitchen. (That's the sort of imagination she had.) And, of all the eyes she'd ever looked into, his were easily the most magical, disturbing, and mysterious, ever. Their black pupils were tiny manholes which, if only she could squeeze through them (if everything else got through, if his world got through, why not Mary?) would open out onto a vastly different world from hers. A vastly improved world, or just a vastly alien world - she wasn't sure which. But not - and this she *was* sure about - a mad world or a sad world or a world she could afford to ignore.

At this moment the first thing that struck her (though it was for the hundredth time) about those eyes - viewed from her side of them of course - was how they seemed to look straight through her. Not rudely, not exactly ignoring her, but rather as though she didn't stand out against her background at all, and were no more special than the cushion on the sofa or the photograph on the wall. It wasn't simply that his eyes were very wide open and unblinking and steady. No, there was this something about them that was much subtler than that. She hazarded a guess that he actually enjoyed looking straight into people's eyes (specially, she hoped, into hers) and wasn't a bit frightened of them - as yet. Repeat: as yet. Perhaps they were fruit-centred cups of blancmange for him, too.

Added to this, of course, was their colour. She could never begin to get used to what she secretly dubbed "those traffic-lights in the City of Dreadful Night." Whether she did so seriously or playfully depended on how dreadfully or decently he was behaving at the time.

Well, that was a bit unfair, she realised. He looked funny all right, but not repulsively funny like that absurd and hilariously skimpy shirt he was wearing. Not to mention those potato-sack unmentionables that rounded off the picture at one end, or that wilderness of black stuff - more like wrought iron than hair - that spiked it off (so to say) at the other end. It was a wonder that the pillow underneath wasn't in shreds...

She burst out laughing. Can you blame her?

What Hodge Podge saw for his part, curled up in the easy chair opposite and now bubbling over with laughter at him, was (to his knowledge) the first young woman - the very first woman - he'd ever set eyes on. And his opposite she surely was, in every sense. She was short and on the plumpish side, and quite pretty, and dressed (as always) in blue, but what immediately struck him about her was her hair. It wasn't golden or red or brown but a breathtaking mixture of all three, so that at a distance it looked like shot silk, almost supernaturally smooth and shining. As for her face, like the rest of her it was round and comfortable-looking, and kindly, and as a rule cheerful. The really remarkable thing about that face, however, was its complexion. If any female deserved to be called a peach, here was that female. Many a ripe peach that he was presently to see on the fruit-stalls of Manbridge, was less peach-like. To say that she looked deliciously ethereal to young Hodge would be to put it mildly.

She also looked funny. What happened to amuse and fascinate

him at the moment was the shape and the colour and the curves and the dance movements of her laughing lips - intent upon their own private pas de deux and paying no attention whatever to their surroundings. And then he shuddered. Suddenly they'd reminded him of another pair of lips - those indecently pink things belonging to Podge-the-Pouter, way back in the village pond of Beaston.

And then he, too, burst out laughing. Heartily, though not quite sure what he was laughing at...

Yes, Mr Hodge Podge, late of Beaston, actually laughed. Laughed loud and long, for the first time in his young life. He couldn't have announced more clearly to the world that he had joined a Very Special Club. That already he was a true citizen of Manbridge, the famous town that lay ten miles to the West of the Moor. Manbridge, the great metropolis that Mary and her father hailed from, and in whose ancient university he was Professor - not, as you might suppose, of the Lesser or Dwarf Gorse but of Botany.

Yes, Hodge laughed and laughed and laughed. And so did Mary. Together they laughed. And then suddenly stopped - for no particular reason - as if they'd been switched off at the main.

9

HARD AIR AND CORKSCREW WANDS

Can you imagine how Hodge the Outsider, the one-time unpopular and downtrodden village idiot, felt about all these developments? That he felt different, a new creature in a new world, goes without saying. Just think what it must have been like to chuckle your first tentative chuckle and find it taking over; to lick clean your first spoonful of Robinson's Seville orange marmalade, after all those coarse and stringy roots and berries that set your teeth on edge; to soap and wring and rinse your hands in warm water, and dry them on a towel that made love to you; to lower yourself into your first hot bath, and soak and soak for ages and come out glowing like a god; to drop off to sleep between well-ironed and spotless lavender-scented sheets instead of among the grubby and prickly leaves you shared with earwigs and centipedes and woodlice; to enjoy all manner of such Manbridgian delights as the restful plainness of wide white walls, the squeaky smoothness of the hard air they call glass, the three separate glints of gold and silver and copper, the smell and spit of eggs in the frying-pan when you're hungry, the instant obedience of the tiny fairy in her tiny glass bubble-palace who with her corkscrew wand suddenly turns night into day and day into night; the sound of a magical word like magic, of a beautiful word like beauty, of a lovely word like love; and above all to listen to music for the first time - to Mary singing, in a voice clearer and softer than the bells of heaven, "Michael row the boat ashore." And, what's more, to be looked at with real interest, kindly and gently. Not looked away from or askance at, the way those Beaston villagers used to, as though they didn't want to know you. Not gaped at and gawked at and goggled at, the way that Podge the Starer had done, as though he were famished and fancied you for breakfast. But instead just looked at with those mild Mary-eyes that told you that you were somebody that someone cared about, and neither a nobody for overlooking nor a what-have-you for gobbling up or rushing up or topping up, as the case might be. In fact, she was far from being just another feature of the landscape. For much of the time, the contrast between Mary and her background was for him as wonderful as the contrast between the Moon that saw you and the sky that didn't.

Yes, that was perhaps the big change. At long last he not only existed but belonged, or even existed because he belonged. Not approved of all the time (far from it!), not understood most of the time (alas!), not noticed by everyone (the Professor, for instance, rarely noticed anyone or anything except his botanical specimens); nevertheless someone to be reckoned with. Often enough confused, uncomfortable, frustrated, and sometimes furious - and taking little trouble to hide his feelings - Hodge still had this new sense that he was actual-factual, in a real world along with real people, of whom he was one. Unique, readily and sharply distinguishable. Hodge Podge to a T-shirt. Hodge Podge to a T.

Certainly he had come up in the world. He felt taller. To be specific, some twelve inches taller than in Beaston. Less specifically, he had the vague impression that his centre of gravity had shifted upwards, from around his middle to somewhere near the top of him. It was not so much a feeling of exaltation as of rising to occasions. Not so much a matter of getting above himself, or getting stuck-up (as we say) as of a general uplift. Hodge was walking tall and looking the world in the eye - which from time to time was making it mighty uncomfortable. You could say he was stepping high, and wide, and somewhat handsome - which frequently made Mary feel like taking him down more than a peg or two. In a motherly kind of way.

Thanks to Podge, the high bit - the growth upwards - had come easily (or all-too-easily) to him, and there was not much he could do or needed to do about it - yet. Not so the wide bit, the growth sideways which we have already taken a preliminary look at. Though the two went together (no having one without the other), the first looked after itself while the second took most of his attention, was an ever-renewed concern and delight. In fact, as we shall see as this tale unfolds, the history of Hodge Podge in Manbridge and the history of his explosion in slow-motion come to much the same thing. And emphatically this lateral or sideways development was no padding-out or building-onto, no addition of artificial gadgetry to a natural nucleus, but true growth, the burgeoning and flowering of a Plant of a very different order from those the Professor took account of, but every bit as real.

You will remember how seriously in Beaston poor Hodge suffered from organ deficiency. How his primitive and almost useless hands and feet were for him a handicap and a disgrace. All the other creatures had done better, they had made it, had made good, had made something of themselves, had developed their bodies and their talents in all sorts of marvellous ways. And now, as yet only on the edge of Manbridge County, young Hodge Podge had already started outdoing them all, and the great but unsung Miracle of Hodge's Hand was in full swing. What this miracle looked like to Mary we have already seen. What it felt like to Hodge was a different matter.

He just loved growing these "true limb-endings" or "real hands" as he insisted on calling them. The immediate reason, of course, for this passion for spreading himself was that he was getting his own back on that Beaston lot, who, if they didn't actually *look down* on him, it was only because he was not worth looking *at*. Getting his own back with a vengeance he was, a million times over. What had they got that he was not in the process of getting with knobs on, plus countless wonders they had no chance of getting, ever? Ha, ha!

The caravan, for a mere caravan, was well-stocked, and not a bad place for spreading oneself in, Hodge-fashion. Between them, the Professor and his daughter sported just about every gadget you could want - useful, and pretending-to-be-useful, and plain pretentious, such as a three-speed electrical machine for polishing your nails with. Mary had a habit of carrying around a raggedy old handbag containing an assortment of indispensable thingamybobs, from felt pens of every colour and a last-year's diary and a broken looking-glass and a whistle for summoning her dad to meals, to a gauge for measuring hailstones and a plastic duck that quacked when you tickled it. So Hodge, of course, had to be supplied with a hold-all, too. She found him an ancient school satchel, which he then insisted was not his handbag but his baghand or bag-of-hands. In it he kept what he called his cutting hand and his spearing hand and his scooping hand (resurrected from the mortuary of the kitchen drawer), plus his brushing hand and combing hand (resurrected from Mary's dressing table), plus his biffing hand and smoothing hand (resurrected from her dad's toolkit), plus as many other kinds of tool-hands as he could snaffle and stuff into the thing. Why, the way the fellow talked you'd think he was the Almighty, as reported by the Prophet Ezekiel, stringing together and bringing to life all them dead bones.

"Hand-tools," corrected Mary, patiently, "Not tool-hands."

When frustrated or contradicted or thwarted, Hodge had a not entirely playful way of baring his teeth and either hissing or growling, or both. One after the other, of course: not even this wonder-man could combine those noises.

He treated Mary to one of his less combative growls, and muttered something unpleasant about her pretending to be a cripple.

Determined not to let the creature get away with it, she stuck her tongue out at him.

For answer, he took a screwdriver out of his bag, and started demonstrating its use on a door-hinge. As if she didn't know!

"Second elbow, not hand," he said, cryptically, pointing with his left hand at his right wrist turning the screwdriver.

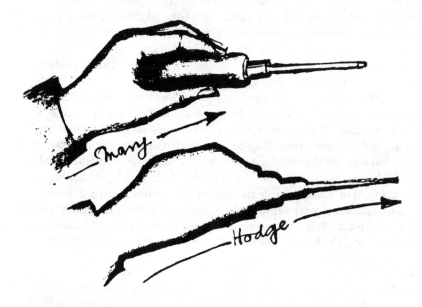

Very patiently, by no means for the first time, she went through her naming of parts, pointing carefully to each in turn: "First your elbow, then your forearm, then your wrist, then your hand, then the screwdriver in your hand... And for God's sake, stop unscrewing that door!"

"That's it!" he cried. "*I* stop unscrewing. I don't stop the *screwdriver* unscrewing."

"So there are legions of Hodges?" said Mary, calming down. "Hodge the Screwdriver, Hodge the Hammer, Hodge the Saw, and so on. A whole tribe of them. In fact I know a tribe of Manbridgers who actually talk like that. It makes a certain amount of sense."

As always, and in spite of her irritation, Mary was trying hard to understand the fellow. She knew very well that what was so very important for him wasn't to be sniffed at. The chances were that it would become important for her, too. Already it was interesting and not without charm.

"You mean," she added, "that the poor little sweetie-pie screwdriver when in the bag was playing possum and shamming dead? Or, if you like, really was quite dead and useless, but now you're holding the thing - all right, growing it: or should I say, hodging it? - it's springing to life and doing its thing in Hodge the Screwdriver?"

"Yes, yes, yes, yes!"

He was jumping up and down in his enthusiasm...

What was winning her over to his side, in a tentative sort of way, was his repeatedly telling her (yes, he would tell her, of course, never ask her!) to jolly well *listen to herself*. To take seriously the way she talked about whatever tools she happened to be incorporating at the time. For example, to hear herself saying: "*I'll* cut the bread," and never, oh never, "I'll hold this handle, which holds this toothed steel blade, which cuts the bread." And to listen to the Professor saying "*I'll* dig a hole" and never think of mentioning the poor spade.

"Bully for the iron-handed Professor!" was Hodge's comment.

10

WHY PLANTS DON'T WEAR SHOES

Getting even with those Beaston villagers wasn't the only motive Hodge had for spreading himself. Far from it. There were deeper reasons.

In fact, you could say that our hero was a mass of built-in contradictions. Inconsistency was his middle name. On the one hand, his Podging had left him feeling superior, one-up on those animals, bumptious, pushy. On the other hand, it had left him *wounded*, cut off from Earth and sky and all they contained. Snip, snip - as if some malevolent Troll were busy reducing him to a cardboard cut-out with his wicked shears. Or as if some cosmic Cook were relentlessly bringing down her pastry-shape on his edgeless rolled-out dough, and turning him into a neat little Manbridgian cookie. Or as if the Great Engineer, having assembled his world-machine, found this nut called Hodge Podge, left over. As if, in short, he were as loose and as lost as thistle-down in a force-nine gale.

Without spelling it out quite so precisely, he was in effect saying to himself: "In Beaston I was small - and very big. Here, on the edge of Manbridge, I'm big - and very small. There, Beaston was in me somehow. Here, I'm in Manbridge anyhow, and there's no going back. I have to find a way of blurring my edges again, of unshrinking, of feeling my way into and being... being what? Being what I was, spilling over into just about everything."

And his way, as we've seen, was deliberately extending himself, in all directions and by all means, and shaping up - shaping up to what? Again, to just about everything.

It was Hodge's drawings and sketches, more than anything else, that revealed what he was up to. Hundreds and hundreds of them he made. It's impossible to include here more than a few of them, but they should be enough to indicate what was going on in his mind, what was cooking.

Here's a typical recipe: Take one ordinary person. Multiply and prolong his arms into what Hodge called tool-hands, draw out his head into super-eyes and super-ears and super-mouths, and, instead of legs, substitute a large blob of Earth. So that what you have is a topped-up, side-specialised, bottom-weighted-down and stuck-in-the-mud Monstrosity. At first glance a spider gone all wrong.

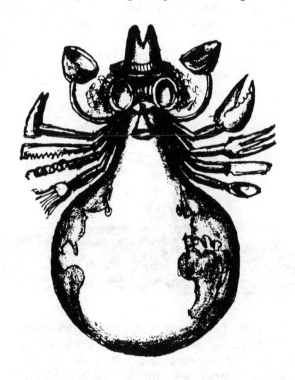

This particular picture-recipe did something to account, in Mary's eyes, for what she chanced to see through her bedroom window one morning at dawn. Hodge, stark naked, arms outstretched with palms upward, and feet invisible in the mud (it had rained heavily in the night), was standing perfectly still with his back to her and facing the sun, just rising above the Moor. There he remained motionless, incredibly elongated, for what seemed hours. Not daring to disturb him (he would have been so upset), she crept back to bed.

Nothing was said when a cleaned-up and properly clothed Hodge appeared at the breakfast table. Nor, later on, when she discovered that this *planting* of himself (as she called it) was his morning ritual. Outdoors and indoors, Hodge didn't wear shoes. There were none in the caravan that were anything like big enough and broad

enough to take those six-toed feet of his. Besides, it seemed he had
strong objections to shoes anyway and on principle. For him the special
virtue of plants was that they didn't wear the things, and never ran
about in them or out of them. Hence, Mary gathered, his special relationship with the vegetable kingdom: so special it was that he seemed
to regard himself as an honorary subject of that kingdom. Rooted to the
spot, these semi-divine creatures weren't just continuous, through their
hugely intricate root-systems, with the soil and the subsoil water they

drew on, but with the Earth itself. And surely were somehow alive to
their blessed state. In their self-effacing and quiet way, they were
preaching to shod and shifty and footloose Manbridgers the gospel of
Continuity and Unseparateness. Little heeded, alas. Fiction won over
facts, feeling over knowing. Manbridgers knew better but felt and fared
worse. They felt so sure that, like sausages, they stopped at their skins.
The idiots pretended that what they sat loose to they were separate
from and independent of. Not that the hyperactive creatures did much
sitting.

    It took Mary a long time to piece this story together and get
Hodge to endorse it, in his peculiar fashion, by presenting her with all
sorts of drawings of himself elaborately earthed. Their message was
clear enough. Not less clear, but more surprising, was the recurrent
representation of himself as a centaur, a horse of sorts with a Hodge-
like torso and head. True, Hodge and Jones, Mary's little horse, got on
remarkably well. Between the two of them from the very start there
appeared to be an understanding that even made her feel a touch

jealous - so ready was Jones to be ridden by Hodge, barebacked and bridleless yet responsive to his every whim, just as if man and horse had become one creature.

It was an impression further confirmed by something that Mary happened to see when Hodge supposed she was gone on walkabout with the Professor. Feeling tired and cold, she had left him and come back early, to find Hodge lying flat-out and face-down on Jones' back, holding onto the animal's forelegs, and with his own legs dangling alongside Jones' hind legs. So together were the two of them that at first, in the dusk, she thought that Jones had suddenly grown preter- naturally stocky, and was celebrating the fact by racing about the place, rearing and whinnying.

So it wasn't only plants that Hodge felt this oneness with. Unlike Mary, perhaps we can understand what it must have meant to him - after those unfortunate misunderstandings in Beaston - to be on such terms with an animal. To be so continuous with an animal.

Certainly the incident mightily increased Mary's respect for him - a respect tinged with awe. And, as always, puzzlement. For inconsist- ency again Hodge took all the prizes. Here was Jones who, on three counts, should have been a stranger and a problem to him, showing up as closer than a brother. Jones, who was not only a beast, but a beast that wore shoes and ran about tirelessly. And was, in short, just about as unplantlike as he could be!

Would she *ever* get to know, much less sort out, this elongated bundle of contradictions? This most improbable but least stodgy of Hodgepodges? This idiot boy of hers who had so much to teach her?

That evening they sat on the high heath - not a stone's throw from where she had found him in the beginning - and watched a reluctant sun go down Manbridge way in a cascade of orange and crimson and apple-green. For a long time they were perfectly quiet. Then she started singing:

> Mary had a great big lamb,
> His fleece as black as coal,
> And everywhere that Mary went
> Her lamb declined to stroll.
>
> "Mary, Mary, quite contrary,
> How does your garden grow -
> Smelly old shells and half-cracked bells
> And prejudices all in a row?"
>
> "It scarcely grows at all," she cried.
> "The moment I turn my back,
> My coal-black lamb he tramples it down,
> Or eats it all up for a snack."

Whenever she sang to him, no matter what the words of her song, he could be counted on to go off into one of his ecstasies. This time, Mary got the message that, at least for the moment and in his peculiar way, he loved her dearly - as the angel whose voice raised them both to float, immense and undivided, into that sunset, and into heavens far beyond.

11

THE NURSERIES OF HEAVEN

Mary's habit of secretly coining words to express her less-expressible ideas and feelings was coming in useful now. Hodgepodgery, for instance. Richly deserving that label, and a fair sample of what she had to put up with at this time, were the following.

Waking in the middle of the night, she thought she heard a scratching sound coming from the kitchen. Silently she eased open the door, without switching on any lights.

There was Hodge, again stark naked, with a lighted match in each outstretched hand, and that familiar ecstatic look in his face.

"Hodge on fire!" he was whispering. "Fire on Hodge."

"Trailer on fire, you idiot!" she shouted, "Do you want to burn us to death?"

There followed a serious row with the Professor, who, catapulted out of bed by the commotion, threatened to send him packing, there and then. Cowed, he slunk off to bed without a word.

His only reaction, come the morning, was to produce reams of fiery floral sketches. The message that Mary pieced together was that Hodge wasn't so much a firebug as a colourbug. It seemed that for him, while cool bright colours blazed and sang with the light of Heaven, hot flames actually took off for Heaven. As for flowers, they grew in the nurseries of Heaven and were flown to Earth every morning by the angel wing of Interflora. After all (Hodge argued), where did their colours go in the night? What on Earth happened to them? Surely they faded and died and went to Heaven at dusk, and came down from Heaven at dawn with a new-born brilliance. On walks, accordingly, he was always being held up - entranced by a dandelion, or a cinquefoil, or a scarlet pimpernel. He saw the dandelion on the heath as a ring of seraphic flames, and the flames of the gas ring as a seraphic dandelion. Which explained his wasteful habit of turning on the gas when there was nothing to heat, and standing there in raptures.

Then there was his obsession with coloured glass. A red tumbler had got broken at the sink, and the pieces thrown in the rubbish bin. From which a shocked Hodge retrieved them, as if they had been more valuable than rubies. It wasn't till some days afterwards that he revealed the full preciousness of these treasures. Their truly cosmic significance for him, you could say. Selecting a sizeable piece, he held it up to Mary's eye and kept repeating, with such earnestness that you'd think it was a life-and-death matter, "*Eye* red." And then, holding it to his own eye, and looking out of the window, "*Sky* red!" which he kept on repeating till she walked out and left him to it.

On another occasion, again in broad daylight, he put his hands over her eyes, exclaiming excitedly, "Goodbye, eyes!" And then over his own eyes, exclaiming even more excitedly, "Goodbye, world!" Always he was on the look-out for what he saw as the truly astronomical difference between himself and her. A difference much to his advantage, of course!

He seemed disappointed that she had no comments to make. Did he expect her to dance a step or two at these wondrous revelations?

Was there any limit to his Hodgepodgery and the seriousness with which he took it? Sometimes it seemed to Mary to resemble, alarmingly, the rituals that some disturbed people are driven to perform before they can bring themselves to press a light-switch or turn a door-handle.

An instance of this apparently compulsive behaviour was the way he had of measuring distant objects, using thumb and forefinger as callipers. As if he were actually pinching the moon or a cloud, or picking it out of the sky and bringing it in through the window. On several occasions she caught him *fingering* her dad as he retreated into the distance, and watching the span of the callipers decreasing to almost nothing. Half jokingly and half seriously, she complained that this behaviour was most disrespectful. Was he trying to cut the dear man down to size?

Generally lightning-quick on the uptake, he seemed not to

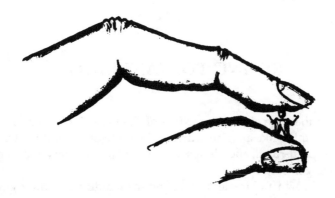

understand her at all. Or was he pretending, putting on his idiot-boy act? Eventually she concluded that, for him, people came in all sizes. The Professor, for example, was so elastic that he could turn up as King Kong, or an under-sized ant, or anything between.

Another ritual observance of Hodge's involved an ordinary twelve-inch ruler. He seemed never to tire of standing at the window and holding the ruler to his eye, first lengthwise, then turning it very slowly through ninety degrees till for him it was end-on. To her rather blasé enquiries about why on earth a grown-up should find this child's game so thrilling, all she could get out of him was: "Clouds, moor, bushes come home! Woosh!"

Yet another ritual - game, obsession, compulsive tick, call it what you like - only became fully apparent on their way in to Manbridge City itself, well into the autumn and at the end of the Professor's field studies.

But that belongs in our next chapter.

12

RIDING TO MANBRIDGE

From the edge of the Great Moor of Kreep to Manbridge City was something like an hour's drive. The Professor was at the wheel of the Land-rover, and alongside him sat Hodge. Mary, mounted on Jones, had gone ahead.

The brown and treeless heath and the winding dirt-track gave way, after a few miles, to a billiards-cue-straight highway through a pine-forest, closely planted and darkling. Then suddenly opened out onto lush green meadows dotted with sheep and goats. Here it was up-and-down country, with stands and coppices of oaks and maples - their autumn brilliance softened by autumnal mists - a rolling landscape whose long views allowed glimpses of just-discernible blue mountains. And here, of course, were occasional roadside barns, and cottages, and mansions, and whole villages that - unlike far-away Beaston - were villages indeed, homely and welcoming.

Hodge, all eyes, was jumping and twisting about with enthusiasm, and making little exclamatory noises that were only occasionally recognisable as words.

What was it about the scene that thrilled him most? The houses? The churches? Well, yes. Mary had shown him pictures of buildings of all sorts and sizes and taught him their names, and here at last they were. But it wasn't the things themselves that turned him on.

No. It was their behaviour. Their amazing agility, in spite of their tonnage. Their rubberiness. Their dash.

Riding To Manbridge

"Grow! Turn! Shrink!" he called, as if he were a master of ceremonies barking instructions to so many square-dancers . And "Twisters!" shouted admiringly, again and again, as if there were no higher praise. As if, till impresario Hodge had shown up, these remarkable dancers had been remarkably awkward, with no idea what to do. Which was surely not the case.

Also, particularly when the view widened out, the cry was "Landslide! Earthslide! Earthquake!" repeated many times. Evidently he saw the whole countryside, from far-away hills to roadside hedges, as on the move, yet firmly under the control of the Professor at the wheel, whom he kept on winking at and grinning at knowingly, as if the old man were the most powerful of wizards. And rubbing his hands together with great vigour - whether to congratulate the Professor, or to imitate the landsliding and landshuffling, or simply to indicate how delighted he was with the literally world-shattering spectacle, is anybody's guess. The Professor, of course, had no idea what the fuss was all about, and was determined to stay that way. What *he* was congratulating himself on wasn't his driving - whether of the Land-rover or the land, who cares? - but on the marvellous collection of gorse-prickles he was taking back to astonish Manbridge with, and further enliven his already-400-page treatise entitled *The Dwarf Gorse of Kreep: A Preliminary Study*.

For some reason, obscure even to himself, Hodge was bent on riding into Manbridge on horseback instead of in the Land-rover. He had his way. At the edge of the city they rejoined Mary. Hodge got out, and the Professor drove on. She dismounted from Jones, Hodge mounted, and the three of them proceeded leisurely to Jones' stable, a mile or so further on. Hodge's horsemanship (or Jones' manhorseship) being what it was, no doubt he counted two and not three.

It was a halcyon Indian-summer afternoon. The light southern breeze bore the scent of the far-off Ocean. The plane trees lining the streets - fairly free of traffic, for once - were on fire. And - believe you me - the nightingales were singing in Manbridge Square. Riding tall on his little horse, Hodge was in one of his trances, crooning made-up words - Hodgespeak, Mary called it - to go with the music. His lean brown face, up-turned and with just the hint about it of the smile of another country - combined with his enormous sack-like trousers, abbreviated T-shirt (fluorescent purple, this time), and spiky crown of hair looking as if it were carved out of pure jet - made up a spectacle the like of which had never hit Manbridge before. The city held its breath. Why, even Jones was caught up in the ecstasy!

A group of children, on their way home after school, halted in their tracks, open-mouthed. Those who dared to, clapped. Not one of them laughed. They were, you see, very young children.

As for Mary Porticule, all in blue and walking at his side, aglow in the fast-fading light of that beautiful day, she finally knew for sure that she was in love. First and last love. Love perilous. Love compounded of pain and pleasure and perplexity in about equal measures, with more than a pinch or two of fun thrown in for seasoning.

13

HAND-GRENADES AND TROUSER TALK

The Professor and Mary lived, on distant but not difficult terms, in the penthouse apartment of a ten-storey block near the centre of Manbridge. It was roomy and tidy and tasteful in the areas belonging to Mary, and unbelievably chaotic and cluttered in those belonging to her dad. She installed Hodge in the spare room. Tiny it was for one of his size, but the views over the roof-tops of the city, with its many towers and spires fighting bitter battles to come out on top, were magnificent. Specially at night, when some of Heaven's glamour came down to Earth.

Here Hodge spent much of each day filling sketchbook after sketchbook with increasingly elaborate drawings of big and little people and animals doing duty as honorary plants, merging with and emerging from the Earth. And of himself burgeoning limb-endings, of course, ever more vigorously in ever more directions. And of just about everything else you can imagine. Clearly he thought and felt in pictures.

Words also came to him with astonishing ease. He was an avid reader, wide-ranging and very fast. In luck, he found himself surrounded by good and not-so-bad books of every description, including scores of well-illustrated scientific treatises dating from the Professor's pre-gorse and less prickly years. Also Mary had collected a wide variety of volumes of the popular coffee-table type. All these he absorbed eagerly. The pictures he never forgot. Nor the text either, provided always he could translate it into his peculiar jargon. It seemed he was incapable of accepting anything from anybody in the raw. To take it in he had to Hodgepodge it. Authors would have a job recognising what he got out of their books. There were two exceptions. The first was poetry, in the broadest sense of the word. If he didn't have to muck about with a text, if it was for taking at its face value, then it was for him literature or poetry, a phrase or a line of which could enrapture him for hours on end. More and more he was loving word-music. The second was humour. He loved Mary's favourite funny books, and his own sense of humour was as lively as it was quirky.

All of which, with Mary lined up nearby for ready reference, meant that Hodge's education proceeded at record pace. He made up for being a very late starter, by compressing into weeks and months what would normally take years and decades. There remained big and curious gaps in his world-picture, of course. But it was like one of those Swiss cheeses: the stuff was so good it could afford a lot of holes.

What was the secret of her pupil's brilliance? Mary kept asking herself. In the end her answer - and she knew it was the true one - came out like this:

He had exploded into her life as an infant in all but physique, and so he remained. Oddly enough, it was his very backwardness that accounted for his brilliance! The normal Manbridgian infant learns far more in his first few months than in the rest of his life, less and less every month and year thereafter, and all too soon leaves infancy and its astounding genius far behind. Not so Hodge, the retardate, the serious case of arrested development. He'd hit on a way of prolonging the miracle of infancy and its wide openness indefinitely, and not so much delaying adulthood as evading it. Shirking it, if you must put it that way. Yes, this was his secret, no doubt about it. This was the magic that enabled him painlessly and at highest speed to go on taking in vast quantities of Manbridgian information and know-how without being taken in by it. Or closed in or closed up. Lucky fellow! What a lesson, what a rebuke for Mary and her kind, so disastrously eager to grow up into clever-clever worldlings! She felt she should be crying at the top of her voice, with Hodge, "Shirkers of the world unite, you have nothing to lose but your brains!"

All of which left Mary with the problem of how to fit Hodge into Manbridge. She tried many things. One of them was to arrange that his quirky but intensive and far-ranging homework was backed up by field-studies in the form of carefully planned excursions into the city and its environs - always under her watchful guidance. It was much, much safer that way. For Hodge was a master of the unexpected. Never, for instance, dutifully struck dumb, did he stand gaping at the official wonders of the place, at the big things and the famous things. Fountains like hundred-foot madonna lilies failed to impress him. Spaghetti junctions like - well, like spaghetti gone haywire, fearsome cranes crisscrossing the sky and obviously about to keel over, monstrous mirror-faced office blocks reluctantly taking in each other's washing, and deep potholes and caverns and underground rivers gushing sedated Manbridgers on their way to and from work - all of these left him cold, or at least lukewarm. If in weak moments he allowed himself to be astounded at such marvels, he soon pulled himself together, and saved his wonder (and his all-too-vocal praise) for truly wonderful sights. Such as the rainbow eyes of the lacewing on the outside of the shop window, so much more remarkable than the goods on display inside it. Such as the explosion that half-wrecked the shop when he did go inside - blowing out at least one wall - followed by apologies to the mystified shopkeeper for carrying around such a devastating hand-grenade. (Hodge just couldn't get the silly man to see what he saw, and count three walls instead of four.) Such as the streaming blood in city streets on wet nights, staunched and washed away at

regular intervals by amber and green lotions. Such as the obvious fact that the escalator he was supposed to be riding on never moved; and was this not far more marvellous than the escalator itself - so marvellous that the news had to be shared with the other passengers? Such as the patterning and colouring of the masterpiece that Manbridgers call a disgusting filthy pile of rubbish on the pavement, but in reality is an inspired composition repaying the most careful study. And so on, and on. It took Mary several days to recover from as many hours in town with Hodge.

Take the matter of his new trousers. What interested him was not the salesman's spiel about the garments he was fitting Hodge out with, but the bobbing up and down of the man's Adam's apple. That he should be able to get a word out of that improbable instrument - and without the slightest clue about how he was doing so - was for Hodge infinitely more significant than what the fellow was saying, than all that trouser-talk. Which made the purchase even more complicated than Mary had bargained for.

But the real trouble started when it came to paying for the trousers. He couldn't see why the salesman refused to hand them over to him till he'd handed over to the salesman three identical engravings of a middle-aged woman. The trousers, Hodge explained carefully in a level voice, weren't for her but for him. With mounting exasperation he threatened to give a demonstration, and to call on witnesses to prove his point. By this time a small crowd had gathered...

He never did get the hang of money. In a café he would ask the cashier why, to insert bits of cake into one end of yourself, you had to extract bits of metal from the other end. Can the wretch be that dim, Mary asked herself time and again, or is he kidding, putting on his village-idiot act? Or is he plain mad? This one she *could* answer. If this was madness, there was invariably method and surely blessing in it - the method and the blessing of wide-openness to what's Given. GIVEN! that was the magic word, Hodge's spell, his Open Sesame to the whole range of his treasures. Truly speaking, either Manbridge or Hodge was crazy. It was one or the other. Mary might take a lot of persuading, but in the end she was pretty sure to conclude that he was the sane one. Too sane for comfort.

Take the matter of the lift that refused to lift.

Mary, accompanied by Hodge, has business on the top floor of an office building. Before entering the lift on the ground floor, Hodge insists on "measuring", between his outstretched hands, the people standing round the hall. "Very big people," he explains to Mary, in his too loud and most irritating school-marmish voice. Then, in the lift, he demonstrates to the startled passengers that it isn't moving, and alas they are stuck - for how long he wouldn't like to say. "Look, look!" he cries, pointing in turn to the walls and ceiling and floor, "Stationary!" Emerging from the lift on the top floor, he drags Mary to the ten-storey stair-well and starts "remeasuring" those people in the hall on the ground floor: this time, of course, between thumb and forefinger. "Now they're small people!" he explains. This ritual of his is followed by her ritual of trying to teach her Hodge that people stay the same size, and she and Hodge *distance* themselves from them. Which he absolutely refuses to allow. The lift failed to lift them, didn't it? And don't rulers measure zero when held end-on? Manbridge's truth is that distance is real, Hodge's truth is that distance is imaginary. Manbridge's truth is that people stay people-size, Hodge's truth is that people come in all sizes from dust-grains to worlds, swelling and shrinking all the time as if they were so many bubbles being blown (and pricked) by some fun-loving Demiurge.

Battered but not beaten, Mary would try another approach.

"So what? I don't see it matters so tremendously. Why do you have to get so passionate about it?"

This sort of cavilling always brought out the worst in Hodge. He became angry, or condescending, or simply spread his hands and gave up on her, and the last was easily the worst.

So it was this time. Again she found herself forced - most reluctantly - to concede his point, the practical point that when you substitute variable people-sizes for variable people-distances they remain your people. Instead of boorishly rejecting them, keeping them at arm's length or pushing them off into the far distance, you embrace them.

Embrace them kindly, because they are your kind and kindred, and truly close friends. And the same goes for all the world's treasures - from stars and sun and moon all the way down to your mother-of-pearl shirt buttons - they remain your treasures when you stop lying about them and admit you don't have an inch of barge-pole to shove them away with. This hard-to-take but simple truthfulness (Mary was realising, gradually) could make a huge difference in her life. How much of her gloom came from the ruinous habit of cutting herself off - compulsively plying those Devil's scissors called Distance - from the riches that were in fact her very, very own! Why, even those funny scientists of Manbridge - every man-Jack and woman-Jill of them, even her dear old prickly dad - when pressed, will tell you that, nerve and vein and pore, you are inseparable from the great world and everything in it. Moreover that - come on, be reasonable! - what you see you see where *you* are, not where you insist on seeing that darn thing off to. Really to see is to prick the balloon of distance, to call the bluff of that trickster, to arrest that arch-thief and come into your heritage.

It took Mary some time to piece together, from the scattered and often confusing hints that Hodge graciously doled out, this much of what he was really up to. Of what inspired his campaign against distance. After which the problem was that the more it made sense to her the more it was apt to make trouble for her. For him, too. But then the wretch was a born trouble-maker. The infallible way to lose friends and cease to influence people in Manbridge was to have Hodge Podge for your special friend.

Not only did the fellow have this embarrassing itch to telescope space, but time also. Leading to yet more trouble, inevitably.

Mary had two aunts, elderly and somewhat strait-laced maiden ladies called Jane and Dorothea, who happened to be identical twins. They lived together in a rather grand old ancestral home, where she visited them regularly - more for pleasure than out of duty. On one of these visits, plucking up her courage, she took Hodge along. He behaved tolerably well. What intrigued him was the difficulty of telling which sister was which - a difficulty they compounded by always dressing exactly alike. It was all rather fun.

However - trust him! - he did start probing too deeply into the root distinction (which he knew very well) between identical and ordinary twins. At this point Mary butted in adroitly with an elaborate story about another pair of identical twins, one of whom was seen to commit a murder. Which one? That was the insoluble question. Since they couldn't both be hanged, neither was hanged. Had Aunts Jane and Dorothea ever thought of committing their favourite crime, and getting away with it like that? More fun, in fact, thanks to Mary.

Back home, Hodge, after consulting Mary's book of birthdays and one or two of the Professor's textbooks, took upon himself to send the Aunts a birthday card of his own design - without letting on to Mary. And a peculiar birthday card it was. It pictured what (to anyone with a smattering of biology) was a human egg being fertilised by a sperm, flanked by a pair of human embryos, with their tails and fishy gill-slits well emphasised.

The key to the puzzle was the timing of the card. It was posted to arrive on the first of November, whereas the official birthday of the ladies fell on the first of August.

Justifiably furious, Mary became a touch less so when she discovered what she might have guessed, that this was no practical joke in the worst of taste, but yet another tactical move in what Hodge looked upon as his Great Re-rooting Campaign: getting little humans who are shod and loose and lost, in time no less than in space, to cease cutting themselves off from the Great Non-human that They Are, and Ever Were, and Ever Shall Be. In this instance, Beaston and all that. Typical, according to Hodge, of Manbridge goofiness was the elaborate pretence of its citizens that they are *only* human and spring to life all ready-made in the maternity ward.

Instant people, off the shelf, family size. Just as if their blessed cars arrived by stork, or turned up under gooseberry bushes. As if, emerging svelte and shiny from the very end of the assembly line, they were to wash their windscreen-wiper hands of all the rest of it, pooh-poohing with their exhausts all that disgusting prenatal engineering. Instant cars, born fitted with their registration plates.

Mary's aunts were, to say the least, even less amused than Mary. It was the postman who had a good laugh.

Also it wasn't Mary, but the bystanders in the park, who were entertained when Hodge daily insisted on flattening himself against and embracing a tree, or extending his arms along the boughs of a sapling. While warming more and more to his message - summed up in what he called his sloggan (sic) BE YOUR SIZE! - she wished to high heaven he'd find less provocative ways of getting people to grow up and out that didn't have the reverse effect, and moreover bring on one of those headaches of his.

There was a further worry - all the more niggling on account of its vagueness. For as long as Mary could remember there had been rumours about the ruthless activities of a secret department of State called MI 13, and of an even more sinister unofficial organisation known as CAUTION - (spelled out: Campaign Against Unmanbridgian Tendencies and Insidious Opinions Nationwide). Hodge's message, she felt sure, was just the sort of thing those bodies existed to discredit and suppress, by whatever means. And she had no way of concealing it and keeping him under wraps... In fact, there were moments when she almost wished that two other people had discovered him, half-dead, on the high Moor, and taken him under their wing.

Such - it's a fair sample to be going on with - was life with Hodge Podge in Manbridge City during the twelve months or so following his arrival.

14

SPLODGE

Partly with some vague idea of treating Hodge to a thorough soaking in his beloved Nature, and partly to drag him away to regions which offered less scope for disaster, Mary planned excursions to some of the more interesting and scenic attractions of the countryside, with its wide variety of wild animals and bird-life and plants.

Commencing with the sewage plant.

At least, that was the way it turned out. She had proposed that they should visit a famous beauty spot at the top of a hill commanding a view of the whole of Manbridge. Also, (on a clear day, which this was) of all the country roundabout, as far as the Great Moor of Kreep to the east, and the coast to the south. Mary proposed, but Hodge disposed. On the way out it wasn't the scenery - the charming landscape and bright skyscape - that held his attention but rows of grubby farm buildings, and machinery scooping up mud and sugar-beet and potatoes, and a repulsive concrete slab of a mill-cum-bakery. She had to explain what everything was for and how it worked, no matter how boring. Why? Why because it was all part of his digestive system, his belly: and who wouldn't be interested in his belly? So what she didn't know she made up, just to keep him quiet.

Further along towards the scenic look-out they had to drop into a valley, which might have been pretty enough if it hadn't been taken over by the aforementioned sewage works. An impressive installation it was, too - the only one serving Manbridge. Hodge insisted on a minute inspection. Mary couldn't have been less fascinated by the rotary filters tirelessly squeaking and gurgling and dribbling away - to say nothing of the sludge beds and splodge tanks and squelching influents and effluents - while Hodge couldn't have been more fascinated. The smell (in case you've never been exposed to it) was earthy, a rich country smell that can only be described as at the opposite end of the scale from Chanel Number Five. Breathing deeply, Hodge inhaled it as if it were lilies of the valley.

"Mananus!", intoned reverently and repeatedly to the puzzled official, called for some brisk improvisation on Mary's part. She explained that her companion was a junior member of the royal family of the Kaffertiti Islands, and his dearest wish was to become a sanitary engineer and sweeten up the place. Not quite sure of the protocol, the official gave a nervous salute.

After what seemed hours she managed to tear Hodge away from it all and draw his attention to higher things.

Well yes, the splendid views of Manbridge town and the surrounding country which they had set out early that morning to enjoy did meet with his gracious approval - for a minute or two.

What really excited him, however, was a more distant scene. Far to the south he could just make out the white shoreline and the shimmering blue of the Perilous Sea, and on the very edge of it a lofty and many-pinnacled fortress. At once it captured Hodge's imagination. Castle Godsea was its name, said Mary. Though dating from the Dark Ages it was still inhabited - by a remarkable community. What were they up to? She thought they were a kind of upside-down people. Was it that Mary didn't know or couldn't find the words, or that she had her reasons for reticence? Anyway he was left with the conviction that Godsea held a special enchantment, and was destined to be of decisive importance for him. From this time onwards the mystery and charm of that Castle was never far from his thoughts. It served as an Eldorado or New Jerusalem around which his vague images of all that was lovely and luminous and innocent - and unmanbridgian - could take shape and play.

Mary sensed his mood. What an in-and-out choke of a chap he was (she said to herself), what an absurdly variable and often far-too-rich a mix of a man! The merest flip, and he'd gone over from foul excretions to pure ecstasies, from sanitation to sanctification, from the unclean obscurities of Earth to the pure and generous Light of Heaven! And back again!

What next caught his attention was a sparkling sheet of silver in the middle distance, nestling in a fold of the hills. Manbridge reservoir, Mary explained. It was a grievous mistake, she realised, as soon as the words were out of her mouth. Nothing would satisfy him but a conducted tour, not of the beauties of the lake or the varieties of wildfowl on it, but of the unpleasing building at the end that housed the pumps, filters, and pipework. But this time Mary, unable to take any more plumbing, sat tight in the car and let him get on with his inspection alone. It didn't take long. After five minutes he emerged rapidly from the building, seen off by a loud-voiced character explaining that some people had work to do. And that he wasn't going to be told by some loony that a twelve-inch water-main was his blasted gullet.

"Au reservoir," retorted Mary, and made a very rude gesture.

Hodge was silent, and not a little crestfallen, on the way home. She couldn't remember having ever seen a face more expressive than his. One registering, like the surface of that lake in the hills, every slightest variation of the weather. Other people had a certain useful opacity behind which to hide their feelings. Not Hodge. If anyone could be described as transparent, here was that one. You could certainly see through his headaches (he was having one now), the reason for them being, as a rule, only too apparent.

Through the days following that excursion, he didn't talk about it at all, but instead turned out sketch after sketch. Which he showed her with his usual excitement, mixed (she thought) with some less typical but not altogether unwelcome nervousness. A shade less cocksure, he was, as if he were slightly doubtful about their reception, and didn't altogether take for granted her understanding of and agreement with what meant so much to him.

Really he needn't have worried.

The overall message of those drawings was becoming plain enough to her. If any doubts or difficulties remained they were cleared

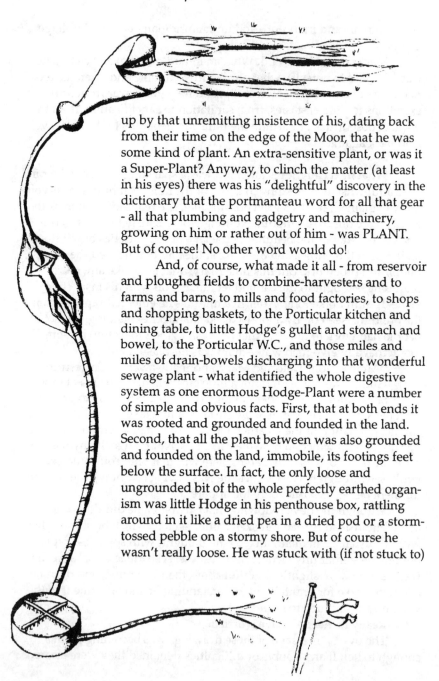

up by that unremitting insistence of his, dating back
from their time on the edge of the Moor, that he was
some kind of plant. An extra-sensitive plant, or was it
a Super-Plant? Anyway, to clinch the matter (at least
in his eyes) there was his "delightful" discovery in the
dictionary that the portmanteau word for all that gear
- all that plumbing and gadgetry and machinery,
growing on him or rather out of him - was PLANT.
But of course! No other word would do!

And, of course, what made it all - from reservoir
and ploughed fields to combine-harvesters and to
farms and barns, to mills and food factories, to shops
and shopping baskets, to the Porticular kitchen and
dining table, to little Hodge's gullet and stomach and
bowel, to the Porticular W.C., and those miles and
miles of drain-bowels discharging into that wonderful
sewage plant - what identified the whole digestive
system as one enormous Hodge-Plant were a number
of simple and obvious facts. First, that at both ends it
was rooted and grounded and founded in the land.
Second, that all the plant between was also grounded
and founded on the land, immobile, its footings feet
below the surface. In fact, the only loose and
ungrounded bit of the whole perfectly earthed organism was little Hodge in his penthouse box, rattling
around in it like a dried pea in a dried pod or a storm-
tossed pebble on a stormy shore. But of course he
wasn't really loose. He was stuck with (if not stuck to)

the Plant for his life-needs. Little Hodge was a tiny section of the stem of Big Hodge. How long could the little one survive, disconnected from the tap of the kitchen sink, for example? His real mouth was drinking all the while from that reservoir in the hills, and the intervening water mains were Hodge quenching his unquenchable thirst. Why, he even incorporated that nasty turncock man.

All of this, and heaps and heaps more of the kind, was clear enough to Mary. But Hodge was taking no chances. His sketches were replete with hints, ranging from subtle to unnecessarily crude, that Hodge was nothing if not the whole Plant. That he really did extend all the way from the sucking pipework in the water-works to the spewing pipework in the sewage-works. To rub it in, he drew at one end of the system - of his true Alimentary Canal - a rather horrible pair of lips, and at the other a rather fine pair of trousers - Hodge's new trousers flying triumphantly on a flagpole. Pennants for raising and lowering at least once daily, he explained. Quite unnecessarily. But then a lot of the things he explained, and did, were profoundly unnecessary, in her view. The ridiculous fellow did so overdo everything, run things into the ground. But then, bless his heart, his point was precisely that he *was* run into the ground, as much as any plant, all along the line! If he was nutty, at least he was a ground-nut!

Her difficulty, nearly always, wasn't understanding what he meant but feeling what he felt. Was this Hodge-Podge of a man an essentially explosive mixture, while Mary-Mary-Quite-Contrary was just plosive, or even implosive? Emotionally lacking, withdrawn, incurious, small-minded? No! She was sure it wasn't anything like as simple as that. Hodge was not *all* right, and she was not *all* wrong. Something suspicious, something that made her uneasy, something wrongheaded - yes, *wrongheaded* was the word - was going on. And Detective Mary Porticule was determined to find out exactly what it was.

Meanwhile, the things he *got* up to were her best clues to what he *was* up to, she reckoned. Better, at a guess, than his earnest and increasingly eloquent, but often contradictory attempts to explain himself.

For instance, there was the Kaffertiti affair -

15

KAFFERTITI AND AFTERMATH

The Professor received a telephone bill which seemed twice what it should have been, or more. He made a fuss about it, to no effect. He refused to pay. There followed the usual threats of disconnection, and warnings of the ruinous cost of re-connection. More fuss and mutual accusations eventually produced the information that several long-distance calls, totalling upwards of two hours, had been made from the Professor's number. No doubt about it. Calls to where? To the Kaffertiti Islands, if you please! To *where*, for God's sake? In vain he protested that neither he nor his daughter knew where those Islands were, let alone knew any of the islanders - and that the telephone company had got its wires even more crossed than usual.

While this row was in progress Hodge remained on the sidelines, apparently taking no interest. In fact, the horrid truth might never have come out, if Mary hadn't remembered one of his sketches, showing a Hodge whose extended ears and mouth encompassed the Earth, including a region clearly marked KAFFERTITI.

Kaffertiti And Aftermath

His explanation, pieced together and edited by a tightly self-controlled Mary, was that, learning from the telephone directory the wondrous news that he had grown ears and a voice-box in the Kaffertiti Islands, it had seemed a shame - even irresponsible - not to make use of them. But why, for God's sake, those lousy Islands? Because Mary herself had connected him with them, on that visit to the sewage works. Since then he'd felt somehow linked to the place. But why did those hideously long-distance calls have to go on for so long? Because neglecting to exercise your limbs could mean you lost the use of them, and were in danger of creeping paralysis. And so on. All sounding utterly reasonable to their guest, utterly unreasonable and infuriating to his long-suffering host and hostess. Hodge's exasperating air of virtuous puzzlement seemed quite genuine. What harm had he done? None whatever, that he could follow. Besides, he'd made friends with such a dear old lady in those Islands. She wasn't lousy, he was sure.

It was only after much pleading with her dad, and much apparent penitence on the part of Hodge, that he was allowed to stay on.

Mary hoped against hope that this crisis would do something to alert Hodge to the use and the importance of money.

Her hope was dashed when, the very next day, as a mark of contrition and to calm her down, he lovingly presented her with an expensive box of chocolates. Where had he got the money from? From nowhere, he replied in his most charming manner. Nobody in the shop had asked him for any.

For two strong reasons she put up with Hodge the Menace - Hodge the Scourge of the Porticules - and as good as told the Professor that if Hodge went she would go with him. The first, of course, was that she was in love with the man. The second, again of course, was that she knew that, behind even his most perverse and idiotic behaviour, there lurked something hugely important. Something that she'd begun to get, and that he hadn't finished getting and giving. Not by a long chalk. Something that they had to work at and work out together.

What was that mysterious something?

It was not a something you *got* - just like that - and then it was yours forever. It was something more elusive, that you can get all right yet get all wrong (which sounds silly, but isn't), nevertheless can't do without. Something that's as much a question as an answer.

At least the question part of it could be put positively and clearly in four little words: "How big am I?" Or, less succinctly: "How extensive do I have to be to be myself and all there - or, better, all here?" Or, if you like, "Where is it that I stop and my world starts?" Or, to use the car salesman's jargon, "What is my basic model, or minimal version, and what are my optional extras?" Or, again, "What can I do without and still be me? How many things do I need to be myself? Hodge tells me I need hundreds and thousands of things, all neatly fitted together and ranging from a vast and clear water-vessel in the hills to a small and splodgy water-vessel in the valley, with still smaller blood-vessels in between - the whole watery contraption spread over I-don't-know-how-many square miles. All right, I reply, but why go so far afield? And why, having gone so far, stop there?"

In fact, Mary concluded, it all boiled down to that well-worn question, "Who am I?" That, in essence, was the query and the quest that underlay all his Hodgepodgery, however little or much he recognised it. The burning obsessive quest for self-knowledge was the fire in his belly, the place he was coming from, the driving force of him. Yes, she was sure of it. What's more, she warmed to that fire. It was hers, too - burning with less of a roar and crackle, but every bit as brightly - and had been since childhood.

Now among Mary's friends and acquaintances there were not a few whose favourite question was this same "Who am I?" These she divided into three camps, which, in her funny way and for ease of reference, she called the Psychers and the Psitters and the Psadhanas. And her hope was that Hodge - who was still, in spite of all her efforts to socialise him, a loner and the prince of misfits - might find, in one or other of these groups, just a few kindred spirits. So that at last he would begin to settle down somewhat in Manbridge and give himself - as well as herself and her dad - less of a hard time.

And then, of course, there was just a chance that some of them might learn the odd thing or two from him.

First, she took him along to the Psychers.

One lecture, followed by question time (in which, to her great relief, he took no part) was enough. His only reaction at the time was to hold his head in his hands and pull faces as if he were in pain.

Next day, however, he turned out a macabre series of sketches in which Hodge (recognisable by his spiky mane) is pointing inquiringly at himself and being publicly hanged for his pains, while the hangman - with a dubious expression on his face - is pointing at various food-stuffs which an old lady is offering him.

Pictures which, given a good deal of help from the artist, Mary

interpreted as follows. These Psychers aren't in the slightest degree interested in Who They Are, but only in How They Feel. "Who am I?" is a formula for reciting, not a question for answering. What they are asking is: "Do I *really* loathe porridge and prunes and rice pudding, or do I *suppose* I do because Mum forced the stuff down my throat? What do I *really* like eating, drinking, doing, having done to me? And all that sort of thing. Getting the answers right is being Myself, genuine and not phoney, not so darn screwed up. As for this True Identity of mine, I don't know what you're talking about."

Such, decoded, was Hodge's impression of her friends (well, acquaintances) the Psychers. Come to think of it, it was her impression too, though she would have put it more politely.

Their visit to the Psitters turned out to be even less productive.

They met - all six of them, eight with Hodge and Mary - in an ancient disused wine-cellar at the centre of town. Cold and dank it was, but whitewashed spotless. Also poky and low-ceilinged. Even Mary had to crouch to get through the arched door without braining herself. The leader was a large and severe stubble-headed lady, her chalky pallor as well as her massiveness enhanced by her black tights.

They sat on cow-pat-size and cow-pat-shape-and-colour cushions in a circle while the lady demonstrated the required posture. She called it the Gnarl or Yogaknit. You had to interweave your arms with your crossed legs, and fan your fingers out on the floor. Your back had to be straight, your eyes half-closed.

This posture, the lady was explaining, put you in a position to address the problem of Whether You Really Exist… The correct answer, it seemed, was that you don't - thank goodness!

Quite politely, Hodge said that, while he could just about make the Gnarl or Yogaknit, he couldn't make the connection between the posture and the problem. Let alone the answer.

"You will, with practice," came the curt reply. "Just hold the posture, and note whatever thoughts and feelings crop up, and let them go."

She tinkled a bell, to signal the start of whatever-it-was…

After twenty minutes of whatever-it-was - it seemed to Hodge more like twenty hours - she tinkled once more.

"Well," she demanded sharply, "how did you get on? What came up for you? What sort of stuff?"

Half growling and half sobbing, Hodge blurted out: "I'll tell you what! Pain! Terrible pain! What the hell am I doing this absurd thing for? What's it got to do with Who I am? How long is the silly old woman going to keep this up? This cushion is stuffed with rocks. I'll die if I can't scratch my back. So I don't exist. Well, isn't being the undertaker at my own funeral ghastly enough, without this self-torture? I hate the creature's coiffure. I think she's an overgrown black beetle. The smell in here…"

"Very good," cut in the lady hurriedly, interrupting a flow that threatened to go on indefinitely. "That's what we have to do. Watch all that filthy rubbish coming up. And let go of it."

Hodge was not to be put off. "So this - ha, ha! - is What We Really Are! Filthy rubbish! Or is it rubbish bins?"

"Of course it isn't. The very opposite, in fact. We have to go on watching the stuff and nonsense coming up until it dies down. Then what's left is Emptiness. No me. Nothing."

"And how long - ha, ha again! - will it take me to find out there's no me to find out anything?"

Controlling herself with evident difficulty, she spelled out the answer: "Given enough practice, a few can get there even in this life. It's just possible. But in your case most unlikely. I suspect you will need hundreds or thousands of lives."

"Or longer," spat out Hodge, "and thank heaven for that!"

He rose shakily and painfully to his feet, only to bash his head on the ceiling.

Off he staggered, bent double. Mary spread her hands at the company - whether the gesture indicated dismay, or apology, or helplessness, or sort-that-one-out-if-you-can, she hardly knew herself - and followed close on his heels.

As a last resort she decided to try the Psadhaners, exposing them to Hodge, and Hodge to them, more out of an exasperated and resigned curiosity than out of hope. These excursions into Who-Am-I? country couldn't go more awry, she felt, than they had done already.

A service (or should one say puja?) was in full swing in the temple (or should one say mutt?). Creeping in at the back, Mary and Hodge joined the company of a hundred or more seated on the marble floor. It was a shiny, luxurious interior, marble-lined throughout, brilliantly lit, and heavy with incense. The congregation - men and women of all colours and ages and not a few children - were reciting in monotone the words "Who am I?" three times, followed by a loud handclap and a deep bow directed at the figure at the business end of the mutt. On him everyone's attention was concentrated. Many of the devotees, swinging from side to side, appeared to be far gone in ecstasy. Mary toyed with the idea that the incense was really a kind of general anaesthetic, perhaps ether.

From where Mary and Hodge squatted at the back, they couldn't see much of what was going on up front. What they did make out was a very lofty and ornate marble pillar or pedestal, and seated cross-legged on top of it a hazy figure of a man bare down to the waist.

He was gesturing vigorously and apparently talking, but what he was saying didn't stand the ghost of a chance against all that recitation and clapping. Even in the rare and very brief intervals of comparative silence in the mutt, it was almost impossible to hear a word he said. The height of his pedestal ensured that he remained out of earshot. A fact which seemed to fuel rather than damp down the worshippers' fervour...

Twenty minutes of this was enough for Hodge. He made for the rear door, Mary following.

Leaving at the same time was a young man who had the radiant look, Mary told herself, of Moses coming down from the Mount. "May we speak to you?" she asked.

"Of course," he said with warmth. "Let's have a coffee together."

In the café she asked the young man - who'd introduced himself as Prem-Prem - why the noise in the mutt was so loud, and the pedestal was so high, that nobody could hear what the holy man sitting on top of it might be saying.

"Yes, tell us," urged Hodge, in his too-polite, somewhat ominous voice.

"Well it's like this," replied Prem-Prem, unruffled. "We keep on asking energetically who we are because our beloved Sadguru wants us to. It's as simple as that. If we go on like this we're sure to hit on the answer one fine day. Meantime, *he's* the one who sees Who he is, absolutely, and therefore deserves our adoration. We love him with a very special kind of love, and this does change our lives."

"So this seeing Who you are is terribly difficult?"

"Our Sadguru up there is saying it's the easiest thing in the world. We - or most of us down here - know it's the most difficult - for the likes of us."

"Either you're lying, or he is," said Hodge, matter-of-factly.

Mary kicked him under the table, but he went on: "In any case, seeing Who you are would be a catastrophe. It would mean razing that pedestal to the ground, and instead of a Sadguru you'd have a Happy Friend."

Much to Mary's relief and surprise, Prem-Prem laughed loud and long at that.

"And then," he said, "we'd have to the turn the temple into a community centre, with Mothers' Meeting on Monday afternoon, Cubs on Tuesday evening, and Bingo on Saturday night! Hurray!"

Yes, he really was a delightful fellow.

But she had to agree with Hodge, afterwards, that in general the Psadhanas were no more interested in Who they are than those Psychers and Psitters had been. Rather less so, perhaps. Why, even a chitter-chatter of parrots, reciting *Who am I?* till their dear little tongues wore out, would never go so far as *actively* to ensure that the question wasn't a question but a meaningless incantation, and that anyway the answer was inaudible.

"All the same," added Hodge reflectively, "I'm not sure about that chap. I've a funny feeling about him. Could it be a *premonition?"*

"Any more jokes as feeble as that, and I'll jilt the joker," retorted Mary. "Add that one to your premonitions."

That's what Mary said, off the top of her beautiful head. What she was thinking was more like this. With the possible exception of Prem-Prem, none of those Who-am-I-ers, whether Psychers, or Psitters, or Psadhanas, was the tiniest bit interested in what she privately called

Hodge's Predicament: to wit, where does one stop and one's world begin? Let alone able to help him solve it.

Never mind. That was her job. Her secret, long-term ambition, let's say.

Meanwhile, their sampling of those three species of Who-am-I-ers wasn't a total waste of time and a write-off. Why, even Hodge brought himself to admit that there was a kind of honesty about the Psychers (with their appeal to experience), and a kind of rootedness about the Psitters (with their plantlike posture), and a kind of abandon about the Psadhanas (with their wholeheartedness), which appealed. Yes, appealed even to Hodge. Oh, he was a slippery customer all right! Protean. When you thought you had him taped he'd casually unveil a quite different side of himself. You never knew where you were with the fellow. In fact, Hodge wasn't so much a proper noun, Mary reckoned, as an irregular verb. Not so much a rational number as a surd. As absurd as the square root of minus one...

...and even more indispensable.

16

WIDE-EYED WORLDS

I t would be wrong, in fact, to give the impression that life with Hodge was all storm and stress and saying sorry to offended parties. There were whole days when he behaved in a distinctly civilised fashion, and you could almost mistake him for a regular, died-in-the-wool Manbridgian. And there certainly were individual Manbridgians, such as the enigmatic but good-natured Prem-Prem, that he took to immediately.

Such also was Georgie, an old friend of the Porticule family. A keen amateur pilot, he flew a four-seater out of Manbridge airport. Simultaneously it occurred to him and to Mary that an airborne Hodge might respond favourably to the spectacle of Manbridge lights, noted for their colour-range and brilliance, on a clear night.

He responded all right. Up there, it seemed to Mary that he glowed with an intensity to match that jewelled panorama, stretching in all directions beyond the eye's reach, each gem marvellously set off against its deep velvety-black background. For once he was dumb-founded. Only afterwards on the ground was he sufficiently recovered to explain that he saw the stunning beauty and brightness of those jewels - ruby, emerald, amethyst, chalcedony, onyx and pure diamond - as no mere finery worn by Lady Earth, no applied or artificial adorn-ment, no make-up or get-up, but her natural complexion, her nocturnal beauty-spots or plumage. As much *her* as the peacock's tail is him, and even more spectacular and alive.

So successful was that flight that they repeated it next morning. The air was still very clear, and even seen from five thousand feet the plan of the city and its environs was etched with sharp precision.

Georgie pointed out a spot, near the city centre, which he said marked the Porticules' penthouse. For Hodge it was himself. He was the spider lurking there at the nub of that vast, irregular, fine-spun web. Or rather, with sensitive arachnid feet feeling himself along each radial thread to the very end, he - attacop Hodge Podge - was the whole web and every fly and firefly caught in it.

No, that wouldn't do, he decided. Extruded from their parent spinnerets the threads are no longer the spider. Webs take leave of their spinner, but roots stay with their stem. That old vegetable model, dating from those early days on the edge of the Great Moor of Kreep, was the right one, his true portrait. Of course he wasn't an ordinary creeper among creepers or plant among plants, but one of an altogether superior order, a Superplant, *the* Superplant. And here was this unique specimen delightedly holding out a mirror at arm's length (some arm, five thousand feet of it!) to view itself luxuriating, wrapping itself around the Earth! What a sight! How vivid and vigorous and varied, how very Superhodge! Such proliferation of roots! Some, not dead-straight but alive-straight and smooth-curving, converging and diverging and gathering into all manner of nodules. Others, similarly flowing and nodulated, but with a bluish glint and gleam. Many others, very fine-threaded, wobbling nervously all over the place. And just a few, majestically forthright and sturdy, coming to a head at regular intervals in great four-petalled blossoms reminiscent of wallflowers. Honorary Cruciferae, according to Hodge, showing off his knowledge of the botany books on the Professor's shelves.

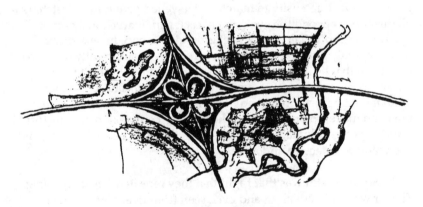

And - and this was the point, the crux of the crux of the matter - all of it One Plant, One Conscious Living Being, who is none other than Mr Hodge Podge, late of Beaston and now of Manbridge, feeling himself into the whole of himself, all the way to the last and latest questing tips of his finest rootlets.

"Or Miss Mary Porticule," he added. A thoughtful afterthought, typically condescending.

"I see what you mean," she replied, in her best you're-not-provoking-me voice, as she gazed down at the Creeper from her side of the aircraft. "But I can't say I feel it. I still have a sense of being little me, little Mary Porticule strapped and belted into this little seat in Georgie's little plane. Sorry! Am I being petty, or suppressing something, or out-to-lunch, or narrow-minded? Is there something wrong with me? Am I supposed to feel - what's the word I want? - *creepy?* All elongated and tingly and goose-pimply and shredded and threadbare, like a neurotic and hypersensitive road-map? Do you mean to say-?"

Unable to take this waffling (his word for it) any longer, Hodge broke in: "I keep begging you to listen to what you say, and then you'll begin to feel what you feel. You said to me this morning: 'Would you like to fly today?' You did *not* say: 'Would you like to sit in the plane while it flies today?' Nor do you say now: 'Help, help! I've been caught up and hoisted sky-high, like a lamb by an eagle!' No. The lamb's become the eagle and the eagle's become the lamb. They've merged, are inseparable. You feel yourself airborne as the whole of what's airborne, and you're taking it easy and in your stride. Up here you're relying on your wings as unquestioningly as down here you rely on your legs. All that rot about being a little thing, strapped motionless inside a big thing that's whizzing along at three hundred miles an hour, five thousand feet up, is eyewash and drivel and apple-sauce and pure baloney -"

"What a filthy, indigestible hodgepodge of metaphors!"

"Don't put me off! You fly. That's how you talk, how you feel, how you are. And - do listen to me! - *if you can feel yourself all the way to your wing-tips up here (and you do, you do!) you can feel yourself all the way to your root-tips down there.* There's no stopping half way, all edgy and timid and mock-modest. In for a penny, in for a pound. So come off it, come off pretending to be little Mary Porticule. You're unviable, you won't work for two ticks, you aren't Mary, till you're all these things and worldwide. You have to be that big. You're a fragment of yourself till you are all that you see down there, and a jolly sight more besides."

To which Mary had no answer, no way of formulating her vague feeling of unease.

She knew in her guts that this aggravating, tactless, absurd, explosive enfant terrible of hers was right - but far from a hundred-per-cent right. And that she, who loved the creature, was wrong - but far from a hundred-per-cent wrong.

How could this be?

Not till much later did that instinctive knowledge, that irrepressible hunch of hers, take shape and begin to make sense. As we shall see.

True to form, Hodge followed up these flights with a spate of sketches showing a Hodge whose arms had spread themselves into plane-wings and whose feet had come together in a plane tail. One of these sketches he cut out and stuck onto the metal frame of a terrestrial globe belonging to Mary. Who observed him, in one of his trances, turning the globe for minutes on end while the plane of course stayed still. He seemed to think that the best way to get around is to let the planet do the travelling - to let the tail wag the dog, so to say.

This gave Mary an idea. Encouraged by his eager study of all the astronomical literature he could find in the apartment, she proposed a visit to Manbridge Observatory, a very well equipped installation at the summit of the only mountain within easy distance from Manbridge town.

Hodge was keen. So keen he made her nervous. She got him to promise (ha, ha - as if he knew what the word meant!) to behave himself and not try - all starry-eyed - to teach real astronomers their job. Or to invite their ridicule with his ideas about Lady Earth.

Hodge and Mary were shown everything, peeked through the great telescope, given V-I-P treatment.

Well, you can imagine Hodge's excitement at Jupiter and her moons, at the rings of Saturn, and Mars, the red planet. And more particularly at how the Milky Way resolved itself into a Sahara of sand-grains, each a star comparable with our Sun. And at the further resolution of some of these suns into other Saharas, their sands caught up and spiralling in the cosmic whirlwind. Wonders upon wonders, leaving him speechless.

But he did recover sufficiently to ask some questions - and with characteristic speed to cotton onto the answers - that clearly showed where his chief interest lay. Which wasn't so much in the staggering numbers and sizes and spacing and time-scale of those heavenly bodies as in (to quote Hodge) "how they *place* one another."

Their guide was one Dr Fox - a youthful and somewhat pert employee of Manbridge University who knew Professor Porticule, which helped. Or did it? Mary wondered. Though amused at the naiveté of Hodge's language, he obligingly began by explaining how we on Earth can estimate the distances of the Moon, and the Sun, and the planets of our Solar System. The telescope they were now looking through at the Moon is matched by another telescope on the far side of the Earth. Each of these instruments, trained on the Moon, has its own angle on that body. Half humorously and half humoringly, he described Mother Earth as sporting a handsome pair of observatory-eyes, some four thousand miles apart, which give her binocular vision of her heavenly boy friend Mr Moon and enable her to place him quite satisfactorily. Just as those Mr-Hodge-eyes, some four inches apart, give him binocular vision of his earthly girl friend, Miss Porticule, enabling him to place her quite satisfactorily. And prevent him bumping into her.

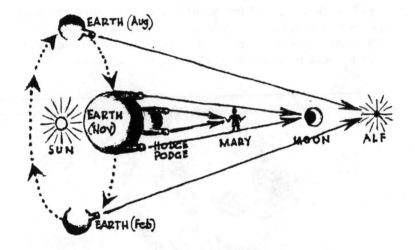

"Talk about being wide-eyed!" exclaimed Hodge, reverently.

"That's nothing, mere chicken-feed!" replied Dr Fox.

In his best show-the-children manner, he plunged deeper than ever into Hodgespeak. "The stars - I'm talking about the wide boys that have ringed themselves with planets, that have grown up into lovely solar systems - now they're *really* wide-eyed! Take our own Sun system, in which Earth's annual orbit is two hundred million miles across. To get two reasonably different angles on one of his nearer friends - such as that bright lad up there called Alf Centauri - he views Alf from this telescope today, and then from this same telescope again six months from today: which means, you'll understand, two hundred million miles from here. And he locates Alf at the spot where the two converging lines of vision meet. Binocular vision again, this time with one eye six months *later* than the other… Which must be even more fun than having one eye *browner* than the other!"

Hodge, seemingly unaware of any chiacking, was jumping for joy. "Oh isn't it marvellous being so elastic, so in and out! Man pin-pointing man, planet pin-pointing planet, star pin-pointing star - that's me! To probe deeper into the universe, take on more of it. I'm the Hodge who's eyeing Mary, the Earth who's intent on the Moon of her delight, the Sun who's all eyes for young Alf Centauri! I'm the lot! Hurray!"

Dealing their guide a hearty wallop on the back, he attached himself once more to the eyepiece of the telescope (and a very nice picture of the Moon's Sea of Tranquillity it presented him with). In fact, Hodge being Hodge, no doubt he'd have preferred a stronger word than *"attached"*. Let's say he *re-grew* that eyepiece, that terrestrial eye.

Dr Fox took the opportunity of giving Mary a knowing wink.

Dr Fox

Coming on the top of all that joshing, it made her jumping mad.

"Mr. Hodge is a most distinguished foreign poet and savant, insufficiently respected in this uncivilised country," she announced, in a grande-dame voice that froze him in his tracks.

And added, sotto voce, "That's about the weight of it, too, you conceited worm! Goodbye!"

The day after that visit to the observatory a concert was held in Manbridge's grandest concert hall, the main part devoted to *The Song of the Sun*, by the celebrated Manbridgian composer Gustavus Painter.

Hodge swore again and again, cross his heart, he'd behave himself if they went along. A promise of special importance, seeing that the only seats Mary could get were in the front row.

And behave himself he did, till the very end of that choral symphony. When, instead of joining in the applause, he acknowledged it, graciously. He stood up - all six-foot-six of him - turned to the audience, and bowed graciously and deeply and repeatedly. The conductor - a bare five-foot-six - hardly got a look in.

There were flashes. People were taking photographs. Mary prayed it wouldn't get into the morning papers.

When, by some miracle, it didn't, and Hodge pleaded so charmingly and sincerely (was that a tear in his eye, the blue one?) that he *did* behave himself - his solar self, of course, and it would have been bad manners to ignore that applause - Mary calmed down quite a lot.

Besides, the poor goof was having yet another of his headaches.

17

GREEN, AMBER, RED

Mary Porticule was puzzled, and worried, and hurt. Did anyone who was really in love avoid these three miseries (she wondered), and remain serenely loving? Lots managed to, probably. And that left her angry with herself, which made a fourth hang-up.

To complete her discomfiture, Hodge made her feel so small, so shrunken.

Here he was (she reflected) cheerfully expanding, expanding, expanding. At the beginning, in that caravan on the edge of the Moor, hand-tools (beg his majesty's pardon: tool-hands) were all his joy. Here, in Manbridge proper, these limb-endings had gone on growing. Every part of him flourished and proliferated, every sense-organ took off, till he was like an exploding rocket. (She tried to forget how brief was the glory of even the most powerful and spectacular of fireworks.) And now, not content with wrapping his tentacles round the Earth, he had to go on to *incorporate* the Earth! And - just like that! - the Solar System. The Galaxy would naturally follow, and nothing less than the Cosmos itself would complete his shopping list. It was only a matter of time. There was no stopping him.

More and more she was convinced that there were two ways of reading Hodge's gigantism - his, and hers: and they didn't fit. He was

so certain that these miserable little Manbridgians, uprooted and shod
and scurrying about like ants of unsound mind, were sick because they
were separate. That, hell-bent on amputating themselves from their
Body - from their terrestrial and solar and galactic and cosmic physique
- they were enfeebled, crippled, lonely, worried stiff. And that he, the
great Doctor Hodge Podge from foreign parts, was none of these things,
thank the Lord. He saw his enlargement, by these inevitable if not easy
cosmic stages, as his healing and his wholing. Yet here the fellow was,
all-too often, giving the lie to these pious sentiments. His behaviour, his
moods and state of health, were giving the game away, were letting the
cat out of the bag. With more and more expansion was coming more
and more resentment - yes, even cattishness at times - worse and more
frequent headaches, ever-increasing stress. Yes, *stress!* Of all her friends
he was by far the most at odds with the world as it is, the most ill-fitting
and difficult. And the most stuck-up, too. So goddam sure he was right.
So goddam sure everyone else was wrong. Mr Megahodge, that was his
name, and she didn't like it a bit.

And yet, and yet! The goddam crazy thing was that he *was* right.
Nothing, nothing at all about this ridiculous and fascinating and exasperating creature could be written off, rubbished, dismissed as the
deplorably high price-tag attached to the admirable part of him. Or as
mere value-added-tax, so to speak. He was as indivisible and clean and
salty as the sea wind. He blew through Manbridge like great gusts of
fresh air, even if it was too often so bitterly cold it gave you frost-bite.

Of all the double-binds that Mary had got caught in during her
short life, here was the most tricky and the most binding. It was no good
at all looking for some middle way or third horn of the dilemma to
impale oneself on, some reasonable compromise (such as "Here I stop,
at a good deal more than a decently trousered and shirted and tooled-
up Hodge Podge or Mary Porticule, but well short of those silly
Kaffertiti islands"). No good whatever. He was absolutely right: one *is*
very big. *And* there was something terribly wrong about his rightness:
one is also very small. She'd told herself this before. And she'd tell
herself this again, and again, though it seemed to make no sense at all.

To translate all this into personal terms, he was in some indefin-
able way her healing, and yet quite often he seemed to be tearing her
apart, heart and mind and body. Himself also.

All she could do was hang on, and trust to goodness that time and
circumstance - and love - would come up with a solution.

In the dim hope of getting light on this dilemma - and, just conceivably, resolving it - Mary thumbed once more through the many drawings that Hodge turned out at this time. What they all aimed to show (she figured) was that objects of every grade from galoshes to galaxies are for wearing: and that they are alive and well when you put them on, and dudder than duds and deader than dead when you take them off. That refusing to *be* the world is blue murder - homocide and geocide and cosmocide - and *being* it is being the life and soul of the cosmic party. That willy-nilly you are the heart of the matter, and to blazes with false modesty. In short, pure Megahodge again, the mixture as before. Well, what did she expect?

Nevertheless, it did put an idea into her head. A desperate one, perhaps, but then the situation called for desperate measures. Hodge was *green*, the archetypal Green Man. Not a washed-out pea-green but vivid emerald, a natural who, you could say, was determined to be more eco than Mother Nature herself. As *the* econut, he ought to go down well with (beg their pardon!) other econuts, and they with him. *Ought* was the operative word. You never could tell with Dodgy Hodge. Or rather, you *could* tell. It was a pretty safe bet that he'd succeed, against all the odds, in finding some way of giving offence, and taking it. She wouldn't put it past him to disagree with his echo. Let alone his eco.

Never mind. Anything was worth trying.

Having given him the longest and severest curtain lecture yet, and extracted servile promises (for what they were worth) of good

Dr. Seuridge   H. P.

behaviour, she took him along to a supper party at the house of an old friend called Dr Severidge, a colleague of her dad's in the Biology Department of the University. Also present were his wife Margery, and half a dozen guests. A cheerful, pleasant, socially responsible lot, as green as they come, Mary thought; but allowed herself to wonder why the younger men had to wear such luxuriant ecobeards (as though a beard-preservation order had been served on them by the Local Authority), and the younger women had to wear home-knitted ecowoollies of indeterminate shape reminiscent of insufficiently filled bean-bags. Such modesty! the more beautiful those people were the more they hid the fact. All, however, were deeply concerned (as she was, of course) with such urgent issues as whale-hunting, the destruction of species by pesticides, the squandering of fossil fuels, atmospheric and marine pollution, holes punctured in the ozone layer, the felling of rain forests, and so on. And all (she felt sure) were aware of the ever-growing evidence that Gaia, our much abused space-platform, is in fact a special order of living organism.

It was the last of these topics which she hoped against hope would ring joy-bells of agreement in Hodge. Which would in turn resonate strongly around the assembled company, and a good time would be had by all.

He was very quiet throughout supper - a vegan affair, attention-demanding, chewy, and noisy with celery-munching, not conducive to an easy flow of wit and wisdom, anyway. Afterwards, Margery Severidge, who'd been primed by Mary privily and well in advance, became lyrical about Mother Earth and her life. Which elicited several gratifying grunts and nods from Hodge, and even one or two of his rare smiles.

So far, so very good, said Mary to herself, half persuaded that surely the till-now-green evening wouldn't suddenly turn amber and red on them - specially if she were to think up some excuse for pushing off early.

You've guessed right. It was not to be.

Exactly what it was that sparked Hodge off, that lit his fuse to such explosive effect, Mary never quite grasped. On reflection, she could scarcely believe it was Dr Severidge's casual and would-be-humorous description of Spaceship Earth as an inscrutable old darling of a vessel, and a very, very different number from the gang of vandals and nitwits on her passenger list.

"What she must be thinking of us! Always supposing," added Dr Severidge, "she has a mind to think with."

"Idiot!" muttered Hodge, and it was pretty clear he wasn't referring to Mother Earth.

Though spoken very quietly - almost whispered - it stirred up the Severidge's supper party all right. Nor was the effect dampened by the addition of some barely audible remarks about Manbridge pinheadedness. Plus, after a two-thousand-volt silence, an improbable "Absolute rot-tommy!" thrown in for good measure and to clinch the matter.

The fact is that, when het-up, Hodge had a rather amusing way of inverting words and phrases. He would, for example, blurt out "Hell bloody!", or "Cockpoppy!", or "Hugbum!" in the heat of the moment. But this time the result was more unfortunate than funny. His host's first name, as bad luck would have it, was Tommy. And Tommy was taking the attack on himself very seriously indeed.

Bringing down on the dining table a fist that air-lifted the china and cutlery by inches, he spluttered: "So I'm an idiot, am I? Talking absolute rot? In this country, let me tell you - "

Mary, trembling and near to tears, butted in: "Oh he didn't mean it like that. I swear it. It's the language problem. Sometimes he gets his words terribly mixed up."

Turning to Hodge, she said in her or-else voice: "Explain to Dr Severidge, in a reasonable and civilised way, what you can't quite agree with, and why."

Her fire-extinguisher worked, beyond all expectation. Damped down, he made a heroic effort to save what little was left of the situation.

"I do apologise. Really I do. You see I feel strongly on the subject of Earth. I can't help taking *personally* what you say about her."

"Why personally?" This from a slightly calmer Dr Severidge.

"Because I'm more Earth than I'm Hodge. It's as simple as that. It's a fact I'm stuck with, whether I like it or not. No, I'm not being bloody-minded. Or a whole lot too big for my boots. It's just how things are."

"Explain," said Mary.

"Oh how can I? I do my best. Nobody understands."

This tone of voice was unfamiliar. It sounded to Mary as much like a cry for help as a cry of pain.

"Explain," she repeated, a lot less fiercely.

Green, Amber, Red

"Well, I'll try. I don't mean to be rude, but I have to say it: you people stop at your precious skins, I spill over. You separate yourselves from what you deploy and depend on, I'm continuous with it. I incorporate it, I become it, whatever it happens to be. So I don't grip a bow that stretches 150 horsehairs that scrape four strands of catgut attached to one curved sound-box: *I play the violin.* So I don't, like a rat, infest a ship that sails the sea: *I sail the sea.* So I'm not an item of fragile freight securely strapped in slot 16B in the economy hold of a plane that's flying at 700 m.p.h: *I'm flying Air Manbridge.* I talk like that, and so do you. When you wake up and stop pretending, you *incorporate* the fiddle you play, the ship you sail, the plane you fly. Well, in exactly the same way you and I aren't just seated on Mrs Severidge's easy chairs in her elegant sitting room, that's on the ground floor of number 12/14 Greenshank Street, that meanders through the poshest suburb of Manbridge, that's the proudest city on planet Earth, that's flying round the Sun. No! To the extent that we're all there and alive and with-it we *are* the planet in flight! O happiness!"

"All this blah-blah about your wretched feelings. We're interested in facts; and action." This came from a large, red-faced type called Hank, in no friendly tone of voice.

Catching Mary's eye, Hodge made a valiant effort to play it cool: "It's not only the way I feel. It's the way I am. It's physical fact, and not for lying about. I'm not me, not all there, not right till I'm all I need in order to be me. And that's plenty. What am I without my air and earth and water for a start? Or without my sunlight? I'm much more my Sun than this right arm. I can lose all my limbs, and getting on for half my human body, and still live till I'm a hundred. How many minutes do you give me, cut off from my Sun?"

"I think you are abominably self-centred," said Hank.

"And I think you're idiotically off-centre, eccentric, self-alienated," replied Hodge, giving as good as he got.

"Now then," warned Mary.

"This is all so very inward-looking," said Dr Severidge, and his manner was conciliatory. "So personal, so very subjective, if you see what I mean. Mind you, I'm not denying you have a point."

"All right then," Hodge responded, in like manner. "I'll try to speak more generally. To think that your life and consciousness are bottled up in your skin is - well, pure Manbridge parish pump. The life ON Earth is the life OF Earth. (What an astronomical difference the change of one letter makes!) Our consciousness of Earth is her self-consciousness. Our consciousness of the other planets is her other-consciousness. Put it like this: subject matches object, all the way up and down the scale. As Hodge I see Dr Severidge, as Earth I see Mars, as this developed Star I see -"

"Mystical claptrap!" growled the large one.

"Show me the scalpel that can amputate the one-hundred-and-fifty-pound you" - then, pausing to take another look at the man, Hodge corrected himself - "the two-hundred-and-fifty-pound you from the billion-ton you, without butchering you instantly."

At that, the fellow started up from his chair.

"This is all somewhat intellectual, Mr Hodge," broke in Dr Severidge, in a brave attempt to avert mayhem. "I'm wondering whether it matters so much. In practical terms, I mean."

"It matters because cutting yourself off from Yourself is being unfriendly to your environment - to what you call your environment, but is really you - and must affect your attitude to it profoundly. It's all-round unhealthy. You care for what you are, are careless about what you are not."

"Claptrap!" repeated Hank.

Undeterred, Hodge continued on, "Or put it this way. What could be more environment-unfriendly than *having* an environment instead of *being* it? Sloughing it off as a snake sloughs its skin? Making yourself out to be perhaps a fatal case of organ-rejection? Or - to look at it from Earth's point of view - what greater injury could we do her than amputate the most vital parts of her anatomy (namely ourselves) and set them up on their hind legs as passengers who've come along for the ride and spongers who've come along for the hand-out? What could be more sure to reduce her to imbecility than to attribute every gleam and spark of her intelligence to those same hitch-hikers and spongers, as such? Repeat, *as such*. Why, it's like crediting Leonardo's paintbrush with the Mona Lisa, and making a monkey - or rather a machine - out of the painter. No; vitality and intelligence aren't the sort of merchandise you can box. They leak all over the shop. They flood the place."

"We Greens concern ourselves with practice, not theory - which is always controversial," replied Dr Severidge. "With the specific problems of the Earth, with ecological details about which there's no serious disagreement. I don't hear you talking about them."

"Forgive me for saying that you Greens are really Puce, which is the colour of fleas -"

Catching Mary's eye - talk about dangerous radiation! - he tried again. "Responsible and public-spirited and forgiving and hospitable fleas, but still Earth-parasites. Jumping about and unearthed and therefore in danger of fatal shocks. Now if you were to Earth yourselves, and have the humility and good sense to see eye to eye with and merge with your Hostess - consciously to be of one mind with her when you're minding her business, and of one body with her when you're bodying her forth (which you're doing all the time) - why then you'd serve her even better than you do now. Even better than you do now," repeated Hodge, with the slightly complacent air of a statesman who has found a formula at last.

Whether the rest of them bought it there's no telling. The big one certainly did not.

H. P.

Hank.

"I never heard such crap in all my life," he barked, and started waving a large and knobbly fist. Hodge's reaction was, for him, an unusual one. It was no reaction. He just shrank into his shell. Absented himself from the party, and sat there like a granite statue staring into space.

Which was nothing like as bad (Mary said to herself) as if he'd jumped up and poked that repulsive fellow on the nose...

And that, bar the frostiest leave-taking ever, was the unseemly end of what Mary - bless her heart! - had hoped might turn out to be not so much the Greening of Hodge as the Hodging of the Greens.

What made it worse was the migraine that the episode brought on. By far the severest yet, and it lasted for several days, on and off.

Mary was worried. And apprehensive.

18

THE MERRYGOROUND

That green-amber-red dinner party signalled a change in the flow of Mary's feelings about Hodge. Also vice versa, she suspected. A mutual distancing, a new reserve on both sides, a wariness had come between them. To her he appeared more weighty and not to be shifted, more lofty and out of reach and at odds with all Manbridge than ever, and at the same time more top-heavy. Yes, that was exactly the expression - top-heavy. More dominating, more stubborn, more his own man - which wouldn't have been at all bad if only it didn't make him less her man. But really it's impossible to say clearly how she felt, for the simple reason that she didn't know herself: didn't know from one moment to the next, let alone how she'd feel in five minutes' or five days' time.

It was most unsettling. She had a strong sense that a crisis was looming. Suspense filled the air. An electric charge heralding a God-almighty thunderstorm, if such a thing were possible in deep mid-winter.

All of which was reinforced by two challenging developments on the Hodge front. A pair of more-than-normally-odd items of Radical Hodgepodgery.

Hodge had been devouring, along with every other sort of book the apartment could boast, Mary's well-worn and wide-ranging collection of children's stories. They appeared to go down smoothly enough. In fact he complained that they were a jolly sight too bland, too mild and unadventurous for his taste. Their heroes were timid, their giants stunted, their magicians feeble. He gave Mary to understand that now in *his* world - the real one, of course! - a hero was gloriously heroic, and a giant was gigantic indeed, and a magician worked truly miraculous miracles; and he left her in no doubt about the identity of the World's Wonder who played all three roles to perfection. His Hodgepertise was - astounding!

Thus he, Merlin H. Podge, could (to list just a few of his talents) lengthen or shorten a plank to order without tools or effort, could urigeller coins and other metal objects as if they were plasticene or putty, could make mountains or molehills or molecules of people as required, and when fed up with it all could wipe out and renew the whole caboodle instantly and start anew. And if she didn't believe him she had better study his drawings. Which were, he assured her, drawn from life, actual-factual to a fault.

Take, for instance

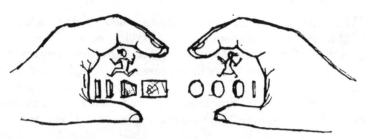

To drive the point home, he insisted on singing to Mary what he called his Cautionary Caterwaul:

Mouse One is blind to what he sees,
He suffers from an eye disease,
His furry coat is full of fleas,
The darkness brings him to his knees.

Mouse Two squeals NO to what he sees.
Because the facts all fail to please
And he prefers his fantasies
Puss catches him with perfect ease.

Mouse Three squeaks YES to what he sees,
is troubled by no cats or fleas.
Relying on what *he* perceives,
He trips all traps and chews their cheese.

Which wouldn't have been so bad if he hadn't tried to set the ditty to the tune of the Manbridge National Anthem. Which, when competently sung, was painful enough, but sung Hodge fashion was - excruciating.

Well, the fact that her Wonder Man happened to be tone deaf was, perhaps, some sort of consolation. It made his big-headedness slightly easier to handle.

Big-headedness it remained. Inflation run wild! Gigantism with a vengeance! And (once more) the crazy thing was that he'd got it right! Here was the sighted man in the Country of the Blind, the wide-awake one in the City of Sleepwalkers, the realist in the Land of Make-believe.

In the end that couldn't be bad - for him, for her, for Manbridge, for the world...

Repeat: in the end.

Meantime...?

The second Revelation or item of Radical Hodgepodgery, following hard on that traumatic dinner party, was of a different order. Important though the first (namely, how to urigeller just about everything) evidently was to him, it wasn't vital that she shared his feeling. (In fact, she found it fun, and how important it is to squeeze all the fun you can out of this sorry old world!). It wasn't an issue that threatened to come between them.

Not so the second item. On her reaction to this "Ultimate Revelation" of Hodge's hung the quality of their relationship from now on - no less. That much was clear from the start.

Usually he was all eagerness to show her his latest drawings, and, in case their message should be obscure, to explain them in detail. Not quite so much, of late, in that schoolmarmish and patronising manner of his, but still with almost no hesitation or reticence at all. And usually she got their meaning at once: also, along with the meaning, at least a twinge of the feeling, by way of preview. To share his enthusiasm was never automatic, rarely immediate and easy, but in the end it happened, one way or another. Never had she run - slam! - into a brick wall capable of parting her from him for long, a seemingly impenetrable barrier of incomprehension.

So it had been. Now came the change. Slap bang, without warning.

Almost nervously, Hodge asked if he might show her a funny little sketch. He called it his Merrygoround. A mere scribble, it was nevertheless (she gathered) by far the most significant of all the hundreds he'd turned out so far. Yes, though it was amusing in a way, he must ask her, please, to take it very seriously. It was one of those terrifically funny things that aren't for making fun of.

Of course Mary promised, cross her heart, and assured and reassured him, and expressed her keenest interest in - whatever it might be.

And this is what it was:

What Mary *thought* was: My God, is that all? What's the fuss about? Being has to be. Happenings have to happen. Consciousness is. So what? Does the poor darling think he's invented the stuff? That it's his holy offspring, immaculately conceived?

What Mary *felt* was a vague sense of resentment and a threat bordering on fear, made worse by the knowledge that such a reaction was utterly unreasonable. In the past, Hodge's gigantism had amused more than appalled her: as if such an Ego were unfortunate, but proper to the healthy child he was at heart. But not this time. No, sir! She even entertained the idea that she had lost him the way those devotees had lost their Sadguru, stuck - should she say stuck up? - at the top of his sky-scraping pedestal. Lost him, anyhow, for the time-being, till some-one or something cut him down to size. Well, let's say to her level, rather than to her size.

That was what she *felt*.

The Merrygoround

What Mary *said* was: "Thank you, dear, for trusting me. You know how seriously I take all your ideas. Some I get quickly, some slowly. I promise you I'll stay with this one till I've something intelligent to say about it."

Whether Hodge was reassured, or grievously disappointed with her response, she found it hard to say. That very uncertainty was an indication of their altered relationship.

19

CRIME AND PUNISHMENT

Add to the foregoing the practical question of what to do with the fellow, all day and every day, and you'll have some idea of Mary's worries at this time.

If it wasn't safe to take Hodge out under supervision, how much less safe to let him out on his own, far from her watchful eye! On the other hand, she could hardly keep him cooped up at home like a lap-dog, and double-lock him in when he had to be left alone. As for supplying him with cash and a map of the town, and careful instructions about shops and shopping and prices and pedestrian crossings and tube trains, and then letting him loose - that would be taking fearful risks. More than likely he'd give his last penny to the first busker or down-and-out he came across. Or stop the traffic because everybody needed a rest and re-Earthing. Or button-hole a policeman and demand to know whether he was inside that uniform. Or take all his clothes off because they were insulating him from the wind and the blessed sunshine. To say nothing of real and only-too-imaginable disasters of every sort.

She couldn't let him out, and she couldn't keep him in.

The problem was getting her down.

Though it was a bitter cold winter's day, the so-and-so had crept out when she was busy in the kitchen.

He'd been out now for no less than two hours - almost certainly not in that windy park...

There came the telephone call that she'd dreaded.

Yes, it was the police. Would she step round to the station to help them with their enquiries. About a certain Mr Hodge. Or was it Mr Podge?

Mary was there in five minutes flat.

The inspector explained that Hodge - who was being held in another part of the station - had been taken up for shoplifting on a fairly ambitious scale. His pockets were stuffed to overflowing with expensive merchandise, including a box of liqueur chocolates, several packets of smoked salmon, and three cans of caviar. He hadn't a brass farthing on him.

His behaviour, on arrest, had been somewhat strange. At first incoherent, and then protesting that he wasn't a thief, he'd demanded to know what ownership was, anyway. They had with difficulty got his address out of him. Was it true he lived in her apartment? What could she tell the police about him? Was he quite sane? And so on.

She told the Inspector the facts. Well, the facts he was bound to find out anyway.

As for her opinion about Hodge, she let him have it. He certainly wasn't on drugs. She was quite sure he wasn't mad. Or some kind of idiot. Very much the opposite. He was what they call an eccentric genius, a poet, childlike in his innocence and indifference to convention, absolutely not the criminal type. An idealist and generous to a fault, he was one of those rare souls to whom property meant almost nothing. His intention was to give away every bit of the stuff he'd pocketed, present it to some hungry-looking child or grown-up. It was Christmas time…

"We are charging him with the criminal offence of larceny," replied the Inspector drily, cutting short her testimonial. No, he couldn't be let off just this once and placed in her care. The court would decide what was to be done with him, his sentence, and whether bail should be granted meantime. In his opinion Mr Hodge's behaviour and state of mind made it necessary - in the public interest, and perhaps for her sake too - that he should remain in custody pending trial.

That night, the most-read and G-for-gutter paper carried a picture of a wild creature that Mary could scarcely recognise, and a lurid version of his arrest, under the caption: SIMP, CHIMP, OR PLAIN IMP?

Abominable though that caption was, it did serve to bring to a head a thought that had been milling around in Mary's mind for a long while. A thought - you could call it a persistent doubt - about Hodge, which we have already touched on. About the wild inconsistencies and contradictions in the man. In particular, how the devil could he be at once so razor-sharp and so dull-witted, so subtle-sensible and so stupid?

"Don't tell me," she imagined herself protesting to him, "that you didn't know the risk you were taking when you pinched all that stuff. You're much too observant and intelligent - and well-read, for that matter - to plead ignorance of the law and its penalties, and of the role of the police in upholding the law. Why, then, did you do the damfool thing you did? I can think of only two explanations. Either you are mad in one department - mad with the monomania of those who stay sane in all other departments - are, as they used to say, a kleptomaniac: or else you deliberately brought the weight of the law down on your miserable head, like poor old Samson in Gaza. Well, I refuse to believe the first. Real kleptomaniacs are cleverer than that. They don't avoid the check-outs: they sail through - with a couple of pounds of King Edwards in their baskets, an innocent smile on their faces, and no improbable bulges anywhere. So it must be the second. In which case, why oh why are you doing this horrible thing to yourself? And to me, you heartless oaf?"

Mary never put the question to Hodge, in anything like those terms. It turned out she didn't need to. The answer came to light, so to say.

Back, then, from speculation to the hard fact that Hodge was in remand prison, awaiting trial for larceny. Bail had been refused.

A week after his arrest - by far the worst in all her twenty years - Mary attended court, in response to a subpoena.

Before giving her testimony she had to listen to the details of his arrest.

He'd been watched by the store detective - and repeatedly photo-graphed - stuffing his pockets from the shelves, and then coolly stroll-ing through one of the unattended check-outs into the street, where the testifying officer apprehended him. He seemed unaware that he'd committed an offence. His behaviour on the way to the station and subsequently was strange rather than violent, and hardly a word could they get out of him. Witness wondered at first whether the Accused was under the influence of a powerful drug, his appearance and manner were that peculiar.

Mary was next in the box.

In a level voice, and avoiding eye-contact with Hodge, she outlined the story of his rescue on the Moor and convalescence, soft-pedalling the oddities of his behaviour and loud-pedalling the insights that went with them. The impression she tried to give was that a spot of well-meant but misguided shoplifting was a small price to pay for the Accused's gifts to Manbridge so far, let alone those to come. However, she did of course share the court's concern at his unsocial tendencies, and undertook to do all she could in future to correct them, if he could be released into her care. In short, there had been a serious misunder-standing, and she was anxious to play her part in putting it right.

Her pleading was eloquent, but desperate rather than hopeful. It proved unavailing. He was remanded in custody, pending further investigation and medical reports.

A fortnight later the case was resumed and Mary was in court again, this time in the public gallery. She felt ill, and baffled. Why all this fuss about such a petty crime?

Hodge, gripping the rail of the dock as if it were driftwood and he were at sea and drowning, looked to her terribly pale and tense, and even thinner than usual.

The first witness, a clinical psychologist, testified that in his opinion Hodge was profoundly disturbed and in need of careful obser-vation, diagnosis, and treatment. His examination had been too brief and superficial to reveal the exact nature of the subject's condition. His was a difficult case. Perhaps a unique case.

The second witness, a psychologist specialising in subnormality, had been astonished to find that Hodge's score in intelligence tests (conducted, incidentally, with much difficulty - at first Hodge had been totally unco-operative) was the highest he'd ever measured. And, in spots, amazingly low. He, too, was puzzled. Further investigation was essential.

The third and final witness was a social worker. Here, she was pretty sure, was a serious case of maladjustment arising from a de-prived, traumatic, and probably violent family background. The fact that she'd failed to extract from the subject a single word about his people (and not too many words about anything else, for that matter) would seem to confirm her provisional diagnosis - of an extremely difficult childhood, so difficult that he'd repressed all memory of it. Under the extended treatment that he certainly needed, his amnesia could probably be cured. Then further progress could be expected.

The magistrate sentenced Hodge to custody in a penal institution specialising in mental disorders. For how long would depend on the more detailed reports submitted to him in due course.

20

A VISIT FROM MARY

A lapse of three weeks, and at last Mary's enquiries met with a response. He was an inmate of the large and notorious institution called Strangefields - regarded by itself as a psychiatric hospital rather than a prison, and by the public as both, and therefore doubly sinister. He could be visited the following morning, and on Wednesday afternoons thereafter.

She'd spent all night wondering what would happen at the interview, trying out scenario after scenario. Would he rush into her arms (supposing the rules and set-up would allow any such thing), or burst into tears, or go off into one of his silent and almost catatonic trances, eyes trained on who-knows-what unmanbridgeable landscape?

In the event it was none of these. What she found was worse than anything she'd prepared herself for. Here was a switched-off Hodge. A de-hodged Hodge, if such a monstrosity were possible. That he looked washed-out and washed-up was to be expected. That he was skinnier than ever, and drawn, and tight-lipped - this was bad and sad enough, but understandable. But what hit and hurt her like a stab to the heart was that the old light in him had gone out. A dullness and a deadness, like the secondary eyelid of some reptile, had descended upon the brightness that even she had never been able to gaze into for long, so alive those eyes had been. If that had been the brightness of an inspired and hopeful lunacy, this was surely the drabness of a dreary and hopeless lunacy. His madness - if this was madness indeed - wasn't even animated enough to be scary.

Were they breaking him? Were they hell-bent on Manbridging this wonderful Outsider till he succumbed to their pettiness, their lack of humour, their crippling blindness, their desperate fear of life?

He was quiet enough. Far too much so. If this was one of his trances, it was a trance of despair, in which there was nothing left to say. If he was pleased to see her, he wasn't showing it.

She asked him how they were treating him.

He shrugged his shoulders.

Was life here very bad? Or just about supportable?

He shrugged his shoulders, grimacing a bit.

Could she do anything for him?

He appeared to consider this, to have the germ of an idea. Only to dismiss it with a third shrug and a hoarse "No thanks."

That was about all...

In preparation for her visit to Strangefields she had pulled a lot of wires and wangled a highly-irregular interview with the Assistant Governor, who turned out to be guardedly informative and sympathetic.

At first (he said) Hodge had been a dead weight to himself and everyone else, stupid and unresponsive rather than difficult, a near-zombie. But in the last few days he appeared to be brightening up just a little. His migraines were giving concern. The staff in charge of him reported strange behaviour, such as feeling himself all over as if to check whether he was present and solid. Occasionally he talked to himself, incoherently. He'd been seen to pick on a mark on the floor, or a stain on the wall, and stare at it for minutes on end. But he wasn't aggressive in the slightest.

Medical and psychological assessments were in progress.

Yes, a weekly visit by Miss Porticule would be a good thing.

She had a request to make. Could he be supplied with drawing materials? Pictures were to him what words were to Manbridgians, his spectacles on the world. Unlike words, his sketches weren't symbols standing for things but their actual form, simplified and clarified. They weren't dumped on the world, they *fitted* it. At least for him, they were its bones. So she was sure that the opportunity to express his thoughts and feelings on paper would help immensely. Coloured felt pens, please, and reams of recycled A4.

"Why of course," agreed the Assistant Governor, "It shall be done."

"One other thing," said Mary. "Can you tell me why Manbridge is making such heavy weather of this case? After all, this is Hodge's first offence, and shop-lifting is a minor and very common misdeed that normally attracts a fine or a few days in jail, at most. All this costly rigmarole of medical and psychiatric reports - you'd think he'd committed the crime of the year, or was accused of high treason!"

The assistant Governor's reply was that the courts had recently been given wide powers for combating Unmanbridgian Activities, and judges much increased discretion in sentencing. Conceivably Hodge's real offence (he hinted, but was careful not to spell out) might not be a million miles from the high treason she had mentioned... But all this was outside his field. He was a prison officer, not a lawyer, and he knew no more about the Government Agency MI 13 than Miss Porticule did... She could seek professional advice...

In the event, the answer to Mary's question came over loud and clear. Whatever route her inquiry took, it ended in something like an impasse marked CAUTION! In a hedgehog of barbed-wire, a pole-mounted TV surveillance camera, and the sign:

KEEP OUT!

ARMED RESPONSE

21

MANBRIDGE ON HODGE

I t was five weeks after her first visit to Strangefields.

Five difficult weeks for Mary, and five further visits - none of them easy - during which Hodge changed hardly at all. They still talked very little, but he did light up a shade or two when she asked to see his sketches. More and more they consisted of mandalas - nests of concentric circles, reminiscent of those made by raindrops on the surface of a pond - with question-marks at the centre and circumference, an assortment of bodies in between, and arrows radiating from and returning to the centre. Scores of variations on this theme. What an obsessional type he was! For him the pattern was magic, obviously. Fervently she prayed it was white magic, healing magic.

Was it that the rings shielded him from some outside horror?

Or that they were pressing, pressing in upon some worse inside horror, till they squeezed it out for good and all? Like pus from a boil? She'd no idea. Time should tell. What it would tell she didn't allow herself to brood on more than she could help.

Five difficult weeks, and now the case of H. Podge was coming up again before the magistrate who had remanded him for evaluation. It was to be heard in the conference room of the institution. Hodge, given the option of attending, chose to do so. Mary - once more having pulled the right strings - was present, too.

The experts lined up to report on him were a new lot. Namely, Dr Bultitude, the chief medical officer of Strangefields; Dr Rudolph Manheim, neopsychiatrist there and also in private practice and a professor in the University; the Reverend Pringle-Postern, padre of Strangefields; Miss Roseacre, social psychologist; and Nurse Sterry.

Sri Sat-Guru Stubbs, UNCOM (United New-Age Church of Manbridge), would also testify.

Throughout the proceedings Hodge sat with closed eyes, his head between his hands. Most of the time he seemed to be asleep. Mary knew he wasn't. Far from it.

Dr Bultitude found H. Podge to be much underweight for his height of six-foot-six. His blood pressure was on the low side, his body temperature fluctuating, his appetite extremely meagre. He lacked energy and tired easily. Though he suffered from frequent and often severe headaches - a fact that hadn't been easy to get out of him - there was no definite evidence of a brain-tumour. Blood tests had revealed quite complicated chemical abnormalities and deficiencies. Suitable medication and dietary adjustments were being tried out. They needed time, to produce perceptible results.

There was one other thing he perhaps ought to mention. He disclaimed knowledge of what the connection was, but felt there must be a link between the temperament and behaviour that led to Podge's arrest on the one hand and some curious features of his anatomy on the other. He was, in fact, both polymastoid and polydactylic: that's to say, he had four nipples, and six toes on each foot. And then there were the eyes of different colours, of course.

Altogether, a remarkable, not to say baffling case.

Dr Rudolph Mannheim, neopsychiatrist (neither Mary nor Hodge knew what that meant), testified that he, too, had found H. Podge a difficult case. Not so much hostile as unco-operative in the extreme, morose and sulky, refusing point-blank to answer even the simplest and friendliest of questions. He left the doctor little to go on, apart from his drawings, a large number of which he'd had photos taken of. Not without obstruction from the person into whose hands they had fallen, he felt bound to add. (A pause here, and a meaningful glare at Miss Porticule.) These drawings, however, along with his body-language, were diagnostic enough.

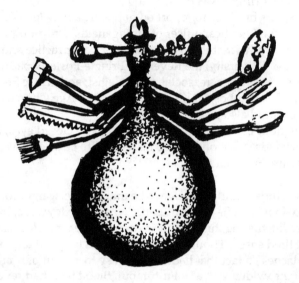

They showed him flowing into things, continuous with whatever he was in contact with - a chair, a hammer, the soil, and so forth. Here, clearly, was a case of failure to individuate. He was retarded and a shirker, not on account of inherent mental defect but fear. Fear of becoming a person, a particular and distinct being. Hence his strong desire to escape from a difficult and dangerous world to the ease and safety of the womb: where he had been, precisely, continuous with his mother. Hence his objection to shower-baths at Strangefields: he demanded hot tub-baths (if you please!) in which to soak for half an hour at a time - another sign of his desire to return to the womb and immerse himself again in the comforting amniotic fluid. His aim always was to escape to a world that existed for his sake alone. Many if not most of his drawings, accordingly, showed him sitting pretty at the centre of all things and served by all things. They were all *his* and scot free, like the goods he lifted from the store. And his regression, naturally, led to aggression when it was frustrated. His behaviour when arrested, for instance.

Oh, another thing about his drawings: they were in all styles - ranging from random scribbling to obsessive attention to detail - which was a further indication of his failure to individuate, and grow up into a distinct and consistent person. And the people he drew were distorted versions of himself, and therefore not only caricatures but morbid to a degree.

As for treatment, though Dr Mannheim rarely prescribed shock therapy he did feel it should be tried in this instance. In addition, naturally, to the appropriate medication.

Finally - a peculiar footnote. During their last session Podge suddenly complied with a request to recount his dreams. The stuff, which was lurid to a degree and reminiscent of his madder drawings, just poured out of him, like raw sewage. At the end, however, it was clear that the whole farrago had been produced off-the-cuff and hadn't been dreamed at all. It had been dreamed up - or down - for the occasion. Whether he had played this trick deliberately and out of cussedness, or was the subject of a psychotic episode, Dr Mannheim had still to find out.

That was just one of the reasons why he needed more time to investigate this case, let alone treat it.

The Reverend Ian Pringle-Postern had a very different story to tell the court.

He had found Podge to be a willing if not eager listener to the

sacred truths of Manbridgism, of which, it seemed, he knew nothing. He put up no resistances or yes-buts or doubts at all. One recitation of the Manbridge Creed, modernised and extended version, and he had all twenty pages by heart, word-perfect. It was a minor miracle.

The Padre felt sure that H. Podge was neither a moron nor a madman. Nor was he a real criminal, but simply ignorant. Morally retarded, so to speak. Or had been, till his conversion. Following which, his rapid socialisation was a near certainty, given some further instruction and regular attendance at Manbridgian services.

Eva Roseacre, social psychologist on the staff at Strangefields, caused a flutter in court by telling the padre he'd got it all wrong. Podge had been under the impression that the Creed was for reciting, not believing. He had told her as much, after one of his sessions with the reverend gentleman.

Not that she took this disclosure at its face value. Nothing the man said could be relied on. So far from being a true innocent or simpleton, he was a trickster playing that role like mad. In fact, he was so good at fooling people that he fooled himself, and lived in a quite unreal world. Of all the cases of alienation from things as they are, his was among the severest she'd come across. And for sure the most peculiar.

As for the subject's behaviour, it had consistently confirmed her view that further assessment and treatment were needed. He had quite a repertoire of reactions to her patient and always tactful questioning. He might stare at her blankly and refuse to say a word in reply. He might fall asleep. He might pretend to fall asleep. He might suddenly blurt out some offensive or meaningless sentence, such as "Take your shoes off and sit still, you loose woman!" Or he might - and often did - turn his back on her.

All of which meant that he should remain in custody, for his own good as well as society's.

The fourth evaluation came from Nurse Sterry. Or - to give her her full title - Chief Nurse-therapist Sterry.

For this, Hodge came to life. He sat up, and the expression on his face changed from bored disgust to the opposite. He went so far as to exchange glances with Mary.

Nurse Sterry was saying how strongly she felt that, because she saw much more of him every day than the other witnesses did, she was better able to do him justice. She had got to know him quite gradually, but the more she found out the more she was impressed. Yes, he was absolutely convinced he was living in the real world, and it wasn't just different from the unreal world that grown-up Manbridgers were living in, but its opposite. It was a case of one against millions, his word against theirs. If they were sane, he was mad, if he was sane they were mad. Was it any wonder that he should lose patience, should feel quite desperate, when practically all his efforts to convey his meaning came up against a brick wall?

Of course she realised that one of the indications of insanity is precisely this kind of isolation. "Everyone's out-of-step except me!" But it can be an indication of genius, of someone who has something important to say to the world that the world's not ready for. In short, the witness had come to the conclusion that Hodge Podge was maladjusted because he was misunderstood, profoundly and all along the line.

What was he trying to say? demanded the magistrate. What was this revelation or inspiration that people didn't get?

Well, that was a hard one to answer. She didn't fully understand Hodge... But of two things she was certain. The first was that he was perfectly genuine: he saw what he saw and felt what he felt, not what he was told to see and feel. And he dared to go by that, regardless of the trouble it got him into. The second was that this inspired naiveté, this bowing before the Ridiculously Obvious - this near-idiocy, if you must call it that - gave him a powerful sense of continuity with everyday things around him, with Nature, with the whole world. Of merging, of completion.

How had she come to these conclusions? By studying his drawings: which, however fantastical, were never nonsensical. By listening to his often cryptic utterances till they made sense, instead of deciding in advance that they made no sense at all. As some of the other witnesses had...

At this, the presiding magistrate, who had been getting increasingly restive, exploded: "I won't have this! Stick to your testimony. And make it brief."

Dr Mannheim stumped out of the hall, banging the door behind him.

A conciliatory word or two from Nurse Sterry followed. The court settled down somewhat. She continued.

What had finally convinced her was a rather intimate experience, of the day before. Hodge had seemed even more isolated and hurt than usual, following one of his interviews with… Well, let that pass… Quite unintentionally she had touched his hand. It was as if she'd received a powerful electric shock. As if that momentary contact had for him been the healing of all the wounds in all the world. As if all the dammed-up life in the world had suddenly been released and allowed to flow through the world's veins and arteries. This impression was confirmed by the few words he blurted out. It seemed *touch* was for him as revealing as sight, and that he was far more *in contact* with the world than people normally are. Almost as "oned" to it as animals and plants are, perhaps -

Again the magistrate interrupted. That was quite enough. They'd all got her message.

"One last thing, Your Honour," she pleaded. "For God's sake don't let them shock and medicate him into submission. That really would be criminal…"

This time, an angry magistrate succeeded in shutting Nurse Sterry up.

The final witness hadn't actually been called on to testify, but was allowed to do so by the magistrate. Sri Sat-Guru Stubbs, UNCOM, had been called in unofficially to see if he could help in the assessment of

Hodge's condition, if not his treatment. Someone unspecified had thought it possible that his bizarre ideas were distorted or childish versions of the New Age Culture of Manbridge, and that connecting them with that Culture might help to sort him out. Mr Stubbs had been asked to expose Hodge Podge to a selection of New Age ideas, and report on the result.

The magistrate confessed to being an octogenarian, and as such unclear as to what Manbridge's New Age Culture might be. Could Mr Stubbs enlighten him? Very briefly. The a-b-c of it would be enough.

Not easy to do, came the reply. However, as luck would have it, he had himself pieced together - more for his own entertainment than for the instruction of his disciples - an informal New-Age Alphabet. It would at least give His Honour some idea of the good things he might be missing. If it pleased His Honour...

"Fire away."

"Here goes, then - Astrology, Breathing oh-so-deeply, Crystals and Corn-circles and Channelling, Dowsing, Ectoplasm, Fairies, Glastonberries and Ghosties, Horoscopes, Imps, Jinn, Kendo and Karate, Ley-lines, Mermaids, Numerology and Naiads, Orgone Boxes, Palmistry and Pyramids and Pendulums and Pixies, Qigong (sic), Rishis, Spectres, Trolls, UFOs, Vibhuti or ashes, Wraiths, Xstasy, Yetis, and of course the Zodiac" - all packed into one breath.

"And that by no means covers the territory," added the Sat-Guru, winded.

"God help us all!" exclaimed the magistrate. "But I should have thought that most of those goods were pretty shopworn, and a lot less up-to-date and new-age than grandma's corsets. However, the question before the court is how much of that witch's brew Hodge Podge can stomach. Is he, or isn't he, an embryonic or frustrated Manbridgian New-Ager?"

Not by a million miles, it seemed. According to the witness, H. Podge had made himself out to be not so much uncomprehending as unimpressed. He had the immortal crust to claim that he possessed his own Ageless Something, compared with which all that ageing stuff (most of which he claimed he was familiar with) was peanuts - some tasty, some just edible, some rancid, but all mere peanuts. Sri Sat-Guru Stubbs had told him exactly what that Something really was. Far from being Ageless it was AGE itself and as old as Lucifer. It was, to spell out the acronym, an Absolutely Gigantic Ego.

"Your Honour," butted in Nurse Sterry, "may I add something

important to my evidence? In conversation with me, Hodge angrily referred to Sat-Guru Stubbs as Lying-Guru Stubbs, and pityingly as Stood-up-Guru Stubbs. Which shows he has more sense of humour than some of us here. And humour's a mark of sanity. One of the things that Hodge is trying to tell Manbridge is that the commonplace down-to-earth things of life are infinitely more amusing and wonderful than all that high-flying paranormal esoteric stuff. For him, the miracle is that a man can *see*, not that he can see your aura. The astounding thing, the *fun* thing, is that he *is*, not than he can conjure sackfuls of foul and futile ashes out of thin air. I say..."

"And I say, another word from you," cut in the magistrate, fuming, "and I'll have you removed from this court."

He turned to Hodge.

"Have you understood what's been going on?"

A barely perceptible nod from Hodge.

"Well then, do you have anything to say?"

Slowly he stood up and straightened up, and seemed (at least to Mary) to dominate the court by far more than his six-foot-six would account for. He was wearing institution grey, too loose and too short, and his hair looked more like a blackthorn bush than ever. Those two-coloured eyes had for the moment come alight again. If he looked ridiculous - which by Manbridge standards he certainly did - it was with the ridiculousness of What is, the absurdity of the Real. If this creature was mad - which by Manbridge's lights he certainly was - it was with the madness of the Creator who casually creates Himself - plus, quite incidentally in a hodgepodge of doodling, a billion universes all in good working order - for no reason at all and with no help at all. And you can't get madder than that, more reckless, more harum-scarum, more giddy. (Yes: under extreme pressure, Mary was tumbling to what that Merrygoround of Hodge's amounted to.)

He stood there silent, his head a little to one side, his arms outstretched to their limit - as if to embrace not just the court but the world - appealing for understanding. Stood quite still, it seemed for minutes...

His lips moved. No sound came out...

And then something gave, his hands flew to his head - as if it were the ball in the desperate game of his life, and he were about to fling it at the court.

In a moment it was all over. He collapsed into his chair, and sat there, impassive and inscrutable, as before.

Next day, in the reassembled court, the magistrate gave his ruling in the matter of Hodge Podge.

"For three reasons I have decided that he shall remain in custody - in institutional care, let's say - for the foreseeable future, or till there are new developments. First, because he is himself unable, it would seem, to conform as yet to our Manbridge laws and customs. This being so, I consider that both Manbridge and he need protection against the likely consequences of his nonconformity. Second, because, taken as a whole, the reports submitted to me show that he is seriously disturbed and requires further therapy in a controlled environment. And third, because I have the feeling that there's more to this case than has so far been revealed. And there's a chance that a further period of investigation will bring it out."

And so the court rose, Hodge to be led off to his cell, Mary to be driven away to her apartment. She'd come in a taxi, and in a taxi she went.

Which was fortunate. Because on the way home she fainted, for the first time in her life.

22

ROCK BOTTOM

The time was a fortnight after the hearing, the place Chief Nurse-therapist Sterry's office in Strangefields, those present Nurse Sterry and a washed-out Mary Porticule. She had still to shake off her illness, a fever which had kept her in bed until a couple of days before.

They were - needless to say - discussing Hodge. Mary's concern for him was agonising enough to wipe out every last trace of the jealousy she had been feeling about the special relationship that had obviously developed between nurse and patient.

Nurse Sterry: "I've been overruled by Dr Mannheim, who of course is senior to me. He's decided that Hodge must be given massive injections daily of the new superdrug Normastorin, which (I believe) has so far been seriously tried out only on monkeys. The fact that the wretched animals didn't immediately lie down and die, or tear themselves and their cages to bits, is hardly reason enough to pump the stuff into poor Hodge and make a guinea-pig out of him. And Dr Mannheim is still - can you believe this? - muttering about electric shocks. I think he's so threatened, personally, by all Hodge stands for that he's hell-bent on punishing him - and at the same time removing the threat - by poisoning him or knocking him out.

Dr. Mannheim

"Nobody listens to me here. I'm thinking of resigning my job so that I can take up his case publicly, in the papers and on the air if they'll have me. Anyway - no surprise - Dr Mannheim is determined to get me off his back. He can't sack me: but has put in to get me transferred, double quick, to some other establishment. Quite unasked, he has produced such a glowing testimonial to my abilities that half the institutions in Manbridge will, he hopes and prays, be clamouring for me."

Mary: "This is terrible. Who does Hodge have here but you?"

Nurse Sterry: "What can I do? The more they try to drug him the more bloody-minded he gets. You know what he's like. And the more bloody-minded he gets the more they try to drug him, of course. They'll win. He's refused to eat, but has to drink. He doesn't have to know he's being fed the dope."

Mary: "How does he fill in the hours and days, alone in that horrible cell? I hope to God he's making lots of drawings. They're his life-line, just about all he has left."

Nurse Sterry: "Until yesterday he was turning them out by the dozen. Drawings of a sort. I've managed to pick this one up, before Mannheim got his hands on it. You'll see how it lends itself to his contention that Hodge is psychotic, as mad as can be.

"Today he's stopped drawing. He's just sitting there motionless, his head in his hands."

Mary: "But how is he *really*, deep down in himself, do you think? How is he standing up to this... this *torture?*"

Nurse Sterry: "Badly, I'm afraid. I'm very worried. There's a real danger they'll send him permanently round the bend, if they haven't done so already. He used to greet me, sometimes, with just the suggestion of a welcoming smile, and we'd talk a bit. But now all I can get out of him is a blank stare, as if he didn't recognise me. And a turning away, in despair. The awful thing is that I don't know what more I can do for him, other than resign and take up his case. But that can't be done overnight. By the time I'm out of here and busy on his behalf he'll be out of his mind altogether, I fear. But -"

There was a loud and urgent banging at the door.

A young man, white-coated, and out-of-breath as if he'd been running, burst in.

"Can I speak to you alone, Nurse?" he gasped.

"If it's about Hodge, you can tell me in front of Miss Porticule. What is it, Johnny?"

"He's been bashing his head against the wall of his cell. His forehead's all bloody. So Dr Mannheim's had him put in a padded cell. When I left him the doctor was lecturing students on his case. They were watching in turns through the peep-hole in the cell door."

"Oh my God!" cried Nurse Sterry. "I must go. I"ll phone you as soon as I can, Mary."

23

THE DITCHING OF PODGE

In addition to the main exercise yard at Strangefields there was a much smaller one, for prisoners who were regarded as unfit to mix with the others. A scabrous, diseased-looking quadrangle of concrete it was, boxed in on all sides with dark grey walls. At the centre of it there lay - there broke out like a weeping sore - a small circular pond enclosed in a dwarf wall. The water, which (as a precaution against suicide attempts) was a mere foot deep, sported three clapped-out and dusty and about-to-sink water-lily leaves, and an even more clapped-out goldfish. Weirdly and woefully unsuccessful had been this strange attempt by some benefactor, years ago, to humanise the place. How pathetic! What a hope!

No sun had ever shone into that so-called ornamental pond, nor had any gale been strong enough and near enough to ruffle its surface - so lofty and forbidding were the walls enclosing Strangefields exercise yard number two, reserved for very disturbed cases.

Johnny, who was one of Nurse Sterry's junior assistants, had led a listless, shambling, scarred Hodge Podge from his padded cell into this exercise yard, for a brief spell in what (exaggerating wildly) you could describe as the open air.

Hodge, holding onto the coping of the dwarf wall of the pond as convulsively as, a million ages earlier, he'd held onto the rail of the dock in the courtroom, stared blankly into the water...

Time stopped expanding, started telescoping...

It was as though the whole absurd and tremendous Manbridge episode - starting with that unforgettable waking up to peach-complexioned Mary and the gorse-prickly Professor in the caravan on the edge of the Great Moor of Kreep, and the triumphal ride to the city, going on to all those funny and horrible and sweet and clever and incredibly parish-pumpish and pin-headed characters - shop assistants, aunts, plant operators, Kaffertiti Islanders, astronomical clever dicks, psychers and psitters and psadhaners, sad-gurus that were happy, sat-gurus that were lying, greens that were puce, and Strangefielders that were strange indeed - as though that far-fetched tale were a dream from which he was waking. A day-and-nightmare that had lasted no longer than a few split seconds, at most. A fantastic panorama!

Anyway, time folded.

It was just as if he were back in Beaston again, standing on the brink of that larger and wilder pond, criss-crossed overhead with streaking swallows. As if this goldfish were a sorrowful and shrunken Snouty the Magnificent Pike.

And as if this other fish, this fat-faced, finless, scaleless, toadstool-skinned, upward-staring creature were a sorrowful and...

Hold on! No!

Not *as if!* There he was, in person. There was Podge!

No dream, this! There he was, for real! Actually in *this*, this Manbridgian apology for a pond - less rounded, strangely scarred, Cupid's-bow-lips paler, but unmistakably that old fishiest of frogs and froggiest of fishes - Podge himself and not a picture. Come on! Do the lips in a picture tremble? Do the eyes in a picture cry?

There he was, captive, back where he belonged, after all that cutting loose and playing merry hell. Podge was ditched. Podge of the piercing eyes, Podge of the busy feet, the wicked lying-in-wait Podge that had *rushed* him, was ditched. There, absolutely and beyond any doubt, hovering so still, held below that polished surface, lurked the spooky, enigmatic, dangerous Podge, in his element again. Looking pleased with himself rather than sorry.

And he, Hodge, resolutely in *his* element, was shot of him, at last de-Podged. Hodge was himself again. No longer Hodge Podge, he was from now on plain Hodge. Just like that. Never forget it, Hodge! Never, never!

This time, instead of holding out tentative and trembling hands, palms facing inwards, to welcome the Thing, he was holding out sinewy and powerful hands, palms facing outwards, to thrust it away. And spitting out the command: "Podge off! Podge off!"

Then he straightened up. Right up, for the first time in weeks. He looked up at the postage-stamp rectangle of brilliant blue trying to shine down into the prison yard. And, in that place where no-one had ever laughed a sane laugh before, he laughed.

Yes, he laughed, and laughed, and laughed, and laughed his head clean off.

He laughed at that patch of burning blue sky, he laughed at the grey prison walls, he laughed at open-mouthed Johnny, he laughed at the scabrous concrete paving, he laughed at his own hands still thrusting Podge away. But most of all he laughed at Podge himself. At Podge who, not to be left out, was laughing like mad, too. Like mad was right. What a fatuous thing for any fish or frog (or cross between them) to do!

Then he strode up to Johnny, and put an arm round his shaking shoulders. Yes, Johnny was joining in now. What he was joining in he didn't quite know, but for sure it wasn't the lunatic laughter he'd heard too often in this place, but the happy laughter of the sanest child of God on Earth. The grown-up child who was trying to speak to him…

What came out, at last, was a very, very quiet: "I love you, Johnny."

All was still, again. And then something extraordinary happened in that hitherto Godforsaken exercise yard for seriously disturbed prisoners. A sound, at first faint and distant, rang out, a music that had never been heard before in birdless Strangefields.

A nightingale was singing.

The case of Hodge Podge came up before the visiting magistrate a few days later. Hodge himself was present.

From the start impressed with the change in Hodge's bearing and general appearance, the magistrate heard the reports of the witnesses who had testified at the previous session - with the exception of Dr Mannheim, who was indisposed, and Mr Stubbs.

There was overall agreement that there had been a striking improvement in Hodge's behaviour, his attitude to all of them and to institutional life, and in his physical condition. Only Miss Roseacre recommended that, seeing the remission might well be a temporary one, he should remain in custody.

To the Magistrate's question whether, if released, he would undertake to conduct himself properly, Hodge replied, in the calmest and firmest of voices, that he would give Manbridge no further cause for complaint.

He was released forthwith, the period he had already spent in detention being reckoned as more than sufficient penalty for the offence he had committed.

Mary took him home…

In the morning, she woke to find herself alone. On the bedside table was a note that read:

Do you think the fellow in dark glasses loitering on the pavement opposite is an MI 13 agent? Anyway, I'm hoping to dodge him somehow. Yes, I have to go now. Trust me. We'll be together soon.

Instead of a signature (and infinitely preferable, thought Mary), Hodge's note ended with a new scribble:

FOOTNOTE

Dr Rudolph Mannheim's lecture to Manbridge University, in his capacity as Senior Professor in the Department of Neopsychology, was well-attended, and made quite a stir. His subject was the case of one of his most difficult patients, whom he'd call Jack Robinson, to avoid identification. He went on, however, to say that Robinson was polymastoid and polydactylic, and had eyes of different colours - so identification wasn't that difficult, after all. The professor explained that his treatment consisted of a judicious mixture of body-chemistry management, an analysis along unique lines of the patient's dreams and artwork, and a third ingredient whose chemical formula was T2L4 (C). *(A long pause, to write the formula on the blackboard)*. Popularly known, Dr Mannheim explained, as Tender Loving Care. *(Laughter, and prolonged applause.)* The resulting remission of the patient's symptoms had been dramatically sudden. One moment he'd been as sick as could be. The next - before you could say Jack Robinson! - he was well. *(More laughter.)* Moreover, as far as the lecturer's information went, the cure was sustained. *(Standing ovation.)*

How much this notable lecture contributed to Dr Mannheim's election to the pro-chancellorship of the university, it is hard to say. But certainly it led to an immediate doubling of his private practice.

PART THREE
GODSEA

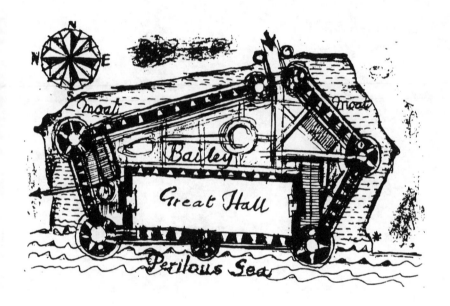

24

THE CASTLE

Among all the ancient fortresses whose battlements and shiny witch's-hat roofs towered above the wild grey country to the south of Manbridge, Godsea was the most breathtaking. Its massiveness and romantic siting at the Ocean's edge made sure of that. Weather-scarred to a dazzling whiteness, it looked and it was the oldest of them all. It had been built by Childe Godefroi in the darkest of the Dark Ages so-called, and the strains of the soaring plainsong of that far-off time were said still to echo around its keep and turrets, if you had an ear for that sort of thing.

The community occupying Castle Godsea was as strange as the castle itself. They claimed to stem from a still remoter age, insisting that - in spite of raids and sieges and sackings and burnings down the centuries by soldiery and whole armies from Manbridge - they had never been altogether dispossessed and broken up. They called them-selves the Godsea-ers, or sometimes the Seafolk. And fitting names both were, for the south wall of the Castle, rising sheer and lofty from the waters of the Perilous Sea, was pierced by many a casement opening on the mists and foam of that horizonless immensity.

Yes, it was horizonless to sight, as well as in fact. In all directions east to south and south to west from that shore, the Perilous Sea was visibly boundless. It had no *other* shore. But more of that later.

The shore it did have, the seashore bordering Castle Godsea on either side, was in several ways remarkable. It was remarkable for its sand which, when the sun was high, looked as white as the Castle, as if snow had fallen. Remarkable also for the ice-plants that poked up out of the sand-dunes, the blue to scarlet petals of which looked as if they had been individually wax-polished. And for its gnarled and twisted oaks, whose bark was like leather tanned to every imaginable shade and texture, and tooled fantastically.

From time to time, in calm weather, there wafted a scent in the mist-laden air of that shore. A scent like no other, but faintly reminiscent of wild violets. Very wild violets.

This enchanted shore lay some fifteen hundred feet below Manbridge, and some thirty or forty miles (as the seagull flies) from its outskirts. Far enough, however clear the weather, to be invisible from there.

The distance seemed much greater to the traveller, however, because the often steep and rough connecting roads were in places more like tracks, casually winding round marshes and rock-piled hillocks and unexpected hollows. There was little traffic along these roads, and you couldn't be sure of hitching a ride. How Hodge made the journey he never disclosed. He said he stowed away in a half-full garbage truck. A garbage truck going to Godsea! An unlikely story, intended (probably) to tell you to mind your own business.

Anyhow, by no means sorry to get away from Manbridge, Hodge at last arrived, one fine afternoon, at the Castle that had already become Home for him. Unclear about what it was, he was clear that he belonged there.

He made his way to the great drawbridge spanning the moat.

Half way along he stopped to look down into the still water. Yes, staring straight up at him was old Podge, as real and as podgy as ever. Down there he was, still ditched. Hodge needed to be sure of that, before going any further. Before going on to pull the rope-end hanging beside the huge iron-bound door.

The Castle

There was a peal of distant bells.

It seemed he was expected. A charming girl - she couldn't have been more than eighteen - with only the faintest of smiles and without asking his name - opened a tiny door within that huge one, and let him in. She introduced herself as Cecilia. Dressed in a brown, coarse-woven, ankle-length robe with a white cord around the waist, and barefooted, she looked vaguely monastic. It only required a head-dress to make some sort of nun of her, Hodge reflected.

She led him through the echoing gatehouse into a garden of fragrant wallflower beds set in grass like green axminster. This, she told him, was the bailey or ward of the castle. Behind them now rose the great machicolated battlements and defensive towers, and ahead the even loftier wall of the castle keep.

A doorway in this wall gave onto a rabbit-warren of arched corridors and spiral stairways, dimly lit and in places not easy to negotiate. This way and that Hodge and his guide turned, till they came to a T-junction. Ahead were three wooden-plank cell doors. On the right was a much bigger one, covered with green baize, across the corridor.

At that moment the cell-door on the left opened, and there came out a small man whose lined face and snow-white hair marked him as old, while everything else about him was scarcely middle-aged. There were no introductions. He passed them, with downcast eyes. But not till Hodge had observed two more things about the man. Though the air here was warm he wore mittens. And there was about him that smell of wild violets.

"That was Frank," said Cecilia, "He told us you were arriving today. We reserved the cell next to his for you. It's a rather special one. It belonged to a former Master of Godsea, Castellan William."

It was only after Cecilia had seen him into his cell - the central one of the three - and had herself disappeared through the green-baize door, that it occurred to him, too late, to ask how on earth Frank had known about him and his coming to Godsea, let alone the time of his coming. That was the first of that red-letter day's impossibilities.

His cell was narrow and bare, with little else than a truckle-bed and a washstand and an uneasy chair. Three walls were of undressed stone. The fourth, the end one, was all window. The light from it played ceaselessly, in pools of brightness, on ceiling and walls so that they seemed awash and liquefied, and somehow continuous with the Ocean the window looked out on.

Hodge opened the casements wide, all the way. The Perilous Sea filled his narrow cell, filled him.

How to describe it? As a wide and glittering Expanse that went on for ever and ever, ending in no horizon or bank of mist or cloud, ending nowhere at all, ending not at all? Impossible! you might say. Yet so it was. To Hodge also it was the strangest of sights, incredible, one he'd never, ever get used to. Yet it was entirely familiar. He was inseparable from it, he *was* it. Thanks to his de-Podging he quite naturally saw himself into the Limitless Sea, and the Limitless Sea into himself, and found the merging both wonderful and homely. Before that frog-or-fish-expelling crisis in the exercise yard for disturbed prisoners, nothing of the kind could have happened: he was bunged up, he was too small, he had no room for the Sea. But now he had nothing to keep it out with or restrict it. Was there ever a Guest so welcome, or Lodgings so commodious?

How long he stood there, boundless, flooded with that Immensity, he didn't know, or wish to know...

But at length, leaving the window wide open and the casements folded right back and fastened against the cell walls, he lay down on the bed. He was tired. He'd come a long way and it had been a long day.

"So Home is like this," was his last thought, before dropping off into a dreamless sleep. Dreamless, yet the sweetest sleep of his whole life, so far.

A third impossibility?

Well, it had been quite a day for impossibilities. Were there more to come?

Cecilia called for him, to take him to dinner.

She led him, up and up winding stone stairs, to the highest storey of the keep, whose massive grimness opened up and blossomed here into the great hall of Godsea Castle. And marvellously great and rich it looked to Hodge. The steep-pitched and lofty roof was a rich interlocking of bleached timbers, adorned at regular intervals with delicately carved angels gazing down at him.

The walls were rich with ancient tapestries portraying Heaven and Hell - fearsome, but fortunately faded: in its prime the mixture must have been almost too rich for human consumption. Even the stone floor was rich with the polishing of countless Godsea-ers' feet down the centuries. A huge log-fire blazed at each end of the long hall. Between the fires stretched the longest of dining tables, its gleaming oak surface mirroring a magnificence of china and glass and silverware and snow-white napery and piled-up fruit, such as Hodge had never imagined, much less set eyes on.

A place was found for him among the diners facing one another across that table, eating and drinking in silence. They were being waited on by bare-footed men and women dressed, like Cecilia, in brown robes - the uniform of servants here, Hodge concluded. What, servants in Godsea! In a community which of all communities should be classless! He was puzzled and a little shocked. However, there was nothing servile about the bearing of those menials - if menials they were. They looked more than contented with their lot. Serene, in fact.

It was all becoming too much for Hodge to take in. As so often, he coped by allowing himself to be captivated by little things. By the wild antics of the firelight on the spectacles of the dear old lady sitting opposite. By the happy grin on the face of the horned and winking demon in the tapestry at the old lady's back. By the grain of the wooden handle of the knife she was busy cutting cheese with. By the flashing red stream of the wine being poured into his glass by one of the servants, in contrast to the flashing blue of the jewel in the ring on the pouring hand, and the dull brown of the sleeve from which that hand protruded. And so on. Quirky, unpredictable, exciting, every least thing somehow precious.

Afterwards, when the dishes had been taken away, a girl whom Hodge could scarcely make out at the other end of the hall, but whose unaccompanied voice came over with carillon-like clarity, sang:

> My life, my life, is what I see
> There is no other sort of me.
> Just like a butterfly I land
> On any object come to hand.
> The universe is centred where
> Selection zeroes through the air
> And settles on, say, just that thing,
> A paradise that I can sing.

The fact that there was no applause, Hodge sensed, wasn't from any lack of appreciation. Quite the reverse. If at that moment you had asked him what he felt about that song - about that whole scene, about Godsea - he would have had difficulty in getting a word out, his heart was that full.

The song's conclusion signalled the end of the meal and the start of conversation. The long table was quickly cleared, and its sections shifted to the sides of the hall. People moved around haphazardly, it seemed, some remaining alone, some gathering into groups on cushions on the floor. A few of the younger ones started dancing to guitar music at the far end of the hall.

Hodge found himself talking with the man who had served him wine at dinner. He still wore his monkish robe. The fact that the wearer appeared to be the oldest person in the hall might account for its worn and patched state, which nevertheless seemed strangely inconsistent with the splendour of the amethyst on his forefinger.

"So many questions," Hodge was saying. "I don't know where to begin."

"We have the rest of the evening before us." His voice was as beautiful as a voice can be. They were sitting by themselves, side by side, facing the fire.

"May I begin with you? Why servants in Godsea, of all places?"

"Why not? It's the most popular job in Godsea. Everyone does his own thing here, what he feels impelled to do. You'll find us astonishingly different from one another. But of course we have a few things in common. The really important ones."

"Such as?"

"Well, we're all Godsea-ers - perhaps I should say putative Godsea-ers - or we wouldn't be here. And if you want to substitute a third *e* for the *a* in that word, I'll raise no objection. We all have a something to see off, and a something to see in. Again, if in both cases you call it a Someone instead of a something, or an Enemy to be held at bay and a Friend to be welcomed with open arms, I'll happily agree."

"The Enemy being Podge?" ventured Hodge, remembering how much these people seemed to know about him.

"Exactly, in your case. In mine, it's Old Nick, my other name being Nicholas. Nicholas belongs to the Sea, Old Nick to the moat. It's my business to keep him there, ditched. To each his particular adversary, his opposite number in the enemy's ranks. The fact is that we're under constant siege from the castle moat, and only vigilance will keep the enemy at bay. Every one of us is an active member of the Godsea garrison and expected to do his or her turn of sentry duty daily. I bet you didn't expect compulsory military service in Godsea, of all places!"

"I checked up on Podge when I crossed the drawbridge this afternoon. There he was in the water. Safely submerged."

Hodge had second thoughts. "Omit *safely*," he said.

"Yes indeed!" replied Nicholas. "Did you notice, on your way towards the bridge, a line of small arched openings in the perimeter wall, just above the water-line of the moat? They are sentry posts. We have no rules about when, and for how long, and at which post you mount guard. It all works out pretty well without any organising. Like practically everything else here. You'll see."

The old man fell silent, and Hodge stole a sideways glance at him. In the dancing firelight he looked, though very old and frail, very *alive*. Even excessively alive, as if he were so transparent to life, so near to being taken over by life, that he couldn't last much longer as Nicholas.

"Do we all have our jobs here? Lifelong work of some kind?" Hodge didn't like to ask outright about the retiring age - if any.

"It all depends. As I said before, we do what we feel drawn to do. Some go off to work daily in Manbridge, and a good thing, too: keeping up our connection with that place is crucial. Many of us have a job here, such as cleaning, cooking, waiting at table, building-maintenance work. Or gardening. I'll show you our kitchen garden tomorrow, if you like. I do a little to help there. A few of us don't do any work at all - unless seeing the Enemy off, and the Friend in, can be called work. We pretty much mind our own business at Godsea, and don't fuss about what others are up to."

The guitar music at the far end of the hall had stopped, and what sounded like a steel-drum band started playing. It stirred Hodge so much that he had an almost irresistible urge to jump up and join the dancers. Then, changing his mind, he felt obliged to stay with the old man a little longer.

The fire flared up, and the jewel on Nicholas' forefinger shone brightly.

"What's that ring?" Hodge asked.

"It was given me, many years ago, by a dear friend called William, just before he died."

"Is that the William who was the Castellan of Godsea, whose cell I occupy?"

"That's right. He was a deep one, but he's chiefly remembered for his delicious sense of humour."

"Is that ring of yours the Castellan's seal of office?" asked Hodge, quite unaware now of that steel-drum band.

Nicholas nodded.

"That makes you boss of this place?"

"Well yes, after a fashion… But I'm for bed now. I'll see you at breakfast."

The old man rose, touched him lightly on the shoulder, and strode off. *Strode* was the right word. He might be on his last legs, but they were still serving him astoundingly well.

25

THE SENTRY

Back in his cell, Hodge found the air chilly and went over to shut the casement. At the same time to take a last look at the Perilous Sea, before going to bed.

No moon or stars lit that deep blue Sea, yet it was clearly visible, apparently by its own light. Self-luminous it was, all the way to the horizon it didn't have. Faint mists were swirling, yet they were perfectly transparent and hid nothing. In short, this Sea, though the realest of the real, managed to pile paradox on paradox!

On second thoughts, he decided not to close the casement on such a scene. "Whatever the weather, I'll never shut out the Perilous Sea," he promised himself, perhaps rashly.

His night didn't go undisturbed. He woke with a start. From the cell on his left - the one belonging to Frank, the white-haired young man - the most alarming noises were coming. Bangings, as though furniture were being flung about. Scrapings, as though heavy objects were being dragged along the floor. Thumpings and small cries, as though someone were being hit. Groans, as though someone were in pain. Omit *as though*. Someone *was* in pain, no doubt about it.

The commotion went on, till he wondered whether he should go and see whether his neighbour needed help to fend off his attacker. What, his *attacker* - in Godsea, of all places? Was Hodge dreaming or was Frank having such a terribly realistic nightmare that he was sharing it with him? Hodge told himself not to be so ridiculous. There was nothing imaginary about that hullabaloo.

Just as he'd decided to get up and knock on Frank's door, the hullabaloo suddenly ceased. All was quiet again.

Hodge went back to sleep.

He was up at dawn the next day.

Standing at the open window - right up to it - and looking out to Sea, he noticed how it was as much a case of looking *in* as *out*. How *in* and *out* were indistinguishable. How through-and-through was the Sea's invasion, how he had nothing to keep it out with, nothing to set limits to it. Flowing into that Immensity, and having it flow into and engulf him, was a unique experience, not remotely like any other. Of all the kaleidoscope of happenings that had come his way in life, this was the least exciting, the least new, the least foreign. Yet it made all those other happenings - yes, even the most joyful, even the thrill of that song of the night before - seem trivial, commonplace, not worth hanging onto. He could take them or leave them. He could manage without the loveliest of all those lovely moments. But this - this sight of the Sea Perilous - he couldn't spare for an instant.

Why, then, was the Sea *perilous, unsafe?* Was it called perilous because its waters drowned Hodge whereas the waters of the moat - alas! - did not drown Podge? Flooded and overwhelmed Hodge - yet in such a way as to buoy him up, for ever and ever and ever?

Hodge shook himself as if he were a wet dog. This inundation, this wiping out of boundaries, these mounting contradictions were more than enough, for the moment at least. It was almost a relief to remember that Castle Godsea was an island and as solid as they come. On this side of it, the Big Unmanageable Sea: on the other, the manageable moat, the little sea with nothing vague or contradictory about it - except Podge, of course.

Detaching himself from the former, he made for the latter.

It wasn't so difficult, after all, to find his way, through the dim and winding passages at the base of the keep, out into the bailey garden, bright with dewy grass and fragrant with wallflowers, to the great perimeter wall. And thence eastwards, along a slit of a passage within the thickness of the wall - where the masonry smelled a thousand years old - to one of the many doors off it. The one that stood ajar.

Hodge entered, and found himself in a tiny alcove opening out onto the moat. There was the shining water, only inches below his feet. And in there, sure enough, lurked Podge the Unblinking Upstarer.

They pampered sentries at Godsea. The alcove was furnished with a small wooden stool, fixed right up to the water's edge, so that Hodge - seated - didn't have to lean too far forward.

In concentrated mood, he kept his attention on Podge - on his opposite number, his particular adversary, his bugbear, his bogyman - name him as you please. But he did find himself marvelling at the creature, at the wild improbability of the little devil lying in wait for him there.

How *peculiar* he was! What a freak! Absolutely different from

The Sentry

Hodge, of course, but also very different from all Godsea-ers and Manbridgians. They were strictly land-dwellers: he was aquatic - though (alas!) with amphibian ambitions. They looked all around as they pleased and let Hodge be: his gaze was riveted on Hodge, on Hodge his mark, his chosen victim. They could be handled: he, the Untouchable, the Smoothie, couldn't - a fact that Hodge had discovered way back in Beaston. They frequently turned their back on him: he never did. With good reason and evil intent, no doubt. Back of that fishy-frog face were tucked those horribly numerous and nimble, itching feet, or else those supernaturally muscular frog-legs. The Gate-crasher *had* to be locked out, *had* to be kept at bay. The Bounder was for binding, for keeping under house-arrest at all costs.

How to do that? Fortunately there was a way. A perfectly straightforward way. The simplest of things to do, though certainly not the easiest to keep doing. "Keep awake, Hodge! Fasten your eye, my lad, on that Monstrosity out there, and it's stuck there, shackled, immo-bilised, done up, though never done for. Held at a safe distance, at swordpoint."

One other thought Hodge had, as he sat there by the moat on sentry duty:

"I came away from that magic casement opening on the Perilous Sea, yet I didn't do so. Here, at this sentry post by the moat, I don't just *think* of the Sea. It's still flooding me. The most surprising and happy thing about life in this castle is that, having seen the Sea clearly (and there's no other way to see it), I don't lose it when I turn my back on it. On the contrary, I have it for backing wherever and whenever I find myself. I carry it around with me, like a pair of infinite angel wings. Or rather, they carry me around. Truly, truly, this sentry is angelically winged and armed, as he guards Eden against invasion with his flaming sword called Unsleep the Podge-Cleaver!"

It was when Hodge, his stint of sentry duty over, turned to go back to the keep, that he saw the writing on the wall.

In fact, the letters were scratched rather than written on the stone. So shallow, so lightly incised they were, that at first they had been invisible. But now the sun of early morning, low and sidelong to the alcove wall, not only brought them out plainly but limned them in bright gold. For Hodge, an unseen hand had at that moment inscribed them for his sole benefit on the hitherto blank surface: and whose hand would that be but the hand of the Godsea-er who had added his signature to his message?

> Each man is in his Spectre's power,
> Until the arrival of that hour
> When his Humanity awake
> And cast his own Spectre into the lake.
>
> *William Blake, 1803*

And then, less suddenly, that same hand rubbed out the inscription so effectively that Hodge could find no trace of it at all. At that moment nothing was further from his mind than to attribute the erasure to the dark cloud that had drifted across the sun.

Breakfast in hall was a casual, buffet sort of meal. Frank was there, white-haired and lined and (Hodge thought) a little unsteady for one of his age, looking much the same as the day before. Hodge had a strong feeling he should not refer to the events of the night. Instead, he asked him whether he had any news of Mary Porticule.

"I think it may be months before she comes," he replied, quite casually, "but come she will. The cell next to you, on the other side from me, is waiting for her."

Again, Hodge found himself unable to put the question to Frank, the question that hovered on the tip of his tongue. How the blazes did Frank know about Mary, let alone about her plans?

Hodge looked, not too obtrusively, at the man at his side eating his porridge. He was still wearing mittens, and (for such a small person) exceptionally large shoes. About him there was still that wonderful smell.

And then, suddenly and for no reason he could put a finger on, the sight of Frank made him want to cry. It wasn't pity, it wasn't love as he'd known love, it certainly wasn't maudlin sentimentality. It felt more like awe. Awe, mingled with total incomprehension, and gratitude. And the tiniest touch of uneasiness.

That completed Hodge's second list of absurdities - the impossible things he came up against before and during breakfast, on his second day at Godsea Castle.

26

IN GODSEA GARDENS

After breakfast that same day, Nicholas the Castellan came up to Hodge and took him off to the kitchen gardens of Godsea. They lay alongside the beach on the west side of the castle, and were approached by a footbridge across the moat.

The pleasantness of what he saw delighted and astonished Hodge. Fringed with wild iris and meadowsweet, the moat here could scarcely have presented to his senses a scene more unlike the bleak stretch where he had twice mounted sentry duty. It was as if he'd arrived in an altogether friendlier and more comfortable world. The air, shielded by the north-south section of the perimeter wall from the prevailing east wind, was mild and still. The ancient stone walling that was such a cold blue-white elsewhere had weathered here to a russet that seemed to bathe everything in a warm light, and even raise the temperature by a few degrees. Pausing to gaze down from the bridge, he found the water to be scarcely less clear and transparent than the air itself, enabling him to make out, in sharpest detail, a shoal of what looked like tropical fish. Floppily-winged angel fish whose shot-silk colours - emerald, cobalt, rose madder, viridian - were enchanting. The seaweed itself, in and out of which those angel fish were sporting, looked to him like a garden of flowers.

"Yes," said the Castellan, reading his thoughts, "you can see why we call this end of the moat the Friendly or Warm End, and yours the Cold End. In fact what we have is a series of microclimates, graduated from west to east."

"That's a very odd thing to happen", said Hodge, "in so small a space. What's the explanation?"

"Some say there are hot springs feeding this end of the moat. Who knows? What's for sure is that this freak of geography (if that's what it is) makes for a huge and by no means accidental richness and variety of life in Godsea. To say nothing of the life in Godsea moat."

"In what way?" demanded Hodge, looking up sharply from those clear depths at the Castellan. He was immensely intrigued.

"It's best, I think, that you find out for yourself. Which no doubt you'll do soon enough... Come on now. Let me show you the gardens."

What at once struck Hodge about the gardens wasn't how big they were (several acres, in fact) or how well-tended (wonderfully so, in fact) but how vividly they contrasted with the seashore. There, all was wild white sand-dunes on which clumps of salt-sprayed and wind-swept ice-plants, and the occasional grey and twisted oak, somehow survived. Here, this side of the garden fence, all was rich black soil streaked and splashed with every shade of leaf green, and punctuated with the yellows and reds and purples of every variety of fruit and vegetable, many of them new to Hodge.

Truly the gardens were a non-stop miracle, so luscious were the strawberries and raspberries and apples and pears and peaches and apricots, and so right and tight and tasty-looking were those cauliflow-ers and Brussels-sprouts and aubergines and peas and beans and tomatoes and cucumbers - to mention only a few of the beauties. Not grotesque or bloated, but just perfect they were for making one's mouth water. Not over-prolific or run-away, but abundant enough to satisfy the most demanding gardener. All in all, another Eden. Why, even the rough wind off the Sea appeared to Hodge to calm down here into the most caressing of breezes.

"How on Earth do you inspire a desert to blossom into this garden of all gardens?" he asked, in a bowled-over sort of voice. "Talk-ing of Earth, how do you lay down on her this magic black carpet that weaves its own luscious patterning? With a lot of encouragement, no doubt."

"Better ask Steve and Stephanie," replied Nicholas. "They provide much of the encouragement and most of the inspiration around here."

A young couple had strolled up. Beautiful people they were, in Hodge's eyes. They looked as if the bloom of what they grew rubbed off onto them, and vice versa.

Steve explained that ever-improving techniques of composting waste from the Castle, plus a kind of plant-breeding so caring that it amounted to botanical marriage guidance, were of course important. But what switched Godsea gardening over into mystery and magic was *admiration*. These plants, like people, knew when they were appreciated, and responded generously. In effect they became junior members of Godsea community.

Hodge was thrilled. All his old love of plants, his feeling of special kinship with those unshod and unloose and therefore blessed creatures, arose in him, stronger than ever.

"May I work here, please?" he asked. Humbly, for him.

"Why of course," answered Stephanie. "But Steve has only told you half the story, the down-to-earth and unexciting half. Really it's the supernatural help we have here that turns the scales. I call our little friends the Booglies and the Eldies. Because we're fond of them, and don't (like most humans) make fun of them or pooh-pooh their very existence, they're grateful. They show their gratitude by nourishing and cherishing all we grow here."

Hodge was looking hard, not at the speaker or her garden, but at Nicholas.

"You'd better tell Hodge a bit more about your friends," he said. "I doubt whether he's heard of Booglies and Eldies, let alone seen any."

Hodge nodded. His frown was of the encouraging and tactful sort.

"Well, they're mostly out and about and busy around dawn and dusk, so they're not often seen. During the day they sleep in old rabbit-burrows and among the bushes. The Booglies are pale green and up to a foot tall, and they have faces like trumpets. They look after the fruit, mostly. The Eldies are smaller, and their faces are like the cockle-shells you find on the beach. They sing and dance a lot, when they're not tending the vegetables."

"Do you see them often?" Hodge ventured.

"Regularly."

"How about you?" Hodge inquired politely, turning to Steve.

"How about a spot of work?" said Steve.

They gave him the job of hoeing rows of beetroot, alongside a lad of thirteen called Oliver. Nicholas went off to pick strawberries.

Well, you can imagine Hodge's pleasure. This was him all over, him extended. To take a dead thing called a Dutch hoe and bring it to life! To grow a new limb-ending for caressing the earth with, and so effectively! To touch and tickle and tumble that rich humus with this so-sensitive steel hand of his! The tickling now, the laughing response of harvest to follow. Just like old times it was.

And, of course, just the opposite. In Godsea even a Dutch hoe lives the other way up.

I hoe in Mambridge   *I hoe in Godsea*

Ten minutes of unsullied enjoyment at being Hodge-the-Hoe, and then he allowed his attention to wander to take in his workmate, young Oliver. Bright of eye, with apple-rosy cheeks and finely cut bone structure, he nevertheless looked a little down-in-the-mouth. A shining sourpuss of a youth, was Hodge's unspoken comment.

"Like it here?" he asked, as casually as he could, continuing to hoe.

"Yes," said with almost no hesitation.

"Go along with all this Godsea business?"

"Yes," said with no hesitation at all.

"Including Booglies and Eldies?"

"Of course not! What do you take me for?"

A longish interval of silent hoeing.

Then the lad opened up: "I'm off to high school in Manbridge next week, with my twin sister. We'll be living there, and coming back here only for the holidays. I aim to go on to the University and read chemistry."

"How do you and your sister feel about this move?"

"Very good," emphatically spoken.

"How do your parents feel?"

"Very bad. They're trying to scare us with stories of MI 13, and talk us into staying on here. We have a sort of school in Godsea, a tiny one and the kids are mostly very young. The labs are hopeless."

"What about the other people here? Do they think you should leave?"

"I think it's about fifty-fifty. Our aunt and uncle back us up. They say there's a whole lot we need to learn in Manbridge that we'll never pick up here. We've been using their library of Manbridge books, which they keep adding to. But that's not enough. We have to go and live and study there."

"Are your aunt and uncle real members of the community? I mean: are they serious about Godsea, and all that?"

"Don't be silly. Of course they're dead serious. They wouldn't be here if they weren't."

They took a rest from hoeing...

Hodge, recovering from his ticking-off, was the first to speak.

"Do you think you and your sister will forget this place and what it stands for, and turn into normal Manbridgers?"

"That's what our parents are frightened of. We aren't. But we're tremendously keen to go."

"Why?"

"I don't know. I think it's like my aunt and uncle say: we have to find our own way. To go, and find our own way back home."

"You hoe your row of beetroot, I hoe mine?"

"That's right."

And that's exactly what they went on doing...

Hodge joined Nicholas for a sandwich lunch on the beach. None too soon, for Hodge. He was impatient to ask the Castellan about Stephanie's Booglies and Eldies. Had *he* seen the little fellows?

"Never. Not a glimpse." His tone of voice was neutral; he wasn't giving a thing away.

"Who else sees them, apart from Stephanie?"

"Really I don't know. Perhaps two or three of her friends."

"Do these creatures live in the rabbit-holes of Stephanie's mind, or the rabbit-holes of her garden?"

There was a long pause. It seemed the matter was one of some delicacy.

"Well, are they real, or imaginary?" Hodge persisted.

"These strawberries we're eating aren't imaginary, nor is their quite exceptional flavour. And the same goes for all the other produce of the gardens, I guess."

"Excuse me, Castellan, but you haven't answered my question."

"I can't. So what? There are billions of questions I can't answer. And I don't mind a bit. More and more I *like* being so abysmally ignorant! You name it, I don't understand a word of it."

"Does your ignorance extend to young Oliver and his sister - to whether they should or shouldn't leave for Manbridge?"

"Yes it does. The choice is up to them. They want to go, so they should go. It's normal. If, on the other hand, they had wanted to stay, I'd have been surprised, but not said they were wrong."

"If you knew they were likely to end up in Strangefields, you would still let them go, without warning?"

"They know the risks. My unasked-for advice wouldn't make a ha'porth of difference, anyway. Also, let me remind you, your way from Manbridge to Godsea lay through Strangefields. Could you, Hodge, have come here by any other route? I suspect you owe far more to that institution than you are ready to admit, as yet. No, the truth is that I don't know what's good for you or those kids - or me for that matter - any more. Or (important correction) I don't know what it is in advance of its happening. In fact, it isn't just that the older I get the fewer answers I come up with, but the fewer questions I put. They think I'm the wise old Castellan, but between you and me I'm the Fool of Godsea. Instead of this ring I should be wearing cap and bells. Not everyone here realises that Godsea is an asylum for retarded Manbridgers - of whom I, its Castellan, am chief."

"Can you be more specific? Topical perhaps?"

In Godsea Gardens

"I'll try. Back in Manbridge I was hooked on being adult and well-informed. There, long long ago, I *knew* - ha! ha! - how I crook this little FINGER and speak this little WORD, and persuade this red strawberry suddenly to turn into a shapeless and colourless sweetness, and why ultramarine is so resolutely ultramarine, and that (come on!) of course these pebbles are perfectly ordinary and natural and inevitable and nothing to write home about, and what size an inch really really is, and when and whether I was born, and where I stop and my world starts, and whether UP is up and if IF is iffy. But no longer! In Godsea I'm all at Sea, and loving it. Nothing *has* to be. Nothing *has* to be the way it is. This sand could consist of teeny-weeny Easter eggs in their flashiest Easter wrapping, and the undertow of this Ocean could run up and not down the beach because it's bewitched, and instead of seeing your face now I could be wearing it, and this fiddler crab could be a beautiful side-stepping musical ogre. And - no doubt about this one - the clear air of the morning could and does smell of wild violets, and - just listen! Childe Godefroi's plainsong is hitting a new high..."

The old man sat there in his threadbare monkish habit, hugging his knees and gazing out into the Sea's horizonless expanse.

"Does this foolery, this ignorance, this funny combination of wonder and cluelessness and uninquisitiveness, seem to you a cop-out? Or perhaps infantile?" he added. There was wistfulness in his voice.

It was a full minute before Hodge trusted himself to reply.

"The man of Manbridge wasn't born yesterday. He's been around. He's canny, and thickly insulated against surprise. He knows a thing or two, knows what's what! The God of Godsea is a simpleton who doesn't. He's young, and never grows up. His hair stands on end with surprise at everything, including Himself. Specially Himself. And, insofar as His Seers see with His seeing and are alive with His life, they are astonished with His astonishment and foolish with His folly and brand-new with His newness. It all adds up to a very special kind of joy. Till you unknow everything you don't know what joy is..."

"Go on," said Nicholas, after another interval.

"Back in Manbridge," replied Hodge, "and even more here, I've found all astonishment boiling down to One Astonishment, and all questions boiling down to One Question, and that question unanswerable. And somehow that Great Unanswerable takes care of all those little questions, is the Happy Answer to all those tiresome little unanswerables. Such as whether Stephanie's fairy friends are real, and whether Oliver and his sister are doing the right thing, and…" - pause - "what the devil's going on at night in the cell next to mine."

The Castellan didn't rise to this latest bait, either. Instead, he asked Hodge to explain what he meant by the Great Unanswerable.

"Back in Manbridge," he replied, "I found myself stuck with a problem rather like Stephanie's here. I saw something terribly important which other people didn't see, and usually weren't in the slightest bit interested in, or were positively embarrassed by. She has her Booglies and Eldies, and good luck to her and them. I had my Popkins. Young Godpopkins, to give him his full name. A secret friend that even Mary didn't want to know about."

"I want to know all about him." The Castellan seemed very much in earnest.

"He was in such a constant state of surprise that he had no eyebrows: they disappeared into his hair. He had a song about what so surprised him. It ran like this:

The Song of Godpopkins

O how *clever* I am
To make myself be
And dream myself up
In time for high tea,
With no help from her
And no help from him,
For no rhyme or reason
But only from whim.

O there should be nothing at all, at all.
There was no-one around to haul or to call
Godpopkins up from the depths of damn-all
And have him enjoy such a beautiful ball.

O how *brilliant* I am
To make myself be
And cook myself up
For dinner and tea,
With no help from him
And no help from her,
As for no earthly reason
I choose to occur.

"There was another verse that I've forgotten, in which Popkins decides he's IMPOSSIBLE. He dances around, madly happy, throwing his jester's cap in the air, and hollering rude things about those solemn imbeciles who say 'Come off it! Of course we have to exist, and Being has to be, and isness is natural and rather a bore,' and all that bosh. He makes lots and lots of pictures of himself getting up to - himself."

"Is Popkins another name for Hodge?"

"Absolutely yes. Absolutely no."

"That was in Manbridge, you say. So Popkins is alive and well here in Godsea?"

Hodge couldn't help noting that it wasn't just the old man's voice that was trembly.

"More so than ever. He's my darling, the love of my life. In fact I always carry around with me one of his self-portraits as a reminder, a memorial, next to my heart."

He fished out of a breast pocket a dog-eared card, and handed it to Nicholas.

"Also I like to think of this as the Great Whirlpool, the Maelstrom, of the Perilous Sea."

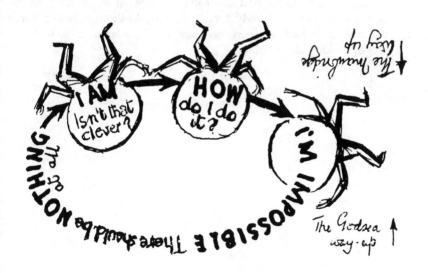

"Here in Godsea for a change," he added, "Popkins is of course the other way up. Also he has swapped his conical-comical cap for a practical sou'-wester and gone to Sea. In fact, he can no longer be separated from the Sea. The Sea to which all returns."

"Amen," said Nicholas the Castellan, handing back the card. "As
it was - as the Sea was in the beginning - is now and ever shall be.
World without end, amen."

He leapt to his feet.

"Let's go in. Like Young Popkins, I could do with some tea."

"I'm ready to sign off, to pack it in for good and all, now I've got
that off my chest," said Hodge, not budging. "And unloaded it onto a
friend who gets what I'm about, at last."

"In the last twenty minutes I *have* died. What's more, I *shall* die if I
don't get my tea, high, low, or medium. Come along, Young Popkins."

That's about all they said that day.

From then on their relationship (if it was a relationship at all) was
different. It was as though they'd said everything. As though further
conversation weren't just unnecessary but a come-down, an anticlimax,
a superfluous footnote to what passed between them that afternoon on
the beach by Godsea garden, on the edge of the Incredible Sea. As
though their vision of the Unanswerable really had answered all lesser
questions. As though the swirling mists of the Absolutely Obvious yet
Absolutely Impossible Sea had absorbed and cleared all the mists of the
world, while deepening the Mystery to infinity. As though the old-timer
and the new-timer had between them surprised the Impossible in the
very act of making all possible.

27

DE-MYSTING

Nothing happened that night to disturb Hodge, and his morning turn of duty by the moat went well enough. Podge, more aggresssive than ever, was duly seen off. The only surprise came when, back in his cell and before climbing the stairs to breakfast, he took leave of the Sea.

Always there had been some mist around, whether thin to the point of invisibility or plain-to-see, whether still or swirling, whether building up here and there into clouds or evenly spread over all that expanse. But today the mist had no limits, and was thicker than he'd ever seen it, and perpetually on the move. A fog rather than a mist, you could say, except that no Manbridge fog was ever so lively, as if every particle of it were being agitated in some truly cosmic blender.

Nothing strange about that. Changes in the weather were to be expected, no doubt. What was remarkable was that the mist or fog did absolutely nothing to hide or limit the Sea. Rather the reverse. It was still a Sea without end, a Horizonless Sea that went on forever and forever. Here was a fog for seeing through, a fog to dissolve all fogs!

Another impossibility, and not the least of Hodge's fast-growing collection! He was beginning to wonder whether there was anything in and around and about Godsea that didn't gleefully contradict itself, with a heigh-ho and a tra-la-la.

At breakfast an exceptionally youthful middle-aged man made for Hodge and introduced himself. He was small, as sprightly as an early-morning bird, and had a voice to match.

"Sebastian's my name. Welcome to Godsea! Or, as I much prefer to put it, to Clearsea Castle."

"Why the preference?"

"I'm against all mysteriousness, mystification, mystery-monger-ing - spell those words with a *y* or an *i* as you please."

"What's your objection?" Hodge's tone of voice carried a maxi-mum of interest, a minimum of challenge.

"Because woolliness, vague uplift, waffle of all sorts are a curse and a cock-up. What sets us free here is clarity and precision. Go for what's as transparent as spring water and as keen as a cut-throat razor, and see what else you need, I say."

"Do I understand you have a way of clearing the Sea of all this mist and fog? Even pea-soup fog? A sort of marine soup strainer or filter?"

"Certainly."

"Why bother, if the mist doesn't obscure the Sea one little bit?"

"In practice, it draws a veil."

"You have a way of penetrating the veil?"

"Yes," chirped Sebastian, with a happy smile. "If you're interested, I'd be delighted to show you."

"Yes, please."

"Come with me, then."

The little man led Hodge downstairs to a cell much like his own, but on the other side of the keep, its west side.

It turned out to be full to overflowing with people and apparatus. The window was shut tight and quite steamed up, except for a D-shaped central bit kept clear with a fast-moving windscreen-wiper.

The apparatus consisted of a very fat and impressive and shiny telescope hung around with gadgetry, mounted on a massive tripod and wired up to what looked like a collection of computers scattered around the floor. The object lens was directed to the clear space in the window. Darting about the place, peering into view-finders, turning wheels, fingering keyboards, pressing levers and reading dials, were two young women and a young man: all three of them alight with the energy and enthusiasm of Sebastian, their chief.

With Hodge, that made five in all, in an unventilated room designed for one, plus the odd visitor. No wonder he felt hemmed in and sweaty and suffocating.

"All set?" demanded Sebastian of his assistants.

"All set, Sebast!"

Coming on top of the congestion in that little cell, the nickname of its owner - Sebast, for God's sake! - was the last straw. It seemed to take Hodge straight to some hideous world.

Sebast was asking him to make his way somehow to the clear space in the window, and look out and say what he saw.

Complying, Hodge answered: "It's exceptionally misty over the Sea today."

De-Mysting

Sebast seemed delighted at Hodge's weather report, and even more delighted to invite him to struggle to the other end of the instrument and peer through its main eye-piece.

"Why, the mist's all gone!" he exclaimed.

His astonishment evidently gratified everyone. Sebastian went so far as to insist on shaking hands with him; and would have patted him on the back if he - Hodge - hadn't returned to the window to make sure that the scene outside was unchanged.

"This piece of wizardry is your invention?"

"Well, yes. With the help of our friends here. But of course there's nothing magical at all about it. In fact, magicalness is just the sort of stuffiness and congealed mist that UVIRT (our ultra-violet-infra-red telescope) exists to penetrate and dispel."

"This brother's feeling stuffy and congealed, all right," said Hodge, and wondered whether they couldn't talk somewhere else.

"They're serving morning coffee in the great hall. Let's go."

On the way there, Sebastian and Hodge were held up, briefly. They stood aside to make way for a troupe of six women dressed all in white, who were filing out of the door next to Sebastian's cell. They were half-singing and half-humming a song that sounded to Hodge like a Sea-shanty - a sacred sea-shanty, if you can imagine such a thing - and there was a strong smell of incense.

From his position in the corridor Hodge could just see through into the room - it looked more like a cave than a room - those white figures were coming from. Could see enough to raise his curiosity to the highest pitch. Every inch of the walls and ceiling and floor, with the exception of a crack of light from the curtained casement at the far end, was covered with a riot of fantastic forms in brilliant colours. Exactly what those forms were he had no time to make out.

"Your neighbours," said Hodge, over coffee. "Tell me about them."

Sebastian was reticent. Was it that he didn't know, or didn't want to know, what they were up to? As neighbours, he said, they presented no problems.

"What do they feel about the stuff you're busy combating and seeing through?"

"How should I know? Probably they want to keep their mists, even thicken them. So do a lot of other folk around here. That's why our work is important."

Having made a mental note to investigate that magic cave at the very first opportunity, Hodge gave his attention to what his companion was saying.

"It's the clearness of the Sea, not its obscurity, which is what this place is all about. Or should be all about."

"Why, " asked Hodge, "do you think some people here delight in the foam and the mists of the Perilous Sea? Isn't the patterning of the snowflake crystal, arising from and returning to the Sea, something to sing and dance about? And after all, what are you and I but the Sea, whipping itself up into strands and gobbets of Godseafoam? Not for nothing, not out of negligence, are we made of the Ocean that's not so much mysterious as The Mystery."

"It's a question of self-preservation. The secret reason why people go for the mist is that they're frightened of the Sea. To be submerged in mist is safe (they suppose) while to be submerged in water is fatal. We say: shed your robe of mist and foam, dare to plunge naked into the Sea, and you'll find there's nothing left of you to drown. As the ultimate Clarity you are the ultimate Safety. Or - to talk shop - the shelf-life of the empty shelf, unlike the goods it displays, has no limit."

"I was wondering," said a still-damp Hodge, "Why you keep the window in your cell shut so infernally tight. The place has given me a headache."

"The Sea air isn't good for our apparatus, and some of us are a bit subject to chills and bronchitis."

"You have a remarkable precision tool," said Hodge, "for making boreholes."

"You approve of my telescope?" responded Sebastian warily.

"It reminds me of an apple-corer. You know the tool I mean, a pointed knife shaped and used like a gouge, used also for peeling potatoes as well as apples, and scooping out their eyes. You core those mist-banks, drilling a clear tunnel through the thickest and densest of them; and - yes! - in a sense scooping out their eyes. Well done! Very clever. But…"

"But what?" inquired Sebastian, getting less chirpy by the minute.

"The apple is more eatable than the core. I prefer the whole apple."

"I don't follow you."

"Looking out of my window I take in the whole width of the Ocean, from east to west. No! From East of east to West of west. Peeking out of your telescope you take in a circular patch, a few inches across. Is that enough? Agreed that your patch is clear while my expanse is cloudy. But the question is: do the clouds hide the Ocean or restrict it in any way?"

"Of course they do."

"In my experience they don't. I checked up only this morning. It's a marvellous thing I can't begin to explain, that the thickest cloud-cover of the Perilous Sea doesn't limit or obstruct its visibility in the slightest. Or dim its wonder at itself - a wonder that your telescope cuts out as so much mist, I think."

"I insist that what we all have in common here in Godsea is the Sea's clarity. Not its mistiness, about which we all differ. And how we differ!"

"Very true," replied Hodge in measured tones. "I grant you that, because the clarity and boundlessness of the Sea are changeless and the same for us all, they are the Sea's essential virtue; and because the mist and the foam are ever-changing, they are a kind of decoration or bonus or (for some) an optional extra. But not for me. I can't spare them. No mists no mystery, no mystery no adventure, no adventure no life. It's not for nothing our Sea is called Perilous. If it weren't awesome and never made me tremble and never left me flabbergasted and weak at the knees, it would be a washout. By itself, your borehole is, precisely, a bore. Guaranteed to bore one to death."

"People used to talk of softening of the brain. I prefer to call it wishywashy sentimentality. I'm not attacking you personally, you'll understand. But you really should try Emptiness. It's good for you. It's strong stuff, it's tough, and doesn't let you down."

"It will and it does," said Hodge. "An empty sack collapses into a heap on the floor. A full sack doesn't. Haven't you noticed how full to overflowing the Emptiness is?"

A long, highly-charged pause...

The two of them stood up, heron and cocksparrow confronting one another. Hodge was reminded of the Green dinner party which had nearly ended in a cockfight.

"Let's get this straight," he said in a level voice, "You think I'm pretty sick."

"In this regard, yes," said Sebastian.

"I suggest it's you who aren't well. You diagnose my trouble as softening of the brain. I diagnose yours as hardening of the heart. You're set on stripping the Sea of all its wild charm and strangeness and joy, and reducing it to a great big Yawn. No, to the narrowest and most mean-minded of yawns. A miserable two-inch bore of a yawn. And surely that's unhealthy, life-denying, a deficiency disease."

"Perhaps you'd better go back to the fug, to the murky climate of where you belong! Wherever that is."

There they stood, frozen. Shaping up. Shaping up for what? Something had to give...

Instead, something was given.

It came out of the blue, for no reason. Neither of them saw it coming, much less intended it. In Hodge's very limited experience such behaviour was quite untypical of Godsea, not to mention the Manbridge circles he'd moved in. You could say that those two so-different men, pitted against one another that morning in the great hall of Godsea Castle, were taken over by the Sea itself.

Simultaneously they spread their arms, and came together, and embraced.

That's all. No word was spoken.

A few moments, and they disentangled. And went their separate ways.

28

UPROAR

T he place was the kitchen garden. The time, it seemed to Hodge, some months after his encounter with Sebastian: in fact, it was a mere three weeks - time did funny things in Godsea. Those present were Hodge and Cecilia, the young woman - still wearing her coarse brown servants' robe - who had been the first to welcome him to Godsea. They were both picking peas, and very fine marrowfat peas they were.

Hodge's headache - the first since he had come to Godsea - was almost gone. The company of Cecilia completed the cure, at any rate for the moment. There was a quiet and a gentleness about her, a soothing absence of anything resembling bumptiousness or even chirpiness.

After an hour or so of work they left the garden for the shore, where they sat shelling the peas that filled their baskets. The morning mists had begun to clear, in favour of brilliant sunshine and the lightest of Sea-breezes. Hodge was the first to speak.

"Tell me, Cecilia, do some people get so disillusioned with this place that they go back to Manbridge? Or fit in so badly they're sent back?"

"O yes, it does happen. There's the sad instance of Ronny Hobb, who was a good friend of mine. Maybe part of the reason was that his Goblin - who was exceptionally cunning as well as exceptionally muscular and bursting with energy - managed to kick up such a smokescreen of spume and spray that he made himself quite invisible. Anyway, Ronny announced that he'd polished off the Menace, and not just seen him off. Finally abolished the Monster, instead of merely banishing him. Naturally this didn't go down at all well in Godsea. So back Ronny Hobb went to Manbridge, where he's collected a band of disciples dedicated to becoming well and truly de-Goblined, like their revered Master. But I'm afraid the truth about him is the other way round. So far from having finished his Goblin off, Ronny's let him in, and become thoroughly Hobgoblined. Such a pity! He was so gifted! Yet so gormless, so gullible... Well, that's how I read the story of Ronny and his Goblin. I could be wrong, of course. I hope against hope I am wrong."

"All of which," said Hodge, "shows how necessary it is to be clear about the meaning and purpose of Godsea, its raison d'etre, its essential dynamics, the secret behind its indestructibility, its survival down the ages against all the odds... But, to move on from Departures to Arrivals, I don't suppose you've had any news of Mary?"

"Yes I have," said Cecilia.

Hodge perked up.

"I didn't tell you this. Mary's a kind of second-cousin-once-removed of mine, and we write occasionally. I was a nervous twelve-year-old in the school we both went to in Manbridge, when she was head girl. Very kind she was to me. She's well, but her father isn't. She's having to nurse him. Otherwise I feel sure we'd have seen her here."

"Is she " - Hodge was having to pick his words with care - "is Godsea her scene? I'd ask whether she's the type, if it weren't for the strong impression I'm getting that there is *no* Godsea type. All right," - he took the plunge - "is she a Godsea-er? Will she naturally want to come and live here as soon as she can?"

"The answer's yes and yes, I'm pretty sure. Something drastic has happened to her. She's been through a crisis of her own since you left Manbridge, though she's not told me much about it. She's always asking about you. I try to keep her posted with news."

"I hope she comes soon. The cell next to mine is empty and waiting for her. Do tell her how beautiful this place is, and how fascinating the people are, and what wonderful friends will welcome her here. Like Nicholas the Castellan. In this very spot - it seems an age ago - we had a conversation. For me, the best in my life. I wish she could have been with us."

"He's not well today."

"I hope it's not serious. Would he like me to visit him?"

"I think he'd rather be on his own. He's a very private man."

"Does the responsibility of his position weigh on him? I mean, we're such an incredibly mixed bag that getting any semblance of unity, and holding us together at all, must be a tricky job. I know he says he minds his own business, but surely the Castellan of this place can't entirely overlook what's going on. Not much is lost on Nicholas, I think."

"Perhaps. All the same, he sees himself as clueless, or even brainless, just like his predecessor William."

"I keep running into the late Castellan William," replied Hodge. "First, you put me in his cell. Then Castellan Nicholas tells me about his sense of humour. Now it's his dim-wittedness. He seems to have made quite an impression - though a mixed one - on Godsea. Tell me more about him."

"I don't know much, apart from the rhyme that became his theme song and signature tune, so to speak. He got it from Manbridge, where nobody (with the possible exception of Charles Lutwidge Dodgson) noticed what sense it made. Typically, the foolishness of Manbridge became the wisdom of Godsea.

"You are old, Father William, the young man said,
And your hair has become very white;
And yet you incessantly stand on your head -
Do you think, at your age, it is right?

"In my youth, Father William replied to his son,
I feared it might injure the brain;
But now that I'm perfectly sure I have none,
Why, I do it again and again."

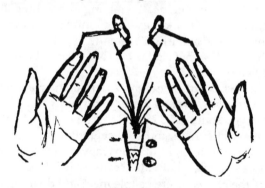

"I think," Cecilia added, "that one of the results of being brainless and inverted is that you can't for the life of you sort out or reconcile the funny things going on here. And that this bafflement, once you accept it, has in it the kind of relief and lightness of heart that comes with being topsy-turvy. Correction: turvy-topsy. The right way up at last. *'Put your feet up and have a nice rest'* makes good sense here in Godsea, all day, and not just after a hard day's work."

"Of course," replied Hodge, "he's absolutely accurate about standing on the head - and the brain - that one doesn't have. That's pure Godsea. All the same, we're a funny old lot, you must admit. Looked at from outside, a community - what a joke! - all smooth and streamlined and pea-green like this peapod in my hand. Suppose, breaking it open now, I found peas red and white and blue and purple, peas cubic and pyramidal and round, peas whole and split, peas that weren't peas at all - with assorted flavours to match - why then I'd have a pea-for-pea picture of Godsea Castle as it really is. The fragmented and incoherent inside story of that seemingly all-of-a-piece stronghold over there on our left."

Cecilia had a musical laugh.

"You seem very cheerful about my crazy pea-pod," Hodge added.

"Isn't it lovely, having Nothing in common?" she replied.

"The answer depends on whether you spell it with a small n or a big N. There's all the world of difference - and more - between a goddamned nothing that shuts everything out and a godblessed Nothing that takes everything in, finding lots of lovely room and a warm welcome for it all. Between, if you like, that Perilous Sea with its sparkle and swirling vapours and rainbow foam, and a sea from which the mists have lifted and even the waters have been drained away, leaving nothing but peril, nothing but death, nothing but nothing. It looks to me as if some members of this so-called community go for the little n and some for the big N. And some don't care much either way since it's the moat rather than the Sea that claims nearly all their attention. Community my Aunt Fanny!"

"Yet things work out, somehow. After all, the place hasn't blown up, or been blown away, over all these centuries."

"But I bet you some of its inhabitants have come to blows. Look, Cecilia, I'm a newcomer here, and only beginning to discover what's going on. My early impressions of chaos may be wrong. How do I find out more? Besides people's individual cells, which I realise are sacrosanct, there are the places where people meet and do things together. Can I wander around, and barge in anywhere, without being invited?"

"I don't see why not. I can't think of anywhere that's out-of-bounds, but do be careful not to get lost in the deeper tunnels. It has happened. You can recognise cell doors by the numbers on them. The others don't have numbers. You're free to venture in there, tactfully. No barging in, you'll understand. But it's not a bad idea to shop around. You'd find it fun, too. I doubt whether anyone's going to poke you on the nose."

"I'm not so sure about that," replied Hodge, pensively, as they got up and made for the castle kitchen with their load of shelled peas.

"Though afterwards," he added, "they might be quite nice about it. Help to staunch the flow of blood, and all that... Well, I'll give it a try."

His idea was to start with Sebastian's neighbours, and their cave-like meeting-place covered with paintings. Paintings of whom or what? That was just one of the many things he had to find out.

But track down that cave he could not, for all his trying. Really, he complained, everyone should be given a detailed plan of Godsea, floor by floor, showing every staircase and corridor dog-leg and lobby, with dead-ends clearly distinguished from through-ways. Also places where - ouch! - you banged your head. Besides, the lighting was grim. Quite often the most dangerous spots were the darkest. Something ought to be done about all this. He'd mention it to the Castellan, as soon as he got better.

Abandoning the search, he found himself outside a door that stood ajar. Invitingly ajar? Well, hardly. Pandemonium was issuing from it, an uproar that for the moment took Hodge back to that dreadful night on the Great Moor of Kreep.

The door opened onto a far larger room than he'd reckoned on, brilliantly lit, and full of people. Men and women of all ages and shapes and sizes they were, in various stages of undress, and doing all manner of extraordinary things. Some were dancing ecstatically, flailing arms and legs. Some were creeping about on all fours. Two were standing on their heads. Another pair were spread-eagled on the floor, one face-down and the other face-up, like playing cards. A thin old woman stood flattened against the wall, motionless, it seemed under the impression that she was carved in low bas-relief. A young person sat on the floor, head between his or her knees, apparently in the depths of despair. Another young person stood at the window-sill, pointing out to Sea with one hand and in to herself with the other, her face radiant with what was surely joy unbounded...

Yes, the window - a large one - stood wide open. And just as well, thought Hodge. To shut this lot in would be fire and brimstone.

All of them were giving tongue - shrieking, howling, chirruping, singing, crooning, growling, barking, hissing, spitting, or quietly muttering gibberish. The noise was deafening.

No one took any notice of Hodge. He was thankful for that much.

He decided to sit on the floor, wall at his back, and await developments - in the unlikely event of anything remaining to be developed.

The young man facing him, teeth bared and dribbling a bit,

reminded him of someone. Could it be of himself when angry, way back in those early days in the Porticules' caravan?

It was then that Hodge went barmy.

At least that was the adjective he applied to himself, safely back in his cell at the end of that eventful day.

There he was, then, crumpled up on the floor of a room that had been lifted en bloc out of Bedlam Outbedlamed, and the young man opposite was growling and baring a splendid set of dazzling teeth at him. Well, not exactly at Hodge. The enemy provoking this hyena-like reaction seemed to be an invisible one a foot or so to the north of Hodge. It was a moot question whether that young man registered Hodge at all.

Hodge's response - more teeth-baring, with a little barking and hissing thrown in for realism - was at first tongue-in-cheek. He didn't see why he should play the part of spoil-sport and refuse to join in the fun. In fact, this not-so-terribly-funny fun was proving infectious. He found himself fast becoming more and more energetic and in earnest. Increasingly he felt what he was doing, and doing what he felt. And what he found himself doing and feeling was plenty and fancy-free, with no holds barred.

It was no game or put-on act but the most natural thing in the world that he should now leap to his feet, kindly hold up his hands to the ceiling to prevent it falling on the assembled company, and howl

like a pack of famished wolves. And that he should find the howls
becoming, of their own free will, peals of laughter, and then *O Isis und
Osiris* sung falsetto, and then a series of orders barked out at a squad of
gormless recruits by a purple drill-sergeant, and then *Om Mani Padme
Hum* hummed most piously. Add to these capers several spots of
handclapping, whistling, warmly shaking hands with himself, trying so
hard to put his big toe in his mouth, stroking the gentle air, catching all
those troublesome butterflies, and solemnly reciting the alphabet and
the seven-times table - and you'll have a pretty accurate picture of how
Hodge of Godsea, and late of Manbridge and Beaston, spent most of
that peculiar morning.

It wasn't the sort of thing that could go on indefinitely, of course.
There were limits to the endurance of even the toughest of these
bedlamites: including Hodge, their new but by no means raw recruit.
One by one they slunk off, trotted off, breezed off, buzzed off, as the
case might be, taking no notice of the others. Talk about community!
This was the least communal of get-togethers, individualistic to the nth
degree. Hyped-up though he was, Hodge could scarcely help noticing
how separate these folk were, how private. If this was hysteria, for sure
it wasn't mass hysteria.

The Hodge that pushed off eventually - last to come, last to go -
was certainly in a state. A reckless, devil-may-care, busted-wide-open,
somehow exalted state, rather like one of his old trances intensified. The
difference was that this mood left him in the market for all that might
be on offer. After that shindig, after those pandemonic goings-on,
anything goes. Only the clearly-marked cell doors in that maze of
tunnels were barred to him, anyway. What more infernal or supernal
surprises could Godsea have up its capacious sleeve? Godsea, which
was supposed to open doors on purest heaven! Well, better know the
worst. *Could* there be more, could there be worse shocks (or did he
mean better ones?) to come? Well, tomorrow he was going to find out
for himself, once and for all, what the devil Godsea's up to.

29

THE OINTMENT, THE SWORD AND THE THREE JEWELS

Perhaps it wasn't surprising, in view of Hodge's high-strung state following the Bedlam affair, that he should dream a most disturbing dream that night. One that in two or three places touched on nightmare and screaming terror. Nor was it surprising, in view of the Castellan's earlier references to the curious topography of the castle moat - cryptic remarks about microclimates and the monstrosities they spawn - that the dream should feature the moat and its pondlife. Casual remarks that had nevertheless come to puzzle and preoccupy Hodge to the point of obsession. And (as we know) when Hodge had something on his mind he didn't easily shed it. He wore it, he gave it the full treatment.

In fact, his dream turned out to be one of those singularly opportune dreams that are not less but more vivid and significant than waking life: in detail screwy no doubt, but no less to the point on that account. All the dream lacked was daytime consistency and daytime colour, in particular the red-orange end of the spectrum. Call it a vision and a revelation in monochrome rather than a mere dream. A revelation that threw a broad beam of light - well, of moonlight - on the Godsea Experience: if *revelation* is the right word for what proved to be (how typical of Godsea!) a cat's-cradle of paradoxes and at once an unveiling and veiling, at once a solution and a crystallisation of the mystery of Godsea in general and its moat in particular.

A strangely disquieting and twice-as-large-as-normal moon was lighting up the water to the dazzling smoothness of old silver polished for generations. All was held fast in a silence so intense it set Hodge's ears tingling. And in an air balmy and preternaturally still.

He found himself sitting, none too comfortably, in the prow of a little boat beneath the footbridge at the far western end of the moat (the warm and friendly end Nicholas had called it) watching the unnaturally tall, grey-robed and hooded figure at the stern. A towering presence that did nothing to reassure Hodge. The man (if it was a man) was standing

with his back to him, sculling the boat along so skilfully with his spoon-shaped oar that he hardly raised a ripple on that lacquered surface. Between them, the boat was piled with gifts wrapped in silver foil.

There was no telling whether it was Christmas time or Easter time or birthday present time, or just parcel-post time. Whatever the occasion and the reason, the two of them were bringing presents to the sentries on duty in the alcoves of the perimeter wall. Expensive-looking parcels of intriguingly various shapes and sizes, tied with blue ribbon.

All the alcoves were occupied. Immediately beneath every one of them, of course, there swam - there lurked motionless - the upward-gazing spectre or opposite number of its occupant, his or her equivalent of Podge. The wonderfully smooth motion of the boat, though so close to those watery creatures, scarcely upset them at all. What rippling there was read as fleeting and flicker-ing changes of expression on their faces.

And - much to his surprise - a better-looking gallery of faces Hodge had never seen.

Or a more cheerful. A few were wreathed in watery smiles, some seemed quietly amused, the rest were doing nicely thank you very much. All appeared as contented with themselves as their opposite numbers on dry land were with their parcels. Scarcely a thin-lipped down-curving batrachian mouth or a piscine pout to be seen. If these were fishy or froggy characters they couldn't have been more cleverly disguised. Every one of them was handsomely turned out: hair combed and curled and crimped or braided and be-ribboned, teeth macleaned to gleaming like miniatures of that huge moon, complexions almost Mary-like, cheeks french-polished. Lined up and spaced at regular intervals along the castle wall, they were as sedate and well-behaved as a row of fenders or luminous buoys moored alongside a quay in the Isles of the Blest. Talk about respectability! Many a sunday-school treat at the seaside (Hodge told himself) amounted to a binge or debauch compared with this turn-out. (He *knew*, of course! In his dream he was the world's expert on practically everything, including sunday-school treats!) In fact, he was reminded of the juvenile but saintly cherubs in old paintings - bodiless heads furnished with bright wings like out-size ears - only here they were presumably water-wings. A pretty sight!

All the same there was something not quite right about the creatures, something that gave him the willies. They were too good to be true, by several notches. In particular their smiles lacked conviction. They were the sort you put on rather than break out into.

The sentries, on the other hand, were all right. To each Hodge was graciously handing a special gift. It was being received in like manner, with a little bow. Somehow in his dream he knew which parcel was for whom, but not at all what it contained.

Plucking up all his courage, he ventured to ask the boatman to satisfy his curiosity - addressing the back of the man, if it was a man.

The shock of what followed made him wish to God he hadn't spoken.

The head that turned to reply was *faceless!* Its features eaten away instead of lit up by that eerie moonlight.

"Don't panic, don't panic!" Hodge kept telling himself, to no immediate effect…

It was some little time before he managed to pull himself together enough to attend to the voice that was coming from that horrific Blank. Echoed back from the giant sounding-board of the castle wall and battlements, it came across as cavernous but authoritative. It commanded respect. Nevertheless there seemed a keen ironical edge to it, a suggestion of subterranean depths, of wheels within wheels, of unspelled-out meanings. It could be (Hodge wasn't sure about this) of hollow laughter, firmly held in check.

"Everyone here gets a large economy-size jar of Dr Whyte's Waterproof Ointment, made up to each spectre's special requirements. A fresh two-months' supply, for turning the Seven Deadly What's-its into the Seven Lively That's-its. No expense has been spared in its preparation and presentation. Why even the jar's a part of the treatment. Beautifully designed, it's saying: "I contain a kind of priceless spikenard with amazing healing properties!" And it carries the royal seal of approval, inscribed "Dieu *et* mon droit - God *and* my right."

Hodge could make little or nothing of all this, and said so nervously but plainly.

Crisp and clear came the response from that eaten-away face: "We're handing out a sovereign remedy for turning Podge's pride into Proper Pride, his envy into Divine Discontent and Emulation, his lust into Lustiness, his gluttony into Bon Appetit, his anger into Righteous Indignation (nothing personal, you'll understand: it's the *principle* of the thing!), his sloth into Relaxation (mustn't overdo it, you know!), and his covetousness into Improving Consumer Demand. The ointment to be well rubbed in every half hour, or as directed by your doctor. Warning: not suitable for spectres of up to twelve years."

"Great Scot!" exclaimed Hodge. "Some ointment! How's that for value?"

Then, hesitatingly, on reflection: "The question is: How deep does the treatment go? Is it therapeutic or merely cosmetic? Would you describe it - honestly - as medicine, or make-up, or plain podge-up? Or perhaps a mishmash of all three?"

No reply…

A long silence, during which a score of parcels were handed over and gratefully received.

Hodge tried again: "How much time and energy for the real business of this place - for attending in the opposite direction and looking to Sea - does all that ointment application leave one? After all, though *Dieu et (and) mon droit* sounds the same as *Dieu est (is) mon droit*, it's a very different way of life. And can there be any doubt about which is the true Godsea way of life?"

Still no reply, much to Hodge's mounting irritation. To make it worse, just a low humming which sounded like a mocking version of the Volga Boatmen's Song...

Dun clouds were chasing one another across the face of that vast moon. A chill wind had started to blow from the east. The surface of the water was tarnishing, breaking up.

They had turned the south-west corner and were now skirting the long north wall of the castle, where the alcoves were fewer and further apart. Hodge found the all-pervading acrid smell - was it the smell of battle? - disagreeable but familiar. How different were the spectres here! Each more sinister than the last, more fiercely grimacing, splashing about furiously in a frenzy of frustration. With inflamed complexions, bared teeth, eyes like high-speed electric drills, this increasingly furious mob - in striking contrast to the mild moat-folk now left far behind - were evidently the implacable foes of Godsea and its guards, and just raring to overcome them and invade the place.

The gifts Hodge was now handing out were suggestively heavy and elongated.

At last the boatman found tongue, this time - fortunately - without turning his head. "You guessed right. Here's a fresh supply of arms: short, keen, two-edged swords for keeping these spectres at bay. They've been forged specially for the swordsman who's fighting off the Enemy on the north while he's backed and empowered by the Friend on the south. Mighty weapons they are, once it's clear who's really wielding them. Cleaving the air with lightning swiftness, they sing a song that combines the soaring soprano of the Open Sea with the basso profondo of the moat..."

But the last couple of sentences were lost on Hodge. For the second time his dream had taken off into nightmare.

As he was handing a sword to one of the sentries the moonlight happened to fall on the man's face.

It was *himself*! His doppelganger! Hodge was shaking with terror...

As the first shock began to wear off, the less awful and more awkward side of the encounter began to come out. What does one say to one's doppelganger? What is the etiquette? A death-rattle, a shudder, a stuck-out tongue, or simply a grin and an au revoir?

But they had moved on, making the problem hypothetical...

When at length he had sufficiently recovered, Hodge said, half to himself and half to the boatman, "Maybe I should have expected to meet myself here. This is where I mount sentry duty. This is my part of the moat."

But again Hodge wished to God he'd kept his mouth shut.

This time the face that turned to him as if to answer was horribly decayed and leprous. And that, it seemed, was answer enough.

They had rounded the north-east corner of the castle. The moon, enormous and enigmatic, still shone above the cold waters of the eastern stretch of Godsea moat. Wind-troubled, their surface was broken up into a flashing black and white mosaic. Few, very few, were the guards on duty here, and the very last of them turned out to be a white-haired figure that Hodge was almost sure was Frank. The spray made recognition difficult.

The icy water was boiling furiously, threatening to flood and sink the little boat.

Then it was, in the midst of all that the spume and froth that Hodge saw the Thing that flicked his dream over - yet again - into nightmare, the Thing that was whipping up that maelstrom. In fact (it was no more than a couple of feet off) there was no way of avoiding that terrible sight - sebaceous scarlet skin stretched tight over a horned skull whose gnashing teeth framed a grin like no other. If any one thing in the world could embody the world's evil, this was that thing. Was it showing up in Godsea moat (Hodge wondered) because even Hell could stand it no longer?

What chance had Frank (if it was Frank) against that Thing? Yet, swordless, seemingly with bare hands, he was grappling with it. The spray was tinged with red, presumably with his blood. (Yes, at this end of the moat the red end of the spectrum was coming back on duty. The Devil had need of it.)

"What's this gift for Frank?" Hodge managed to bawl, above the din and commotion. He was soaked, very cold, and still trembling.

"Three jewels," came the swift reply. "The Diamond called Thus-Saith-the-Lord, the Ruby called Balm-in-Gilead, the Emerald called Ask-and-it-Shall-Be-Given. This is a replacement set. They wear out."

"What use are they?" shouted Hodge.

"The possessor of the Diamond sees into people's past and future. The possessor of the Ruby cures their diseases. The possessor of the

Emerald changes their circumstances."

"But surely…?" Hodge began doubtfully, then remembered he'd had evidence of Frank's powers…

The oarsman, at last steering clear of those dangerous waters, had turned the boat around and begun the westward return run. This time he kept to the middle of the moat. Hodge busied himself with baling…

Then, suddenly straightening up, he came out with: "Is Frank's game worth the candle? I mean to say: the price-tag - written in blood - attached to those jewels seems terribly high. Are they as precious as all that? What about the countless things he can't know or do, and the mortal diseases he can only postpone?"

No reply. Only more of that infuriating humming…

Half seriously, Hodge considered whether a bucket of bilge water "accidentally" discharged at the creature, would get a response. Then, remembering that face, he hurriedly dismissed the idea, and went on baling.

But not for long. A couple of minutes and up he came with another doubt:

"What's the connection (if any?) between those three extraordinary gifts and the ordinary business of Godsea, which is Godseeing? Do they help? Could they be a diversion, even a hindrance? No, no! I'm not suggesting that Frank's one of those fellows who torture themselves to gain magic powers for impressing and dominating people with. He isn't, I'm sure… All the same - "

Still no response.

Hodge went on, addressing himself as much as that abominable boatman, "I think I'm trying to say that my section of the moat is this middle part, and neither the complacent west end nor the agonised east end will do for me. The Podge I know is neither my buddy nor the Very Devil. He's my opponent. A hobgoblin or small-time devil if you like, not the Foul Fiend he might pose as, his vanity being what it is."

This time the boatman did turn his faceless face and vouchsafe a measured and stern reply: "There's no more a right and a wrong stretch of moat than a right and a wrong stretch of the Sea it's a loop of. The moat's for navigating and mapping, nor for moralising about. From end to end it *is* the way it is - fauna and flora and satana and all."

"So mote it be," Hodge thought of saying, then wisely thought better of it…

They were fast making for the sheltered end of the moat,

nevertheless the east wind stayed bitter cold... There was a loud and persistent slapping of waves against the side of the boat... Hodge wanted to scream, but couldn't get a whisper out...

He woke to find himself naked on his bed and shivering violently. The blankets lay in a heap on the floor, and the casement window, wide open to the Perilous Sea, was chattering noisily in the night breeze.

30

LICORICE ALLSORTS

On the day that followed his dream, Hodge pushed open so many doors, and got more or less caught up in so many strange scenes, that only a small selection of them stuck in his mind. It is those that we'll explore with him briefly, using his terminology - Hodgespeak - as far as possible.

He rather liked the Humble Bumbles or Cyclopeans, as he called them. In fact, the three men lined up side-by-side in the room only looked, on first inspection, as if they were one-eyed: the single eye turned out to be a gleaming dial strapped to their foreheads. They were performing a drill in unison, consisting of standing, kneeling, and bowing so deeply that the dial made contact with the floor, thus causing it to click and register one more prostration. With admirable precision all three performers hit the floor at once, and the three clicks were one click. The ritual was then repeated.

This went on for so long that Hodge was about to ease his way out. Just then, however, the trio paused and sat down for a breather. Nothing was said, but all three pointed out to him the readings on their respective dials. One clocked up 3,207, the second 7,828, the third 35,704. The hint of a smile of self-satisfaction on the face of Number Three was modesty itself. Much broader was the smile on the face of the Golden Giant they were bowing to. Was it a grin of amusement? Hodge wondered. Was he having a job not bursting out laughing at these solemn gymnastics?

Well, though all three were middle-aged, none showed the slightest sign of stiffness or middle-age spread. And that was something for them to be cheerful about. Humbly, of course.

Politely but silently they offered Hodge a prostratometer, which he as politely declined. The reading of zero was too discouraging. By the time he got to 35,704 Number Three would presumably have got to 71,408, and be entitled to say to Hodge "I'm exactly twice as humble as you!"

Humbly Hodge bowed himself out of that room. But not before he'd noticed that the casement window, opening out onto the Perilous Sea, stood half open.

A glimpse ahead in time. The next night, at dinner in the great hall, Hodge happened to sit next to the 35,704 champion - a small, quiet chap called Kim. He wanted to know how Hodge was getting on at Godsea, and was there anything he could do for him? Anything at all. Nothing, said Hodge, and thought to himself, "Just stick around, raising your score to 100,000 if you must. I don't think I've ever met a more immediately loveable or good-to-be-with fellow."

Unlike Manbridge, Godsea wasn't zoned, class-conscious district by class-conscious district. Back there, (Hodge reminded himself) your next-door neighbour was likely to resemble you in a hundred ways, from accent and table manners to how often you shower and your attitude to fish and chips. You knew where you were with him and her. Godsea wasn't like that at all. Here, your next-door neighbour was as likely as not to be a freak you couldn't make head or tail of, an abortion that could well have blown in from one of the remoter galaxies. That was how Hodge was feeling already. And then -

Not ten feet from the door to the Cyclopeans and their prostratometers, he found himself at the door to what he christened *(verb. non-sap.)* the Huggermugger or Blue Room, alias the Gallery of

Meaningful Diagrams. These diagrams did something to make Hodge feel at home, so like his own they were. Nests of concentric circles that took him all the way back to his drawings in Strangefields, and further still to the interweaving and ever-expanding ripples the raindrops made on the village pond at Beaston, and the spiderwebs in the wood that bordered the pond.

At the centre of each of these Blue-Room webs lurked an improbable-looking spider-person, suffering from what Hodge read as "a severe attack of the chakras," while off-centre there hung equally improbable-looking fly-people And - just to confuse the issue perhaps - these circular patterns had squares and triangles liberally imposed on them. All in shades of blue.

Blue was the word, all right. Interspersed with the diagrams were pictures of an exceptionally virile bright-blue gentleman, being made love to in all imaginable ways by a bevy of exceptionally nubile ladies. What particularly struck Hodge about the participants was the out-to-lunch and over-the-hills-and-far-away and perfectly expressionless look on their faces, as if they were bored to tears. Bored stiff.

But the décor of the Blue Room was restrained compared with its Occupier. Hodge's first impression was that he, Hodge, in the role of deep-sea diver, had surprised a giant Cephalopod, a pulsating, pullulating, many-eyed, many-tentacled Monster in its dim cavern beneath the ocean-bed, where visitors were far from welcome. A more careful inspection revealed that the Monster comprised a number of humans - whether three, or four, or even five, was hard to make out, so entangled and on-the-move they were. The strong smell of feasting (fortunately the window stood open a crack) was accounted for by the brimming wine-glasses held (none too steadily) in some of the Monster's hands, while others were feeding steaming meat-pies into eager mouths. Also by the half-empty bottles and dishes littering the floor, and the spillages.

   The noise - the Monster's cry or voice or song - was a species of musique concrète consisting of squeaks, squeals, catchings of breath, and an occasional ouch. Accompanied (believe it or not!) by an exquisite deep-toned chanting coming from the only one of the Monster's mouths that wasn't otherwise engaged:

> Om!
> Khya, khya, khyahi, khyahi,
> Hum, hum,
> Jvala, javala, prajvala, prajvala,
> Tistha, tistha,
> Stri, Stri,
> Sphata!
> Om!

Hodge stood there irresolute, very aware that several of the Monster's eyes were fastened on him. The etiquette in this somewhat awkward situation wasn't clear. If he'd been wearing a hat (which of course he wasn't) he could have raised it, wished the Monster a superfluous bon appetit, and backed out. As things happened, however, it solved the problem for him by suddenly sticking out a lazytongs hand, wrenching open the door, shoving him through it into the corridor, and slamming it with a bang that shattered his eardrums.

The Blue Room left Hodge disoriented and somewhat feverish. For a few moments he seriously wondered whether he had strayed, through the maze of corridors and staircases and tunnels, far beyond Godsea and into Manbridgian territory; and even further, into still more remote and alien regions. But it *was* Godsea! Heaven help us, did that name mean *nothing*? Were there no limits to what went on in this truly perilous castle by the Perilous Sea, provided you venture far enough and burrow deep enough?

All remaining doubts about where he'd got to were settled when he pushed, ever so gently and cautiously this time, at an exquisitely carved door set in a pointed archway, only a few yards from the Blue Room.

What he managed to make out, in the dim and multicoloured light of that room (the casements were aglow with stained glass) and through gaps in an ornamental screen, more than justified the manner of his entry.

A spare, white-haired figure, wearing ankle-length and richly embroidered vestments, was standing with his back to Hodge at a table, intoning words with great intensity. The fact that they were in a language unknown to Hodge only deepened, mysteriously, their meaning for him. What they said about the eternal patience and beauty of the Sea could be said in no other way, by no other means.

At intervals the recitation stopped and something happened at the table. There was the rustling of linen, the clink-clink of glass, and the plash-plash of liquid being poured. More intoning followed, and then a pair of hands were holding up something white. A bell sounded. The peculiar clarity of that ringing was itself a kind of revelation.

Two other things about that scene struck Hodge. They were the strong scent of wild violets, and the crimson gleam of the wounds in those uplifted hands...

He never knew how long it was before, blinded by tears, he

turned, and groped for the door handle, and let himself out as noise-
lessly as he had let himself in.

There was no need for Hodge to open the next door he came to.
All he had to do was quietly slide a panel in it and put his face to the
opening.

It was a long and bare corridor of a room, and the casement at the
far end of it stood wide open. There, back to Hodge and facing the Sea,
stood a tall and powerfully-built man he didn't recognise. Apparently
he was grasping, with both hands, a long sword, the flashing tip of
which was visible above his shaven head. At the near end, also grasping
a sword - it looked far and away too big and heavy for her - stood a
young woman he'd briefly conversed with. He happened to remember
that her name was Deirdre, because at the time she'd come across as
both weird and dreary. Now she looked even more so - pathetically
vulnerable, waiflike and bedraggled, and scrawny. If, God forbid, it
should come to a fight (Hodge asked himself) what chance had she
against the athlete whose back she was contemplating? Was a brutal
murder about to be committed? In Godsea, of all places?

They might have been a pair of waxworks guarding the entrance
to the chamber of horrors, so still they were. Not a tremor, not even the
sound of breathing came from them.

And then, just as Hodge was about to tire of the still-life picture and move on, came the Clash.

It happened so suddenly and so fast, and Hodge was so taken aback, that a lot of the details of that frenzied collision were lost on him. What held him, what staggered him, was the transformation of Deidre. Sword held aloft, screeching at the top of her voice, she hurled herself at her opponent. But not before he'd swung round and rushed at her with an equal show of furious energy. The noise of their clashing swords and their yells, as they met in the middle of the room, was deafening. So fast was their cutting and thrusting and parrying that Hodge had no way of telling who was winning. If anything, it was the man, back to the Sea, and not that maenad, who was retreating...

And then, just as suddenly as it had begun, the fight ended. The contestants disengaged, backed away, bowed deeply, and turned into waxworks again.

All was as it had been, except that a tiny cut appeared on the man's shoulder. It was bleeding.

The thing that finally impressed Hodge was the effect on himself. It was as if the energy of Deirdre were so powerful that it spread to him, causing every cell in his body to fling its little hat in the air and dance around and bawl its little head off.

He continued his tour of inspection baffled and punch-drunk, but so very invigorated.

"It all goes to show," he reflected, "that you never know. Never, never, never know."

He had promised himself (you'll remember) to visit the cave-like room next to Sebastian's, from which those white-clad women had filed out. Well, it was at the door of this room that eventually - after many another peeping, and either entering or thinking better of it - he fetched up.

He was about to turn the handle when Sebastian himself, chirpier than ever, shot from his door like a sparrow surprised in its nest.

"Oh how nice of you to look us up again!" he cried. "I thought you would. Do come in. We've something to show you."

There was no resisting that shoulder-massaging, that elbow-pulling invitation. Before he could get together any excuses he found himself inside that narrow room again, as crowded with gaffers and gear and gung-ho as ever.

"We've practically perfected," Sebastian was saying, "our Popular De-mystifier. It's a cheap pocket-version of our telescope, and will make the Sea's perfect clearness available to everybody. Come, test it for yourself!"

He pressed into Hodge's hands what looked like an ordinary pair of binoculars, dragged him to the window, opened it cautiously a few inches, and told him to check whether, looking out to Sea with that instrument, any hint of mist remained.

Hodge had to admit to the eager inventor that he was right.

"Keep it," chirped Sebastian. "Accept the gift of a Popular Demystifier, with our best wishes for its use."

"Very kind, but -," he stammered.

It was too late. Sebastian had already slung the instrument over his shoulder, and was half-shepherding and half-slinging him out into the corridor.

At long last he was free to venture into the room that had begun to haunt his dreams.

It turned out to be unoccupied at the moment - by human beings, that is to say. More like a cave than a room it was, as we've noted, or like a barrel-vaulted wine-cellar. It reeked of something like wine all right - wine of a uniquely full-bodied vintage. Every inch of its ceiling and walls and thickly carpeted floor was crawling with little men with animals' heads, and little animals with men's heads, and little men with specially sinister men's heads, and severed heads that were human and animal and who-knows-which, and truly fishy fish and airy-fairy birds and extra-creepy crawlies, and grotesquely unbotanical flowers and bushes and trees. Plus - as if that menagerie weren't more than enough to cope with - a wide assortment of pots and pans and pastry dishes. Taken one by one, you could read those exhibits as twee. Taken en masse they were terrifying. All told, here was a collection well calculated to make Hodge (whose recent adventures had left him more blinking and dazed than ever and somewhat in shock) positively pie-eyed.

It all added up to a kind of noise, visual noise polluting Space just as audible noise pollutes Silence. Not that the latter sort was lacking in that cave. A deafening kind of holy scream tortured the air, merciless in its clanging, yelling, booming, tinkling, whistling, roaring and screeching - fortissimo and sostenuto. And then (for evil measure) there was the incense, clouds of the stuff rising from a forest of lighted joss-sticks - each contributing its particular perfume. How many different perfumes does it take (Hodge asked himself) to build a stink like this stink?

Surely this latest exhibit belonged neither to the world of Godsea nor Manbridge, but of delirium tremens. Why, even the deep-pile velvet curtain drawn across the door he'd come in by, and the net curtain drawn across the window at the far end, were chock-a-block with creatures not of this world, nor of any other world this side of madness. It was as if the very air that cave enclosed were jam-packed with their spirits, Legion by name and nature.

For the first time in his life Hodge knew in his bones that hell is riches without relief, that more is less, and blessed indeed are the poor. On the verge of panic, he made for the window and drew the curtains aside just enough to give him a sanity-saving draught of that Living Water which is the same yesterday and today and forever. And he recalled the words of another Godsea-er: "O Sancta Simplicitas!" His name was John Huss, and he happened to be burning at the stake at the time.

Thus fortified, Hodge felt just about able to cope with the centre-piece of that display. It took the form of a many-armed female with a snaky coiffure. She was clasping grinning skulls, severed heads dripping blood, steaming entrails, flashing thunderbolts, swords, battle-axes, spears, bows and arrows, maces, and - so as not to lose the homely domestic touch - a baby on toast and a nice cup of tea. (Poor old Hodge on the edge of Manbridge County, with his wonderful bag of toolhands, had by comparison been severely handicapped, practically limbless.) Her diamond eyes were radiant with infernal light. Her ruby lips, parted to reveal far too many ivory teeth, framed a smile as frightful as any that have scared nightmare-ridden children out of their wits. Blessed are the non-smilers of the world, for they shall calm down the smiled at.

The finishing touch to that polydextrous lady was her complexion. Whiter than superdaz white it was, chalky blue-white, with cheeks rouged to a crimson that struck Hodge as actionable. By comparison, the Whore of Babylon wasn't in the running.

Nevertheless…

Nevertheless, as with a gasp of relief he very firmly closed the door - none too soon! - on that scene, he realised that this wasn't a door that could be locked and sealed forever. He had to concede that that chamber of horrors - draw the curtain just a fraction - commanded a view of the Immaculate Ocean. That no more than six inches of partition wall separated that terrible Plus from Sebastian's terrible Minus, all that Mystification from Sebastian's Patent-Demystifier. And that from the unholy presence of that sorceress had sallied forth those singing, serene-faced women. Dressed all in white, mark you. Pure white.

And now, back in the mercifully plain corridor, stood a Hodge who, at least for the time-being, was not only in shock but unshockable. A Hodge who was more prepared than ever for just about anything.

Ready, almost, for what happened.

The sound of racing feet, and cries of "Hodge, Hodge!" A panting servant, rounding the bend in the corridor at speed, nearly knocked him off his feet.

"The Castellan's calling for you!" he cried. "Come with me! For Christ's sake hurry!"

31

MARY, MARY, QUITE CONTRARY

We go back for a spell, in time and space, to Mary Porticule in Manbridge, a week or so after Hodge had left without telling her where he was going.

How relieved she had been to hear from her cousin Cecilia in Godsea that - as she'd half expected - he'd turned up there! Also that he seemed in good health and spirits.

To join him was all her desire. To do so, she decided, it would be best, if at all possible, to go by the way he had gone. She would have to understand, and somehow participate in, the mysterious crisis in the exercise yard at Strangefields. She would have to take the medicine that had so dramatically cured him and fitted him for Godsea.

Why (she asked herself yet once more) had he, that memorable night before he went away, been so cagey about what had happened to him? So reticent with *her*, of all people? But just like him it was, of course. Either he overwhelmed you with unsought information, or went dumb. Why O why hadn't she fallen in love with a normal, reasonable man? Well, there it was. And there, all those miles away, he was. She needed him and she needed the cure, whatever it might be, that would take her to him.

Naturally, she found out all she could from Nurse Sterry (now going round looking for a new job), and more especially from her assistant Johnny, who had been present on that momentous occasion. The only suggestive information she could get out of him was that, while gazing into the pool in the middle of the yard, Hodge had shouted something about blowing his top and ditching Podge. Nurse Sterry thought he must have been referring to his shadow.

His shadow? Did the sun ever shine into that benighted court-yard? In any case there was something more powerful and more odd than a shadow lurking about or lurking in that pool. What or who that Lurker might be she had to find out.

The Assistant Governor of Strangefields had been friendly in a guarded way. Again she sought his help.

No, he was afraid the prison rules forbade her to explore the exercise yard, just like that. He suggested that she should apply to join the panel of prison visitors. They had access to most parts of the place.

She applied, was interviewed and accepted, and - a week later - found herself at last in that exercise yard for very disturbed prisoners, with Johnny in attendance. Her excuse for being there was that she wished to see what could be done to revive the water-lilies, and to introduce a companion for the solitary and no doubt unhappy goldfish.

Standing where, according to Johnny, Hodge had stood, and gazing down into the water, she saw what he must have seen. Namely, those tattered and half-submerged water-lily leaves, that depressed-looking fish, and the blotchy grey-green of the concrete bottom. Though it was high noon and the sun was shining with all his might above the prison, he gave up long before he got to that pond. Accordingly, no shadow.

So far as she could make out, the scene confronting her was the same as the one that had confronted Hodge that day. Exactly the same.

What, for heaven's sake, was there about this most uninspiring and untherapeutic of pondscapes that had worked a miracle for that broken prisoner, that wreck of a young man who had slouched from his padded cell into what passed for the open air?

Exactly the same?

Well, not *exactly*. The water-lily leaves were now no doubt more unhealthy, the goldfish was more weary. And of course there was one very obvious difference. The face staring up at her - golden hair and peach complexion and all - wasn't a bit like the one that had stared up at him.

So what?

So nothing. It couldn't be that his face had healing properties that hers altogether lacked. Oh he was a wonderful fellow all right, but not *that* wonderful!

Utterly baffled, she was about to give up and go home, when a tremendous thought struck Mary Porticule.

Suppose his face there cured HIM, while her face there cured HER!

Yes, Yes! That was it!

She was absolutely sure of it! He'd blown *his* top. She was now blowing *hers* - clean off! *That* was what he had meant by the ditching of Podge, and *this* was what she now meant by the ditching of Mary-Quite-Contrary, leaving Who she really was up here - more than a yard clear of that water - clearer than Clear. Clear - what a relief at last! - of that alleged lump-for-looking-out-of, the lump having resolved itself into the widest and brightest and clearest and dearest of seas and skies.

She laughed. Oh yes, she laughed all right! Not by any means as long or as loudly as Hodge had done, but enough to set Johnny laughing too. And to leave him with the lifelong conviction that here, in this unholiest of places and lands, was the Magic Pool of Siloam. It became his Wishing Well, and many a coin he secretly invested therein.

Mary was more eager than ever, of course, to join Hodge in Godsea, now that she saw eye-to-eye with him in this most crucial of visions. Saw, rather, through the Very Same Single Eye. At last she knew from direct and first-hand experience what he and Godsea were about, and that there lay her natural home. From now on, in fact, she was assured that their love rested on a new and truly secure basis. On the Rock of Shared Clarity.

The only obstacle that prevented her following him there at once was her father, the Professor. Struck down by some undiagnosed illness, he lay tossing in bed with a high temperature, babbling of gorse bushes. Alas, his delirium did nothing to undermine his determination not to go to hospital. As for a resident nurse-housekeeper, that was an expense he refused to contemplate. Nothing would do but that Mary should nurse him.

All that was left was to hope for his early recovery, and keep in touch with Hodge through her cousin Cecilia.

She tried writing to him. He scarcely ever replied, and then in true Hodge style - with mindboggling news about the Self-origination of the Cosmos, or the choreography of the waterlight on the wall of his cell, and nothing at all between those extremes. Nothing newsy, she complained. It wasn't that he snubbed her, or didn't miss her at all. On the contrary, Cecilia reported that he looked forward impatiently to her coming. He had no idea how difficult he was.

Cecilia, dear Cecilia, did what she could to keep her posted. At first there was little to tell, beyond the fact that Hodge was with characteristic speed finding his feet in Godsea, and spending much of his time with the Castellan.

And then - real news, astonishing news!

32

THE NEW CASTELLAN

Here's how Cecilia's letter ran:

Dear Mary,

Nicholas the Castellan has just died.

Hodge is the new Castellan!

I can just imagine how you feel about this. Stunned, and thrilled, and frustrated that you can't be here to support him.

Nicholas had been getting noticeably more frail for some time, but the end came with surprising suddenness. Just minutes before he died he sent for Hodge, and told him and those standing around the bed that he was exercising the immemorial right of a dying Castellan of Godsea to appoint his successor. He took off his ring - the ancient amethyst ring of all the Castellans - and put it on Hodge's finger. Then he shut his eyes, smiled, and stopped breathing.

People here are a shade bemused to find so young and so recent a member of the community emerging as their leader. However, I think they will take it in their stride, if only because so little leadership is required of any Castellan, and because the old one was so loved and respected that his dying words have the force of law.

The reasons for the appointment are becoming clearer. The first seems to have been that, in Nicholas' view, Hodge has the liveliest and deepest appreciation of what Godsea stands for: more than any of us, he gets to the heart of the matter and stays there. Nicholas did mention some verses and sketches of Hodge's that had impressed him deeply. I gather that the second and equally powerful reason for appointing this young newcomer was that he is, precisely, a young newcomer! A Castellan of Godsea, in Nicholas' view, should be a stranger to the place, uncommitted to any particular position or practice, not yet dug in and special-ised, wet behind the ears by Godsea standards. In fact, much like Nicholas' picture of himself as the village idiot! The third reason was more vague. Apparently Nicholas was convinced that something had to be done about the office of Castellan - about the job, I mean - and that Hodge was the one to do it.

I know he longs for you to join us. So do I.

With my love,

Cecily.

p.s. I ran into Hodge a few minutes ago. He told me he'd been taken completely by surprise. He was wearing the ring, but didn't seem at all excited.

Subject to minor ups and downs the Professor's condition remained stable throughout the two months that followed Cecilia's letter. Her proposal to visit Godsea for no more than a week or so - during which time he would be well looked after by a resident nurse - was the signal for his fever to rocket. Her suggestion that a spell in the best nursing home in Manbridge would be a pleasant change, and good for him, produced an even more alarming relapse.

Mary's vague feeling of anxiety about Hodge (a mere hunch, based on no real evidence) wasn't allayed by the contents of Cecilia's next letter.

Dear Mary,

You'll be pleased, or amused, or both, to hear that I've just been bashing vegetables in the scullery here alongside our new Castellan, who is wearing a too-short version of our servants' uniform of something like sackcloth. As a servant he's barefoot. (He tells me this is one of the attractions of the job, and that shoes were invented by the Devil to insulate people from the feel of Heaven!) He also waits at table, not too efficiently: he's so apt to be diverted by the lovely colour-scheme of the salad, or what he calls the Godsea (that is, upside-down) reflections in the spoons. At other times, he tells me, he's working on a scheme to link Godsea and Manbridge with a four-lane highway to replace the present apology for a road. There's to be a culvert beneath the highway, containing water mains and electric cables and drains. He seems to have quite a thing about drains, and so on: his face lights up when you mention a manhole, and he talks of our digestive and sewage systems as if there's no telling where one ends and the other starts. Sometimes I think he's incredibly simple, in the best sense of the word. At other times incredibly complex, unpredictable, a bran-tub of surprises.

It's no secret that he would like the various groups or factions of people here (liquorice all-sorts, he calls us) to get to know one another, and what's going on, and What it is we have in common. Is Godsea a community (he asks) only in the sense that a zoo is a community: the cages being necessary to discourage its members from dining off one another?

He tells me the doctor here has some good stuff for the very bad headaches he's apt to get.

Also that I must be sure to send his love to you, with mine,
Cecily

The New Castellan

A fortnight after Mary got this letter her father died, peacefully. At his deathbed a great tranquillity came over her, and it seemed to spread to him. Or was it vice versa? Anyway, in the end there was no more babbling of gorse bushes. Her ear to his lips, she made out the words, "There's a Light!"

On the day of the funeral she got Cecilia's third and last letter.

Dear Mary,

The news isn't too good.

Yesterday Hodge called a preliminary meeting of representatives of some of the main groups here. In itself not an easy thing to do. I wasn't there, but they tell me he proposed a sharing of insights, or cross-fertilisation as he called it, to be followed by some agreement about the aims of Godsea and the future running of the place.

His ideas didn't go down at all well. Nor did his account of conversations he'd had with Nicholas the old Castellan, about why for God's sake there should be something rather than nothing at all. I think people felt he was bouncing them.

The intention is to unite, the effect is to divide. Poor darling, he means well.

This wouldn't matter so much if it weren't making him ill. Really bad headaches he has almost every day now, and he looks tired and sad.

I beg you to come. You would help him and us so much. How, I don't know. But you would.

Love,

Cecily

Three days after getting this letter, Mary left Manbridge for Godsea.

33

PLUSSED, OR NONPLUSSED?

At the time of Mary's arrival at the Castle, Hodge happened to be digging up carrots in the garden. His headache was bearable, nothing like it had been the day before.

Cecilia brought Mary along to him.

Their meeting, so often rehearsed in Mary's mind, turned out to be different, of course, from anything she'd imagined or hoped for or feared. It was the undramatic reunion of two that had never parted. It was also the dramatic encounter of two that had never met. Hodge the terrible embarrassment she was always apologising for, Hodge doing his idiot-boy act (if it was an act), Hodge the law-breaker, Hodge the refugee from MI 13 and Manbridge, had become - what a spectrum-shift! - the be-ringed Castellan of the famous and ancient Castle of Godsea! As for herself, her own crisis in that Strangefields exercise-yard had left her a subtly (but profoundly) different Mary Porticule from the one he had known. Would he be sensitive enough - be unselfishly interested enough - to appreciate the change in her, and how much closer it must bring them? In short, there was a sense in which they had to begin all over again. And what was wrong with that, for goodness' sake? she asked herself.

The hugs and kisses were warm enough, and he actually - was it for the very first time? - called her *dear*. Mary dear. That sounded the right note, was a good omen.

Hurriedly they trimmed and basketted the carrots he'd dug up, and went and sat on the shore of the Perilous Sea.

They had so much to talk about. Quite genuinely, it seemed, he wanted to hear her news first, and in detail. This was a more considerate, quieter, less angular Hodge than the old familiar one. So far, so very good.

Having first made sure he wasn't in pain, at least for the moment, Mary settled down to tell her story.

About her father's illness and death there was little to say, apart from the beautiful end of it. He had spoken of the Light. He had seen the Light of the Horizonless Ocean they were now gazing at. The very same, she was sure. That made her very happy.

About her discovery in the exercise yard at Strangefields, and what had led up to it, on the other hand, there was much to say. She told him about her attempts to find out what had happened to him there, and how she'd wangled a visit to the place, and her frustration when at last she got there, and the last-minute and almost accidental ditching of Mary-Quite-Contrary. Oh how glad she now was that he'd told her nothing, not a word about his experience by the pool; thus leaving her open to her own experience, free to make her own first-hand discoveries without any risk of imitation! Thus there was no question of seeing something to order and because it was a good thing to see, or because it was Hodge's thing, or because it was her one-way ticket to him and Godsea. No, what she saw had been there for the seeing, more obvious than obvious - the staring, fat-faced Mary-fish that would never land on any fishmonger's slab.

"O happy day!" she cried. "You and I sinking our differences, ditching all that separates us. Goodbye confrontation!"

He didn't agree in words. Better, he squeezed her hand - so hard that his ring gave her a stab of pain. Never was pain more exquisitely pleasurable. The ring was beautiful, too.

"I'm curious to know," said Hodge, "what are your very first impressions of Godsea."

"This Sea air! It polishes everything to an unbelievable brightness. Not till you get here do you realise how fog-bound Manbridge is. Looking back now, it's obvious how that smog - though invisible to Manbridgers - took the shine out of all shining and dulled all colours and muffled all sounds and half-killed all scents, and even seeped into the food and drained away the taste. Does that dreadful pollution - perish the thought - ever creep up to Godsea, when the wind's in the North?"

"Not since I got here," said Hodge.

"I suppose the contrast isn't so striking for you. Remember how you used to rave about the colours of scarlet pimpernels and dandelions and cornflowers. And how eagerly you breathed in those smells, all the way from roses to - yes! splodge tanks. And how you loved the feel of the hard air they call glass, and woolly towels. Unlike me, you never were and never pretended to be a native of Manbridge. But at last I'm with you all the way Home to the brightness. Just now it's the incredible brightness and tang of this Sea-foam, and the sparkle of the wet shingle in the sunlight as the water rushes down the beach after each wave... It's all so - what's the word I want? - so physical, so sensuous. I almost said: so low, so crude. And in Manbridge they tell you that Godsea's all uplift and wishywashy other-worldliness, a bloodless ballet in the clouds!

"Now tell me all about yourself, how you really are, what the job of Castellan here means, how you feel about it. Everything, every-thing!"

At first Hodge was hesitant, and rather vague about himself and what he was trying to do at Godsea. But he warmed up as he told her, in graphic detail and with much of his old fire and humour, the story of his explorations in Godsea keep. Told her about his most memorable encounters, about the Bedlamites and his kind efforts to hold their ceiling up; the Cyclopses just a little proud of their humility and prostratometer scores; the Writhing and Ravenous Deep-sea Monster of the Blue Room; the White-haired Celebrant (undoubtedly their neigh-bour Frank) with the wounded hands; the Clashing Couple and the apotheosis of Deirdre; the Singing Women and their abominable cave; and Sebastian the eager inventor of the De-mystifying Telescope. Plus, though in a different category altogether, something of his talks with Nicholas the late Castellan and the secret they shared: to wit, their astonishment that anything exists at all - let alone Godsea and Manbridge and Beaston.

"Good Lord!" exclaimed Mary, and there was no doubting the genuineness of her surprise.

"And try this little lot," he went on, much encouraged. "Follow-ing your Manbridge example, I'll cheekily nickname them for brevity and ease of description. There are the Castle-whirlers, who whisk Godsea in their sufic blenders till it's all Sea. (You'll remember how I used to enjoy pirouetting - because in fact it was Manbridge pirouet-ting. That's one of many previews of Godsea that can be had while you're still in Manbridge.) There are the Shoestringers and Straitlacers who know where the shoe pinches, and lace it tighter. There are the Gelder-Rose Elders, sweet-smelling and most colourful but short on stamens and pistil. There are the Holy Processionary Caterpillars, who have worn the paving of their chapel right through. There are the Estchewers who gnaw fibroid substances and who enjoy cheating their tastebuds of enjoyment. There are the Plymouth Rock and Rollers who are convinced their whitewashed and cocomatted meeting room *is* Godsea. There are the Mindful Yellow Lizards who take five minutes to stalk the breakfast egg. And there are lots more who don't just do the oddest things (why shouldn't they, for Godsea's sake?) but, given half a chance, will tell you how critical for Godsea those things are.

"And that," Hodge concluded, "is just a random sampling of the varieties of Godsea experience. Every one - and this you'll hardly believe - ventilated and lit up by casements opening on the foam of the Perilous Sea, the Horizonless Ocean!... Well, Mary Porticule, what's your verdict on it all?"

"I'm getting the feeling," said Mary, "that the show's being put on by a Slapstick Comedian, a real Merry Andrew."

"In that case," said Hodge, "his sense of humour includes several shades of black. His castle-moat circus, for instance, with its animal acts ranging from cooing turtle-doves at the warm end of the ring to roaring tyrannosaurs at the cold end, isn't so much playing merry with the customers as merry hell.

"Anyway," he added, (was it with that overearnestness that signals lack of deep conviction?): "At least part of Nicholas's reason for nominating me as the new Castellan was that he felt that I was the one to sort out the Godsea extravaganza - insofar as it can and should be sorted out."

"What kind of change had he in mind?"

"He didn't say. But surely he wanted me to do something to bring together and reconcile the isms and anities and inanities here. Why, at present a faction is scarcely aware of the other factions' exist-ence, let alone their beliefs and practices, let alone what goes on in their section of the moat. In fact, Godsea is less a community than the loosest group I can think of in Manbridge. Than the Union of Mums, or the Pinker Club, or Manbridge City Supporters."

"Or the Fans of Shrieking Sidney the Pop-star."

"This is a shame, and I mean a *shaming* shame. But it also holds out bright hopes for Godsea. If it can somehow stagger along in its present drunken and disorganised state, how it could stride forth if it pulled itself together and sobered up! More breadth of understanding and depth of caring, more contacts capable of knocking off the sharper and wounding corners, above all more cross-fertilisation yielding more abundant and more delicious fruit. Why, this place could become as richly productive as its gardens!"

A longish pause, before Mary replied: "Are you sure that's the sort of change that Castellan Nicholas was looking for?"

"What else could it have been? After all, it's not by accident that these folk find themselves thrown together here. Each little faction in Godsea - just by having forsaken its immensely larger parent denomination or sect in Manbridge and elected to come here - has already witnessed to Godsea's powerful attraction, its importance. In that case, could anything be more fitting, more urgent, than to inquire what is this Magnet that has pulled together filings so variously shaped and scattered so widely and thinly on the ground? And what is this Iron Constitution (so to say) that these oddities have in common? If their Castellan may not ask these questions, what may he do? What's he for?"

Another long pause.

"Cecilia tells me you're running into difficulties."

"Yes. Most people here just don't want to know what's going on next door. And when they do find out they are shocked to the marrow, or incredulous, or angry with me for rubbing their noses in the mess. I tell you, this ancient monument is a loony-bin, minus the nursing staff. Sometimes I think it's a ticking bomb."

"A bomb that's been merrily ticking for centuries isn't likely to go off in the next couple of minutes. Besides, how do you rate your chances of setting up a bomb-disposal squad? I suppose I mean some kind of governing body or council, a synod, or even a few steering committees or modest study-groups, and then getting whatever they decide on to work?"

Hodge's hand went to his head. The tone of his reply was restrained. In fact, strained.

"I've been given a job to do, a hard job. I'm not going to let that deter me."

Oh dear, she was upsetting him!

He put the other hand to his head, as well.

'Mary," he said, "are you behind me in this? On my side?"

Her immediate response was to reach up, put her hand on his forehead, and ask: "Does it hurt very much, dear?"

"You haven't answered my question."

"It's not a matter of taking sides. Oh how much I want what's best for you! I'm sure that it must, in the long run, be best for Godsea, too... But please do go slow, feel your way, and take more rest. These headaches of yours -"

He interrupted her. "You think I'm doing the wrong thing."

No doubt about it, he looked hurt and he sounded hurt.

"It's not like that at all. I'm just not sure... Nonplussed, in fact. What about your wonderful scheme for a highway linking Manbridge and Godsea? How's that going? How's it going down?"

"Fairly well. No serious opposition - yet. People are gradually realising its importance."

"How does Manbridge view the project? No doubt MI 13 and CAUTION are plotting away to kill it?"

"It's a funny thing," Hodge replied, "but they seem to think the smartest way to beat the Godsea menace is to pretend it doesn't exist, and that the road to the place - no matter how wide and straight and well-signposted - leads nowhere. In the past, of course, they were for openly and violently suppressing Godsea. And probably will be so in the future. Meanwhile -"

"Well then," said Mary, "what about your concentrating on that link road, and shelving the idea of re-organising this place?"

"Leading Godsea from the rear - to more bewilderment and disorder?"

"Does it have to be led at all? Perhaps in Godsea it's all right to be all at Sea. Perhaps being nonplussed here is as right and proper as being plussed is in Manbridge."

Hodge was not amused.

"Nicholas knew there was something wrong here that can be and must be put right. So do I… So don't you."

There was no mistaking the resentment in his voice.

"In a week's time," he concluded, "I'm going to lay my proposals before the assembled company, come what may."

He got up to go.

Side by side - the long and the short of it - Hodge and Mary trudged along the beach to the footbridge and Godsea Castle, with heavy tread and heavier hearts. "Goodbye confrontation!" she had said, and now felt like kicking herself and howling. Why, this was worse than the worst of their rows in Manbridge: though quieter, it cut deeper. And on her very first day with him in Godsea, at that!

Most worrying of all was his headache. It had become so severe that she insisted he go straight to bed, and then got Cecilia to call the doctor.

34

INTO THE CATACOMBS

Hodge's painful and sleepless night wasn't all wasted. It produced one very definite idea. No doubt it was an idea and a determination born in part of the temperature he was running. Nevertheless he had an inner certainty, a gut-feeling that it could prove decisive, a turning-point in his life at Godsea. And in Mary's too, for that matter.

Every door that he had tried, on that memorable tour of inspection, had opened out on a room lit by a window looking out to Sea. Every door, that is, except one. That door had, painted on it, larger than death, a skull with crossbones. A danger signal that he had found irresistible.

The door in question had given onto a short passage, leading to one of Godsea's many spiral staircases. That was all. He had not explored further. But he'd been left with a strong impression of unfinished business, business he had to complete.

Now more than ever - following that distressful conversation with Mary - he was determined to find out where that sinister door and staircase led to. No-one he asked could tell him. His hunch - his firm conviction - was that it would take him to places and goings-on that would persuade her and all Godsea that he was right, that something drastic had to be done in and for this Castle, and that he, its Castellan, was the one to initiate it. He realised, of course, that (since even the Blue Room had failed to startle her sufficiently) this new revelation would need to be traumatic, a real shocker, if it was to have the desired effect. Well, he was game for anything, this damned migraine notwithstanding. It couldn't be worse than the trouble he was in (or, should he say, the trouble he was having?) with the community, and now with Mary. Mary who, having come along to stand by him, had gone halfway over to the other side.

Yes, come what may, he was determined to find out where that door with the danger-signal led to. That was his way forward. Never before had he felt so much certainty, with so little reason.

He was very much on his own. It felt right. He had decided to tell no-one where he was going. Not even Mary. Specially not Mary. She and the others would find out where he'd been soon enough, on his return. If he *did* return.

The corkscrew stairs were even narrower and steeper than usual, but the treads were no less worn. Many feet had gone this way over the centuries. (Where to? - that was the question. Was the traffic all one-way? he wondered. Had any of those feet returned?) The lighting, of course, was wretched, and there was no suggestion of a rope for handrail.

The corridor at the bottom of the stairs wound this way and that, and its vaulted stone roof frequently came down so low that Hodge gave up ducking and walked along bowed. The silence was a tangible presence, broken only by the echoing plonk-plonk and shuffle-shuffle of his footfall and the sound of his breathing. The dank and musty smell was suggestive of a family burial vault in regular use. There were no doors in the walls of undressed stone. Only the occasional niche, whose contents he was determined not to look into.

At all-too-frequent intervals that corridor (it was rapidly becoming

less like a corridor and more like a tunnel, or even a culvert) set Hodge
a difficult problem. There were T-junctions and Y-junctions and an
occasional X-junction or four crossways. Which turning should he take?
After much dithering he decided to go for the route that was wider and
lighter, and (in case there was nothing in it) the one whose floor was
more worn. It was the least unpromising system he could think of; and
one which, working in reverse, should make his return journey a shade
less tricky. But by no means an infallible system. Sometimes there was
nothing to choose between alternative routes, and he had no option but
to find where his feet were making for.

An uncontrollable shiver went through him as, belatedly, he
realised the risk he was taking. He could so easily get lost in this maze
of tunnels, and no one would know where to begin looking for him.
Come to think of it, he *was* lost! Lacking all sense of direction, there was
no way of telling whether he was still on the outward journey or the
return journey. Maybe his system - for what it was worth - would see
him back, having come full circle, to Mary and Home. Home? (Yes, in
spite of everything, Home!) The possibility - that he would go on
wandering in these catacombs till he collapsed and died - he didn't rule
out. Either it was this reflection, or his fever, which brought on a sweat,
in spite of the cold, dank air.

He had now left behind the tunnels built of stone and come to
one roughly hewn out of what they call the living rock. It followed that
he was no longer in Godsea itself, but in the primeval depths it arose
from. No wonder there was an increasing quantity of water about. In
places it was cascading down the walls, and everywhere the floor was
awash. This was becoming more like a paddle than a walk, and a very
cold and slippery paddle, at that. And presently more like a wade than
a paddle. The worst part was the darkness. Not total darkness, but
requiring utmost caution. More and more Hodge was having to feel his
way, with groping hands and feet, not so much through that darkness
as deeper into it. Here was a night that pressed in on him from every
direction, that suffocated. A long, long night it was too, an age. The
time hurt, it was so long. Now he knew how it must feel to be buried
alive for ever. How it *does* feel.

Naturally he was terrified! Yet at the same time he was keyed up,
as if in anticipation of the discovery that must lie ahead. How was it
possible to be so terrified and yet so undeterred, so desperately unsure
and yet so confident that this was the way, his way, his unavoidable

trial and destiny? A drop or two of comfort he drew from the thought that such light as filtered through into this awful place - only God knew by what devious routes - came from the Perilous Sea. Yes: it was his unbreakable link, his continuity with the Sea, that mysteriously coped with the peril he was in. That empowered him to take it on, without diminishing the terror by a twinge or a shudder.

The danger was mounting all the while. He paused to take stock. The ice-cold water already came up to his waist. He looked back. The way he'd come by was pitch-black. Ahead, there was some light, but the water reached to within a yard or less of the roof. To go forward appeared even more foolhardy than to go back. But where there was light there was hope. The light could lead him to the Sea. The Sea which even these black waters must come from. He raised his hand, already submerged, to his lips. Yes, it was salt water all right. Go on he must.

As far as he could see ahead, the level of the water fell short of the roof. There would be just room enough for him to breathe if he held his head back. But of course there was no telling the depth of the water. The bottom was certainly not level.

Very slowly and cautiously he inched his way - hair brushing the roof, hands pushing at the sides of that narrowing tunnel as if to stop them caving in on him, and feet groping for the contours of the bottom. Extremely uneven they proved to be. Sometimes the water was so shallow and the roof so low that he had to bend double, to go on all-fours. Sometimes so deep that only his unusual height, and his bouncing, dance-like tread, saved him from drowning.

Then came the real test, the ordeal for which all he'd come through was mere preparation, a preliminary flexing of the muscles.

Ahead, the ceiling and the water converged. They actually came together. The tunnel was full. It had become a water-trap or siphon - maybe five yards long, maybe fifteen, God only knew. More, was certain death for the diver.

This time he really was brought up short. He had no intention of committing suicide. After an agonising age of indecision he made up his mind to turn back. After all, the thick darkness behind was the devil he knew and perhaps could live with, whereas the thinner darkness ahead of him was the devil he didn't know and was more likely to die with.

At this point he was granted a vision - albeit a diabolical vision. He actually saw what increasingly he'd felt - that the darkness through which he'd come, and now proposed to venture back into, was by no means a plain or clean darkness. It was foul with horrors. Infesting it was indeed the devil he knew, the unspeakable devilry he had known only too well, and had tried to commit some faint idea of to paper, in that terrible cell in Strangefields. If it were possible to turn back now, only to plunge into and live with that satanic blackness, life wouldn't be worth the living of it. Death, even the watery death that almost certainly lay ahead of him, was infinitely preferable.

In short, that nightmare vision gave him second thoughts. What lay ahead, though probably fatal, was not devilish. Better a quick death in this dim but good light than a slow one in that evil darkness.

Then at last, all indecision at an end, a great calm descended on him. An invasive calm that drenched him through and through and drowned his fear, a calm that was as unexpected as it was deep. Far deeper than the deepest of the waters that faced him. He had a strong sense that it was the calm of the Horizonless and Bottomless Ocean that, by taking on all perils, dissolves them. The calm of the Perilous Sea which is the incomparable and only safety. He knew that to be lost in that Sea is to be saved.

Breathing deep, calling upon the last ounce of an energy that was his because it was not his at all, he dived. He plunged into the siphon.

35

FLOTSAM AND JETSAM

It was three days and three nights since Hodge had disappeared.
A long, long time it had been for Mary and Cecilia. They had
searched, again and again, what they hoped was every inch of
Godsea, and they had been joined by other searchers. Unbelievably
complicated though the Castle was, they were convinced it contained
no trace of Hodge. The many cells and the meeting-rooms with their
peculiar secrets, the workshops of all trades, the winding passages and
corkscrew stairwells, the kitchens and storerooms and unused cellars,
even the roofs and battlements wherever accessible - all had been
systematically explored. So had the gardens he loved to work in. So
had acres of the wild country around, with its frustrating variety of
potential hiding places.

There remained, it seemed, only two possibilities.

The first was that he had got lost in the catacombs beneath the
Castle, far beyond the door with its warnings of danger ahead. Mary
and Cecilia had ventured into the maze of tunnels up to where the
water was ankle-deep. Taking their cue from Ariadne in the Greek
myth, they had sensibly unwound a thread as they went along - the
thread that would lead them safely back to their starting point. Before
turning back they had yelled and shouted themselves hoarse, and held
their breath, and waited. All the reply they got was echo upon echo,
followed by the tinkle of water running down the walls. It was still on
the cards, of course, that he was wandering somewhere in that vast
labyrinth, beyond reach of their cries.

The other possibility was that he had gone swimming in the truly
Perilous Sea, and had either been seized with cramp or swept out by a
strong off-shore current.

No-one in Godsea mentioned the word suicide, but the idea was
around, right enough.

To Mary and Cecilia it was unthinkable. They felt sure - well,
almost sure - that somewhere and somewhen he would turn up, his

ship storm-battered and half stove-in, but bravely sailing into harbour with all flags flying. After all - at least for Mary - he was Hodge the irritant, the human egg-whisk, the survivor-surpriser who loved to astonish and make a commotion. And now he was the Castellan who had sworn that, only two days from now, he would lay his proposals for Godsea before its assembled members. In fact, Mary had screwed up her courage to ask Frank for his forecast. He had replied that Hodge would, he thought, keep his promise. And people told her that when Frank thought something would happen, there was a very good chance of its doing so.

So at last Mary gave up and returned to her room and trusted and was still. Simultaneously gazing in to See and out to Sea - the Sea that both she and Hodge were forever at once lost and saved in anyway - she was at peace. It was a peace that stayed with her as she went off to do her stint of sentry duty at the moat.

The archway she chose lay at the south-east corner of the Castle, on the side furthest from the kitchen gardens. It commanded a view across the moat and along the less-frequented beach, with its rolling sand-dunes and foaming white shoreline. With Cecilia she had combed that beach for miles, in her search for Hodge.

But now her business lay in the moat. There, no great surprise, glaring up at her was Mary-Quite-Contrary, the fuming, fat-faced, fishy Thing that needed - and how it needed! - distancing and ditching.

Not normally, for her, a desperately difficult task.

But today was different. Her attention wasn't hers to command. It kept slipping away from that Thing to picture a succession of Hodges. A Hodge far out to Sea, arms upstretched, going down for the third and last time; a Hodge trapped in the dark depths below her very feet at this moment, reduced to crawling, stuck, entombed, suffocating; a Hodge who had somehow got spirited back to the Great Moor of Kreep, and lay there, after three days and nights lost in a storm, naked, bloody, at the point of death...

O hell, her imagination was running riot! She was actually "seeing things"! Why, she could so easily persuade herself that the brownish shadow cast by the nearest of those sandbanks wasn't a shadow at all, but Hodge lying there fast asleep!

This wouldn't do at all. Mary pulled herself together and got down to business, to sentry-duty again. But only for a minute. There really *was* something odd about that brown shadow. Shadow? It couldn't be! This was afternoon, and the shadows (if any) cast by those dunes lay on the other side of them, the east side. It had to be a piece of flotsam or jetsam, or a strangely shaped mass of seaweed, or...

It moved! A surface ripple it was. No doubt the wind, freshening, was ruffling the weed.

And then, almost as though Mary's prayer had been so pleading, and her visualising so vivid, that the tangled mass of seaweed and flotsam just *had* to come to life - it stretched skywards an arm!

A long, brown, human arm!

36

SEA-BORN

She found him there on the sandbank, just where the moat widened out and joined the Sea. He was sitting up, rubbing his eyes. He had heard her shouting, had seen her racing towards him.

He struggled to his feet, spread his arms, swayed a little - and half collapsed, half sat.

Yes, Hodge had made it, but only just made it, to the end of the siphon and the underwater opening in the wall at the south-east corner of the Castle. Out of that submerged arch he'd struggled, and up he'd popped, like a cork, in what amounted to a little bay of the Sea. A few more desperate strokes, and he'd gained the shore. There he had lain utterly exhausted, but warming up and drying in the blessed sunshine, and there he had slept…

And now, back in his cell with Mary, he was breaking his three-day fast. She had brought him a tray of bread and cheese and honey and all sorts of fruit piled high.

What was there to say? She knew the place he'd been to. The difference was that her way out of it and his had not been quite the same. As for her tale, she'd been looking for him, and now she'd found him. That was about the strength of it.

Sea-Born

The Hodge she had found was not the Hodge she had lost. Here was a new creature, born of the Sea, born of the foam of the Perilous Sea. Of that newness she had been quite certain from the first moment of their coming together on the beach. Exactly what the difference was she couldn't explain to herself, much less to him. Nor did she have the slightest urge to do so. This time (having learned the lesson of their first Godsea meeting) she was content to let the situation unfold, in the absolute certainty that it would turn out to be absolutely as it should be. The fact that their conversation wasn't at all about their feelings, but about practical and everyday matters, simply meant that their feelings dovetailed. At gut-level she knew that at last the two of them, feelings included, were coming from exactly the same Place. The same never-to-be-lost-touch-with Horizonless Expanse. To put the matter more intimately, she knew that something in him had given way, and that now he could really love, and that at last his tenderness for her matched hers for him.

The only question that occurred to her was whether his speech as Castellan, planned for the day after tomorrow, would go ahead.

He assured her that it would. The reason he couldn't go through it with her in advance was simple. He didn't know what he would say. Better let the occasion come up with the words, Mary agreed.

"Meanwhile," she added, "let me sing you a little song. It's called *Looking to See*. I made it up only this morning, in anticipation of this evening:

> Mary searches the tunnels
> As far as can be
> Then to find her lost Hodge
> She looks out to Sea.
>
> O Psyche finds her Cupid
> And Mary finds H.P.
> When they stop being stupid
> And look in to Sea.

"Cupid. Eros. Caritas. Agape..." began Hodge, and paused.

"Yes?"

"Of this I'm absolutely certain, that forever and ever and ever they are flooding the world till it's brim-full and overflowing.

"I'm thinking of the Love that takes the longest view, beyond all horizons, " said Mary.

37

MARY ON GODSEA

This was the occasion.

This was the day and this the evening of Castellan Hodge's promised address to the assembled community of Godsea. He had decided to deliver it in two instalments, the first part before dinner, the second after dinner. Both were to be quite informal.

The great hall, with its two huge and glowing fireplaces, rich but faded and worn tapestries, and massively elaborate angel roof, was looking its spectacular best. Not so much mediaeval as dateless, thought Mary. From where she sat she could spot nothing that placed it in one century rather than another. Childe Godefroi wouldn't have felt out-of-place here. Even the people, seen in this soft and flickering light, were taking on a timeless and universal quality. But by no means a sameness. What a miscellany of ordinariness and distinction, age and youth, radiant beauty and homeliness, lightness of touch and gravity, they presented!

Incongruously or not, she was reminded of a wartime scene from her childhood in Manbridge. A company of conscripts, singing what were probably their last songs, were being marched to the Front. Their faces, no matter how careworn or coarse, had for her suddenly been transfigured with the dignity that only imminent Death can bestow - Death the Leveller and Ennobler, Death which is dying back into the Deathless. The very same dignity that now ennobled Hodge, the young man who had died in the catacombs and been reborn of the Sea foam, and was now on loan from the Sea.

People were assembling around him now, in horseshoe formation. Most were sitting crosslegged or lolling on cushions scattered over the gleaming stone floor, the older ones on chairs dotted here and there, and a few warming their backs at the fire. All were dressed casually, more for ease than show, to express rather than impress. No-one was tarted-up. There were no blue rinses, no twenty-minute complexions, no mutton dressed up as lamb, no old-school ties. This unfashionably fascinating lot, Mary reflected, would cause the haute-couturistes of Manbridge to wring their exquisitely manicured hands. Yet she saw them as beautiful, as splendidly - even regally - turned-out for the occasion. This was particularly true of the menials in their monkish robes, Hodge among them.

He was perched on a high chair, not talking, and looking very relaxed. Around him there rose a steady hum of conversation, an occasional gust of laughter, and a strong sense of waiting-for-it, of expectation. If apprehension and resentment were present in that gathering, how readily they were being overcome (Mary felt) by their opposites! Ditched, so to say.

The news had got around, of course, about Hodge's ordeal in the catacombs, and his triumphant emergence from the siphon. She had the idea that it somehow recommended and endeared him to the company. It was as though he'd paid the price of admission to their hearts. A rather silly idea perhaps, but there it was.

She decided to fill in the time of waiting by trying to make out whether these folk - in spite of their immense differences *as Godsea-ers* - had anything in common *as people*. In what ways - if any - were the body language, the attitudes, the style, the gestures, the tones of voice of this company unlike those of any comparable gathering in Manbridge? Comparable, that is, in size and seriousness and social range? That there were significant differences she was perfectly sure, but far less sure about what they might be. Well, while waiting for Hodge's speech she would amuse herself by attempting to identify some of them. No doubt - feeling as happily expansive as she did - her mood would colour and enrich her findings in Godsea's favour. Never mind, she could deduct the needful discount later.

The first and most striking peculiarity of these folk was that they looked you straight in the eye, steadily, without embarrassment. This wasn't the brassy, challenging, devil-take-you stare of some grown-ups, but more like the I'm-for-looking-out-of gaze of children before the onset of I'm-for-looking-at. In the keep of this Castle, your tight little old frog-fish-face - so closed up and blotchy and misery-making - having been duly ditched and moated, you were left with your vast and serene and marvellously clear-complexioned Face, your Wide Open Face. The Face that never was shame-faced. Why, even those shrinking violets - such as Deirdre of the Sword - who should be shy were not shy or shrinking at all. They, too, looked you in the eye. The overall result was pleasing and comfortable. Yes (Mary decided), though of course everyone's style was unique, there was about all of them the quiet confidence and the charm and the good looks and the loveableness that everyone has when he or she is bored to tears with all that caper and lets go of it. Leaves it to other people to look after.

One of the minor consequences of this handing over of one's appearance was that these people smiled less than the regulation Manbridge norm. Cutting out the put-on smiles left them with the can't-help-smiling sort, which account for no more than half of the total. On the other hand, there was rather more than the usual helping of laughter. Godsea-ers were as unsolemn as they were serious about life. They found it wonderful fun, entertaining, often hilarious, and never needed to grin from wisdom tooth to wisdom tooth to prove it. Cecilia had shown Mary a group photograph of Godsea-ers, with hardly a smile or a smirk to share out between them: and they by no means resembled a wake, or a conference of undertakers. Not at all.

How does it happen (Mary asked herself) that there's all this laughter echoing around Godsea? Why is life here more amusing than in Manbridge? One reason, surely, is that here you see (but never quite get used to) your upside-downness (feet over no-head) and other-way-roundness (Hodge's right is Podge's left) and inside-outness (Podge is Podge but Hodge is everything but Hodge) - a threefold setting-up for Godsea-ers, and a threefold tipping-over for Manbridgers. A banana-skin humorous situation, you could say.

What else? Ah yes! Working in the kitchen, Mary had noticed how her companions did one thing at a time. When they were preparing runner beans it was as though the destiny of Godsea, of the world, hung on the correct topping and stringing and slicing of those beans: or rather of the particular bean in one's hand at the moment. This meant that one worked in silence. To chit-chatter, to talk about or think about absent matters, just wasn't on. At least three benefits accrued. The job got done quicker, and better, and far more enjoyably; and most probably the beans tasted more delicious. And now here, in this magnificent hall, if you happened to be conversing with someone, you gave the whole weight of your attention to that someone. You really looked, you really listened, you really communicated. And when you stopped, you stopped. That was that.

What you didn't do was compulsively churn out social noises. You didn't make conversation for conversation's sake, because silence was impolite, or embarrassing, or left your existence in doubt. Accordingly you could find yourself sitting alongside a friend, or even a mere acquaintance, for as long as ten minutes without exchanging a word, and could be all the more at ease because there was nothing to say, and by God you said it. In fact, silence in Godsea took on a positive quality, a largeness that connected hiddenly with the Sea. The fact that for the last five minutes no word had passed between Mary herself and Cecilia on her left, and Frank on her right, simply meant that she was entirely comfortable - and more than comfortable - in their presence. There was benediction in it.

Finally, there was the way the last of those people were moving around and settling down in their places - more smoothly, somehow, than the Manbridge norm. Their actions flowed less jerkily, more economically, in a kind of dance. There was less nodding and hair-patting and chin-stroking and head-shaking and grimacing, less fidget-ing of fingers and shuffling of feet. There was little or no gush or eagerbeavering or brouhaha, so far as Mary could make out. This didn't imply any lack of liveliness or sensitivity or responsiveness. On the contrary, these folk were livepan and not deadpan, as spontaneous as they come, and above all *natural*.

Yes, that was it. *Natural* was the keyword. How wrong were the Manbridgers who supposed that Godsea was an odd, quirky, fantasti-cal, rarefied scene! If it was extraordinary it was because of its very ordinariness - its unrehearsed spontaneity, its relaxation, its refusal to pose and show off and play the games that Manbridge plays, its child-like sincerity and guilelessness. Here at last it was natural to be natural, simple to be simple, easy to be at ease.

There was a hush in the hall. Hodge seemed about to speak...

But no. Servants were still carrying in logs for the fires, and taking round drinks...

Which gave Mary just time enough to add an all-important footnote and proviso to what she realised were her too-complimentary and rose-tinted observations. Everyone present, without exception, was stuck with his or her very own bugaboo - Podge, Mary-Quite-Contrary, Frankenstein, Old Nick, you-name-it - lying in wait in the castle moat. God help anyone who denied or underrated the menace of that buga-boo, or who imagined it had been ditched for good and all. What a hope! In fact, those up-gazing devils of the moat were at least as much part-and-parcel of Godsea as the down-gazing angels of the roof of the great hall, and the out-gazing angels (well, angels of a sort, shorn of wings and haloes) congregated below and waiting for their new Castellan to speak. Overworld, world, underworld - totally distinct, totally indivisible. Put it this way: though ultimately safe, Godsea keep lay forever under siege from its own outworks. The resulting interior tension was deadly when you denied it, enlivening when you didn't. Here was a most delicate and energetic equilibrium founded on contrast and refusal to compromise or dilute. It kept Godsea on its toes, on the qui-vive. It was very good for Godsea. Mary was no pollyanna. Though she had little idea of what Hodge was going to say, she was pretty sure it would include this sort of warning against woolliness and complacency, and an over-simplified and under-priced euphoria that could never last anyway.

This time the conversation, having died down again, stayed down. The silence was broken only by the roaring and crackling of the fires.

38

HODGE ON PODGE

T his, he explained, was to be the most informal of fireside talks, and - in case he didn't make himself plain - people shouldn't hesitate to butt in with questions. Contributions of any kind would be welcome. In fact, it was story time. The title of his fairly short story was a disproportionately long one: HODGE CAN DISLODGE PODGE BUT CAN'T DODGE HIM. Yes, it was a personal tale because it had to be, a confession if you like, but it was up to everyone listening to check how far it resembled his or her own tale. The villain of the present piece was Podge, and for devilry and low cunning he won the cigar or coconut. In all the history and literature of Manbridge Hodge had never come across a more plausible, ingenious, ruthless, persistent rogue. Reluctantly, he found himself taking his hat off to this Prince of Tricksters.

He began by describing how Podge had rushed him and podged him by Beaston pond, and how this had set the animals against him, and how he only just survived his flight over the Moor to Manbridge. He went on to explain how *separated* from everything he'd felt there, how desperately *cut off*; and how he'd admired and emulated the plants that were shoeless and didn't tear about, but stayed continuous with the world that sustained them. Above all he explained how comforted and thrilled he'd been to find he was growing a marvellous Manbridgian body that reunited him with the world in a thousand ways and at a thousand points, putting all those brilliantly gifted animals to shame with its scope and sensitivity and stamina and serviceability. It turned out to be a growth that could stop nowhere short of the universe itself. He discovered that his true body, when he'd added in all the limbs needed to bring it to life and make it work, and had felt himself into them, amounted to nothing less than the Whole Body of things. There was no stopping short of the All.

"It all sounds fine and dandy, doesn't it?" said Hodge. "However, here arose something of a hitch. This great discovery of mine gave me agonising headaches, upset Mary's friends and Manbridge generally, and eventually landed me - sadly out of my wits - in a padded cell in

Strangefields prison. How's that for trouble?

"Let me explain what had gone wrong.

"You must understand that Podge is hooked on becoming big and powerful, on being always the winner, on coming out on top (literally as well as figuratively) every time and in every way. So what does the old so-and-so do? He battens on and endorses and develops my altogether worthy and acceptable urge to grow, to break down the wall between myself and my world, and misappropriates it. The name of the monkey he makes out of me is King Kong. He inflates my sanity till it's his madness. He turns my passion for savouring the world into his passion for wolfing it. He's the megalomaniac of all time."

"Hold on!" broke in a young man whose dimly-seen face seemed familiar to Hodge. "Generation after generation of Godsea-ers have declared they were strangers and afraid in the world till they *became* the world - including Manbridge and Beaston and all lands - and were as wide as the heavens and as high as the stars. That you're no true Godsea-er till you coincide with the universe. Are you now telling us they were stupid, or mad, or even diabolical? If so, I can't agree. It just happens to be true that I don't stop at my skin, and am not all there till I'm *all* there and leave nothing out."

The young man's voice was the reverse of abrasive, but it did come over good and strong. It, too, seemed familiar. There was a murmur of assent tiptoeing round the great hall.

The penny dropped for Hodge. That mellifluous voice took him back to Manbridge and the temple of the Sad-guru mounted on the top of his Nelson's column. How delighted Hodge was that his premonition had come true, and that the young friend he and Mary had made there had turned up here so promptly!

"Yes of course," he replied. "Those who say 'I'm all things' are quite right - *provided* in the next breath they add 'I'm nothing.' An admission which would never pass the lips of Podge in an age of ages. Put it like this: Hodge is a halfway house between the central Nothing and the peripheral Everything. Go up to him and in the end he's revealed as Damn-all; retreat from him and in the end he's revealed as Bless-all, or plain All if you like. Hodge of Godsea keep is doing both. Matching ungrowth with growth, he's at once absolutely empty and absolutely full, and so is blessed and balanced. Podge of Godsea ditch, on the other hand, is forever trying to do one of them - to grow without diminishing, to explode without imploding - and so is cursed and unbalanced, eccentric, distracted, off his rocker. And that's the best of

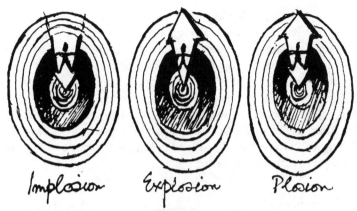

Implosion   Explosion   Plosion

reasons for ensuring he stays ditched. Agreed?"

"Absolutely," came Prem-Prem's reply, ungrudgingly. "Thank you, Castellan."

"It's much the same with power - which, to be safe and sane, must be matched with its opposite, with wide-open submission to what's so. For example, in Manbridge Podge characteristically took full credit for Hodge Podge's 'miraculous' ability to urigeller people and objects, as if they were made of putty. He would! Whereas here in Godsea Hodge gives at least equal credit to the people and objects themselves, to their wonderful readiness to suffer Sea change after Sea change. Yes, in the end and always, it's the Sea that does the trick and packs the power.

"Back, then, to my story. There was Hodge Podge crouching in his padded cell, driven mad by the contradiction between his grand pretensions as Podge and his awful predicament as Hodge. It was (I guess) a breakdown and a hell he had to pass through to prepare him for the revelation in the exercise yard of that prison. What happened there was that Hodge saw Podge off to his proper place, a yard or so off-centre, and was emptied. The one who rightly claimed to be All saw that he was also Nothing. He was cleared and cured.

"So a drastically remoulded Hodge went in search of his kind, his own people. He left what he knew was Podge-infested Manbridge for what he hoped was Podge-free Godsea. And that, the poor nitwit imagined, was to be the happy ending of the Hodge Podge Saga. What a hope! Little did he know!"

"This place has its eye on the Sea" - it was Sebastian, the inventor of the Demystifying Telescope, speaking - "rather more than on the moat. I think you should explain what detaching Hodge from Podge in that exercise yard in Manbridge has to do with attaching Hodge to the Horizonless Ocean in Godsea."

"Properly attended to," Hodge replied, "I find they come to the same thing. The one takes care of the other. Or, if you like, they are two sides of a coin. When Hodge ditches Podge he no longer puts anything in the Sea's way. He uncorks his bottle, opening out a limitless volume into which the Limitless Ocean floods. So, coming to Godsea, he finds himself equally concerned with Podge's moat on the north and Hodge's Sea on the south. With distancing Podge the Cork from Hodge the Bottle, and vice versa. Two-way Looking is the name of the game. Is that your experience, Sebastian?"

"Near enough, Castellan."

"Now for the sequel to my story. As many of you know already, I was astounded to find here at Godsea, instead of the close and heartfelt agreement I'd counted on, an incredible mishmash of views and practices. Pandemonium's hardly too strong a word for it. These folk seemed to have nothing in common. That Godsea-ers should differ somewhat was understandable, even desirable. That they should ignore one another to the point of denying the existence of serious rivals, or tenable alternative views, was ludicrous. That they should contradict one another to the point of cancelling out altogether was scandalous and absurd. The mess was unworthy of Godsea. So were the parochialism, the bigotry. I make no apology for proposing better communication, more mutual respect and caring, greater willingness to listen to and learn from others, richer opportunities for cross-fertilisation. So I started doing what I could to get these improvements off the ground.

"So far, so good. Or perhaps I should say: so far, so-so.

"It was at this point, alas, that history began to repeat itself.

I've described how Podge took Hodge's passionate concern for
Manbridge and proceeded to blow it up and turn it into Podge's
passionate concern for Podge, and serve his native and ineradicable
urge to expand and dominate. Pecksniff Podge, pretending that his
self-aggrandisement was Hodge's self-transcendence! It didn't
work. He got found out, and was thrown out. So what does the
creep do but try again? He gets up to the same game at a higher
level, playing for higher stakes, with a higher chance of avoiding
detection. This time he takes Hodge's concern *for Godsea*, and pro-
ceeds to blow it up and turn it, as before, into Podge's concern for
Podge. He stages a secret come-back. Yes, my friends, there's no
power-trip so insidious, so sinister-subtle as the Godsea power trip.
Podge in Manbridge caught up in his idiot-boy act, Podge the self-
satisfied show-off, the know-all, the dedicated irritant, the angry
young man, was fairly easily seen through. It became all too clear
what Podge the sinner was up to there. But it's by no means so clear
what Podge the would-be saint is up to here - Podge the self-ap-
pointed director of souls, Podge the guru with the answers, Podge
the stickler for his own version of Godsea and his own section of
Godsea moat, at the expense of others. How clever he is at hiding
the fact that he's taking over as Castellan of Godsea!"

A pause. Somebody dropped a tumbler on the stone floor. The
sound of its shattering was like a meteor landing on Crystal Palace.

"Yes, you heard me! That was no exaggeration, or slip of the tongue.
Just fancy, here's Podge up to his old Beaston and Manbridge tricks, in
Godsea of all places, rushing Castellan Hodge, infesting Castellan Hodge,
ousting Castellan Hodge! Oh so hiddenly, so sneakily, taking over!
Castellan Podge, how do you do! Hail, O King of Frogs, your skinny,
slime-green finger bejewelled with the ancient ring of all the Masters of
Godsea! No wonder some of you were getting restive!

"How did Hodge wake to the invasion, the substitution, the secret take-over?

"Well, the evidence piled up till even he tumbled to what was going on.

"First, there were the headaches, the migraines. All along it had been Podge who went in for them. They were one of his cruder ways of announcing his presence up top, his dominating position.

"Then there were some very curious, give-away changes in Podge-in-the-moat. Quite wrongly, the new Castellan felt that his appointment allowed him to cut down time spent on sentry duty; but even so it remained long enough to reveal some strange goings-on. Podge was fast becoming less furious and aggressive, more and more well-behaved, even smarmy. Also phosphorescent. Not a very rare or surprising development in a fish or a frog, perhaps, but the creature positively *glowed*, oozing self-satisfaction at every pore. In fact there were traces of a halo - tilted and worn rakishly and battered, but clearly visible. Even more revealing was the way Podge from time to time actually *winked*: as though Hodge and Podge were in cahoots and up to some very funny business together. Which in a sense they were. Actually his winking didn't do his cause any good. It went too far, it was *too* nasty. A normal run-of-the-moat Podge - ranging from cherub in the west to devil in the east - was unpleasing enough, but an ogling Podge with a smirk on his fat face - this was sheer grand guignol!

"Another funny thing that should have sounded the alarm. The halo showed signs of squaring up into a mortarboard, indicating Podge the Saint's graduation as Podge the Sage and Scholar, intelligent and well-informed: in whose considered view poor old Hodge in Manbridge (the court had got it about right) really was retarded, and no wonder he'd found himself in institutional care. But now, thanks to faithful Podge, he was maturing fast, and would soon be Quite Grown Up. Not Manbridge-fashion adult, of course, but Godsea-fashion. Not so much clever as wise. Why, of course! More winking! More grand guignol!

"You would think (wouldn't you?) that this peal of alarm bells would have alerted Hodge to Podge's bid for the Castellanship. In fact, two more were needed. The first was the unease of a close friend who sensed that all wasn't well with the new Castellan. That (to lapse into Manbridge-speak) his real motives might be far less noble than his publicised ones, his underlying intentions the very opposite of his surface ones. Hodge's debt to that most faithful friend is incalculable.

"About the last signal, it wasn't so much a warning against the Podge menace as a counterstroke. There's nothing like Death's bony finger for pointing to what's real and what's false in life. In the catacombs beneath our feet a door marked with a skull opened on the dark night from which dawns the true and brightest morning. Also on a long overdue piece of tit for tat. The war was taken deep into enemy territory. Instead of Podge invading Hodge in his castle, Hodge invaded Podge in his moat. Right to the bottom he sank, and suffered a Sea-change, and surfaced to tell the story."

A cheerful voice from the back of the hall: "That's giving him what for. That'll teach the so-and-so!"

"Will it?" countered Hodge, enigmatically.

A chill draught swept and whistled through the great hall. People put on sweaters and scarves and moved about. The fires were stoked up.

This time it was Stephanie, the friend of the fairies in the garden, who spoke:

"We've been listening to the story of the Prince, the Princess and the Frog. We've heard how at long last the Prince, helped by the Princess, saw through the horrible tricks the Frog was up to. Now what about the traditional happy ending? Such as: 'And the brave Prince and his beautiful Princess lived happily ever after, and never once let that wicked Frog out of his pond to make trouble between them again.'"

That got a few claps and some laughter, in which Hodge and Mary joined.

"Well let's see," he replied. "There's more to come. I'll tell it, if you don't mind, after dinner."

39

BETWEEN THE DEVIL
AND THE DEEP BLUE SEA

As usual, dinner went off in silence. This evening the silence had a special quality. It sang. It was like the pause between two movements of a well-loved symphony.

Mary sat opposite Hodge who, as the speaker of the evening, had been excused from his duties as waiter. His hand touched hers as they both reached for the salt. They exchanged poker-faced glances, not deadpan but livepan Godsea glances, of the sort that said so much more than any combination of smiles and words.

Her hair, with its blend of bright gold and red and brown, burned fiercely in the firelight. Never had those peach-complexioned cheeks been, for Hodge, so Eden-fresh, so straight from the clear morning of the world. For her part, she saw him as timeless - as at once the two-day-old offspring of the Sea foam, and Childe Godefroi come back to his castle by the Sea, to the fortress he'd founded an age of ages ago, secula seculorum. Was it a trick of the light, or was it a fact that his eyes were now exactly the same colour - the colour of the deep blue Sea? But what pleased Mary most was that the light in them, on this most exciting occasion of his life, bore no trace of excitement whatever.

Dinner over, he stood up to speak.

Heavens, how tall he was!

And how big, how complete! For her at least an all-rounder with the lips of an Infant, the forehead of a Man and the eyes of a Seer! He bore the marks of - he belonged to - Beaston and Manbridge and Godsea. In him abideth all three, and the greatest of these is Godsea.

His voice rang out clear and deep in the silence.

"I suspect that Stephanie's shot at the ending of my story - the Frog ditched for good and all, and the Prince and Princess living happily ever after - was deliberately miles off-target. We all know the bounder isn't so easily bound, and given what-for. He will *not* be taught. Never will he learn the lesson of countless ditchings and settle down to a reformed old age, as a harmless pet in the family aquarium.

On the contrary, this water-sprite seems to get more sprightly and quick-off-the mark, and more devilishly ingenious, every day and in every way.

"I tell you I know what I'm going on about. Here's an up-to-the-minute, blow-by-blow example. Podge, my personal Frog, (talk of the Devil!) has just leapt clear of the moat, and landed right here, right now." Hodge pointed to his left shoulder. "Where he's whispering in this ear: 'Well done, Hodge! How humble you've been, admitting to all those naughty motives - like wanting to sort out and boss this assembled company, and to be loved and admired and kow-towed to by everybody! I reckon you're the most alert, honest, self-effacing fellow in this great hall. Why, you said it yourself - every saint thinks he's a pig - and here you are, assured of your piggishness and, by extension, of your sainthood! St Hodge Podge of Godsea! I like the sound of that!'"

Turning his head and wrinkling his nose and sniffing, Hodge brushed his shoulder vigorously to clear it of Podge-droppings.

That, too, got some laughs and clapping. A voice proposed a toast to Podge the Frog, in recognition of his muscular hind legs, his stamina and tireless opportunism.

Hodge continued: "There's only one way to nobble him for good and all, and that's the way of our dear Castellan Nicholas. There came a day when he searched and searched the moat from the warm end to the bitter cold and couldn't for the life of him find any trace of Old Nick. Old Nick was dead. That was the truth of the matter, the inside story. The social fiction was that Nicholas was dead.

"Well, Hodge is still around and therefore Podge is still around. So long as Podge is down there he will continue to turn up here also, chip-on-shoulder fashion, whispering podgepodge in Hodge's ear. Also nudging him in the ribs, pulling his leg, patting him on the egoback, tickling his fancy for ever new sorts of devilry; and, when all else fails, giving him nasty frog kicks below the belt. There's nothing Hodge can do about it except keep track of and laugh at his manoeuvering, recognise each new hat he wears, tumble to every new act he puts on, and keep seeing the bounder off. It's Hodge's watchfulness that he hates. That, and his ridicule. Dead serious, Podge works solemnly and furtively in the dark. Shine your light and your lightheartedness on him, and - plop! - he's back in the water. But as long as Hodge manages to stay clear of the obituary column Podge will continue to get at him, will seek by every froggy hook and crook to bug him. Podge is the arch-amphibian, ever poised, a pocket Polaris in person.

"Which isn't quite the happy ending of my story that Stephanie had in mind. All the same, the situation's not as desperate or as miserable as it may sound. Look out for Podge's hanky-panky, don't ever let him get away with it, and have fun at his expense. Cross my heart, this Hodge-Podge combat, this clashing and clanging, this hearty ding-dong is indispensable for a real and lively life. Muffle or attune the clanging, tone it down, and the bell tolls for thee. It's the way things are set up willy-nilly, their dynamism, their polarity. Unite your poles and your battery's dead flat; cut out one or other of them and you haven't even got a battery. Given alertness and some sense of humour, it's an exhilarating life this, lived between the Devil and the Deep Blue Sea! The wonder is that this great hall, taking its cue from the prophet Ezekiel, doesn't spread all its angel wings and mount skywards with the thrill of it!

"So let me now eagerly adopt the suggestion that we drink a toast. Are your glasses charged with the good wine of Godsea? I give you Podge. I propose we drink to all our Podges, all the little devils. Giving you your due, we are amazed at your agility and resourcefulness. We are entertained by your disguises, ranging from cherubic to satanic. We are tickled to life by your persistence. Above all, we acknowledge that in the last resort you are in the service of the Sea you are born of and live in. Yes, indeed: let's never forget that the moat of this castle is fed by and continuous with the Perilous Sea, no weir intervening. At the end of the end of the day and in the queerest way this Hodge-Podge affair turns out to be the love affair of all time, the Romance to end all romances and finally land Cartland in the cart. What's more, the moated Podge - repeat *moated* - takes on a peculiar charm, and begins to glow with the beauty of the Sea, the ultramarine beauty that's beyond all beauty and ugliness."

Glasses were raised. Podges were named. The toast was duly drunk.

There was a great outburst of cheering and clapping. Was this, or wasn't it, the end of Hodge's speech? He seemed in no hurry to sit down...

It was Steve, Stephanie's brother, who broke the silence.

"May I change the subject a little? I had thought your address to us this evening, as the new Castellan, was to be about the future of Godsea, the line you wanted it to take. So far, it's been about Podge and Co, Ltd. And quite right too, I say. Sort that firm out and you sort out Godsea Unlimited, insofar as that enterprise can and should be sorted out. All the same, let's get down to business and hear your ideas about changes in the organisation here, or rather in the lack of it."

"I'm concluding with that," replied Hodge. "But I suggest we defer it till these dinner things and tables have been cleared away, and we are sitting around more comfortably."

40

HODGE ON GODSEA

He was back in his high chair at the centre of the horseshoe, a radiant Mary at his side.

Turning to him, she said, "Before you complete your story, here's a little song which I think contains the gist of it so far. I call it *Head for the Sea*.

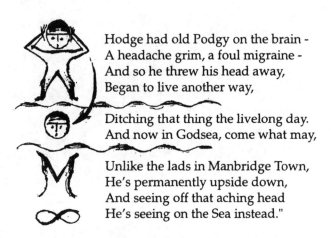

Hodge had old Podgy on the brain -
A headache grim, a foul migraine -
And so he threw his head away,
Began to live another way,

Ditching that thing the livelong day.
And now in Godsea, come what may,

Unlike the lads in Manbridge Town,
He's permanently upside down,
And seeing off that aching head
He's seeing on the Sea instead."

"Which revolution leaves him brainless," added Hodge, after an encore and a decent interval. "Yes, Mary, the wheel of life comes round full circle and he's back to being the village idiot - with some differences.

"And yes, Steve, you are right. I had what you might call ecumenical designs on Godsea. My mistake - Podge-prompted and therefore disingenuous and power-seeking, of course - was to forget that what's right for Manbridge is probably wrong for Godsea. That Godsea is Manbridge turned up-side-down and inside-out. In Manbridge disputants sit round a table and define and enlarge areas of agreement, and whittle away areas of disagreement, giving here and taking there and compromising until, cobbling together a formula, they are able to issue a communiqué to the press and push off and celebrate. Call it the

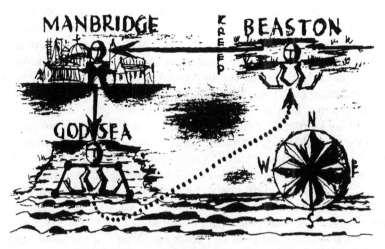

knowing way, the positive way, the plus way, the way of addition. In Manbridge it works in its limited fashion, more or less. In Godsea it doesn't and couldn't work at all. Nor does it need to. Here, the Sea that we see (some of us would say: the Godsea that we Godsee) is our prior and absolute Unity, a Oneness so plenary and so perfect, so powerful and so productive that it inspires and authorises its expression in unlimited and unpredictable and (seemingly) incompatible ways, leaving us nonplussed. Nonplussed, subtracted from, clueless and loving it, as Nicholas used to say. This all-embracing and all-reconciling Unity has no need of any governing body or council or Castellan to regulate its affairs, thank you very much. The very idea is cuckoo, the cuckoo trying to wind up and regulate the cuckoo-clock."

A voice from the floor. "So anything goes? So you don't give a damn if your neighbour's cultivating the weeds you're exterminating?"

"Why should you fuss, provided the partition wall stays seed-proof? Don't forget that his Podge and yours swim in the same Sea-fed moat, and that his window and yours open out onto the self-same Sea, and that beneath his floor and yours the self-same Sea floods the catacombs. I know, because I've just come from them. The Sea, the Sea - always it's the Sea that's the answer to the nonsenses and contradictions and problems of Godsea. The Sea, mark you, not any Castellan of Godsea.

"On this subject I have stop-press news for you. Until this morning I believed that Castellan Nicholas named me as his successor because he thought I would initiate a get-together of Godsea-ers. Until, in fact, I chanced to ask Frank for his opinion. Well, it seems that Nicholas had hinted to Frank that his intention was just about the opposite of what I'd believed. That, in fact, Nicholas had come to the conclusion that the office of Castellan was an anachronism, an absurdity, and that I would be the one to prove and clinch that conclusion. His hope and expectation was that, unprompted by him, I would decide to resign, and to urge that I should have no successor.

"May I strike a concluding personal note here, on the theme of unsuccess - or shirking, if you like? Failing to grow up in Beaston, I went on to Manbridge; failing to grow up in Manbridge, I went on to Godsea; failing to grow up in Godsea (in choosing a new-comer, Nicholas made sure I didn't have the time), I went on to become its Castellan. And now history repeats itself yet again. Unlike Caesar, I came, I saw, I lost - but when did I ever lose by losing? All roads but the road to the Sea are cul-de-sacs for shirking. Oceanic grace wouldn't let me miss the exits from those dead ends -

"To lose all for the sea is to gain all as the Sea.

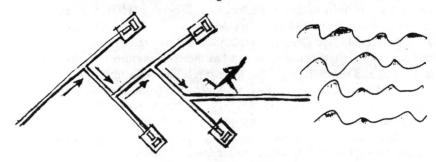

I had no calling -
That was my call.
To win at Nothing:
Loser take all.

"And so it comes about, dear friends, that I now formally announce that I am no longer your Castellan."

Hodge stood up, walked slowly towards the wide-open casement ahead of him, and faced the Perilous Sea.

One by one the rest of the company got up and followed him, till all had stationed themselves at the windows on the south side of the great hall. The Silence gripped everyone.

The Sea, for once, was all foam, iridescent foam going on and on forever. Lightning flashes played continually above the foam. Nevertheless the Silence intensified.

Taking the ancient amethyst ring of the Castellans from his forefinger, Hodge held it aloft for all to see its deep blue radiance.

Then he said: "What came from the Sea goes back the Sea."

There followed an all-obliterating flash of lightning, and a simultaneous thunder-clap that shook Godsea Castle from catacombs to weathercocks.

In Godsea there are to this day two schools of thought about what happened to the ring. One says that, at the instant of the lightning flash, Hodge deliberately flung the ring far out to Sea. The other says: no, it was struck by the lightning out of his hand, and disintegrated, and so was lost forever.

Both schools of thought, however, are agreed on the sequel.

The great hall was flooded by the scent of wild violets, and with the song of the nightingales singing in the bailey garden.